**R.M. LIENAU**

# HOLY GHOST

# R.M. LIENAU

# HOLY GHOST

A Novel

SUNSTONE
PRESS

SANTA FE

Sunstone books may be purchased for educational, business, or sales promotional use. For information please write: Special Markets Department, Sunstone Press, P.O. Box 2321, Santa Fe, New Mexico 87504-2321.

Book design ▷ Vicki Ahl ◁▷ Cover design ▷ Seth Capshaw
Body typeface ▷ Cambria
Printed on acid free paper

Library of Congress Cataloging-in-Publication Data

Lienau, R. M. (Richard M.)
Holy Ghost : a novel / by R.M. Lienau.
p. cm.
ISBN 978-0-86534-803-5 (pbk. : alk. paper)
1. New Mexico--Fiction. I. Title.
PS3562.I4533H65 2011
813'.54--dc22

2011005447

Published in

WWW.SUNSTONEPRESS.COM
SUNSTONE PRESS / POST OFFICE BOX 2321 / SANTA FE, NM 87504-2321 /USA
(505) 988-4418 / ORDERS ONLY (800) 243-5644 / FAX (505) 988-1025

This book is dedicated to all honest members of the Central Intelligence Agency who strive to protect the United States of America from foreign foes, and to those who risk careers and their lives to expose those within the CIA who do not follow the rule of law.

# *1*

Alessandra cranked the wheel left, applied the brakes hard, and her candy-apple red Ford Expedition ground to a dust-raising halt. She had stopped on gravel-covered dirt at the edge of a narrow road that connected to the two-lane highway. She peered through the windshield at a little weathered sign, low in the dirt to the right of the asphalted trace. It admonished travelers that the road beyond was narrow and tortuous; the properties along it private and well-guarded, and not to be trespassed upon. She glanced to her right at the old bridge that spanned the Pecos river, then back at the sign. Behind it, the road rose west into a narrow, rocky, but verdant valley.

Alex, as her friends called her, didn't remember seeing the road or the valley before. She had driven this route several times in the past three years. She had always driven over the new concrete bridge that passed over the river, a part of the highway. Beyond the bridge, it was another quarter mile before the paved road angled steeply up into the Sangre de Cristo mountain range, part of the southern Rockies. She must not have looked to the left before, or committed it to her subconscious, she thought. Now she felt compelled to drive into what seemed forbidden territory. Her stomach twinged deliciously with the notion and she pressed the accelerator pedal.

True to the dry, printed admonitions of the sign, the road, although covered with tarmac, was one lane wide, crowned, eroded, and called for constant attention to the steering wheel as it wound higher into the narrow canyon. Both sides of the track, except for the stream that bore the name of the valley, were crowded with trees, both deciduous and ever-green. A half mile later, she saw the first house off to her right, and she slowed to look. Large, two-story and of dark wood, with a steep pitched roof, it appeared abandoned. Tacked high above the forlorn lean-to porch was a sign proclaiming that trespassers would be dealt with severely. By whom, she wondered. Another half mile of winding way, and subsequent to bridging the stream several times, she saw a meadow to her left. She slowed, pulled to a stop and set the brake. She let the engine idle for another minute as she looked around. She had seen no one; not even another car on her slow, sinuous drive.

She lowered her window and leaned out, supporting her upper body by placing both arms on the windowsill. She surveyed the area. The sun's light dappled the green between the road and the rapidly moving stream. It was high; a few minutes past noon, something her stomach confirmed with increasing intensity.

She had snacked lightly on her trip from the plains of the Texas panhandle. She had left early that morning, bringing crackers, cheese and bottled water. Having left even before Alisa had risen, she was also glad she didn't have to face her husband and his sarcasm about where she was going and with whom she would meet. Her dread of his insinuations had grown of late. She had begun to think she hated her husband, with his snide implications of impropriety severely frowned upon in the "uptight" Bible-belt community where they lived. She strongly suspected he was involved with someone else—perhaps more than one woman—yet she could not bring herself to face him about it and his resultant wrath. There were her parents and children to consider.

He had left the previous day, claiming to have out-of-town business which he had failed to discuss with her—not that it mattered anymore. Her decision to leave was spontaneous, yet she knew openly that her act fell into the category of childish and passive-aggressive. But she didn't care; certainly not at this moment.

Alex sighed, shook off her disturbing thoughts and opened the door. She grabbed her camera, a plastic bottle from the cooler, a paper sack on the floor behind her seat, and headed for the brook. She found an immense, smooth, thick log that lay alongside the creek, long ago debarked by weather and time. Near one end of the dead tree was a flat depression where she sat after smoothing her blue denim dress beneath her. She fancied it had been carved for her, as she arranged her paper napkin table. After consuming the better part of a fat, green chile beef burrito purchased at the country store in the village of Pecos, she slumped into a relaxed state. She stared at the trees above her and drank the last of the cold protein drink she had brought from home in the cooler.

She heard the sound of the first and only vehicle since leaving the two-lane highway that followed the Pecos River. She turned to see a green truck; half pickup, half maintenance vehicle, as it slowed to a stop alongside the grassy area. It had been traveling up into the canyon. There was an official-looking, shield-shaped logo with a white background on the door.

A woman, in a uniform nearly the color of the truck, was at the wheel. She rolled her window down and leaned out. She smiled. "Hello," she said.

Alex answered. "Hello."

"Everything okay?" the woman asked.

"Yes. Is it okay to sit here?"

"Of course. Just checking to see if you're okay. Enjoy your day."

"Thank you."

The woman, still smiling in an official manner, rolled her window up, waved, and drove slowly away.

It was then that Alex realized she was in dire need of relieving herself.

She stood and looked about. The area between the stream and the road for more than a hundred feet in both directions was open grass, with no place for privacy. She frowned. It was at times like these, she thought, that she could use at least one masculine physical trait. Alex peered across the racing water. Privacy could be enjoyed on the other side, but she saw no way to cross.

She rolled her lunch remains into a ball and placed them on the ground, picked up her camera, moved to the water's edge, leaned down and stuck her hand in the miniature rapids. The water was ice cold and shimmering clear. She straightened, then walked gingerly upstream, threading her way past rocks, branches, dead wood and lapping water. Around a tight bend not twenty feet away, she saw a series of large rocks whose flat tops protruded from the flow. They seemed to have been placed there to bridge the stream. Necessity driving her, she hopped successfully from stone to stone across the water, her camera swinging wildly. She leaped the last four feet to the sandy shore and into a willow thicket. She caught her balance, spread the spring-like branches of the light green tree, and crouched through its branches. Beyond the willow was a ten foot diameter clearing surrounded by a ponderosa, more willows and other brushy foliage she couldn't identify.

She looked in every direction, saw no one through the boughs, and heard no sound but that of the frigid water tumbling along the rocky course. Wasting no more time, she lay the camera on the ground, pulled two tissues from the pocket of her dress, raised it, pulled her underpants down and squatted. Thirty seconds later, she shoved the tissues under a rock, stood and straightened her clothes. It was then she noticed movement out of the corner of her eye and swung to her left.

He stood six feet tall, and was dressed in a red and black plaid shirt, the sleeves rolled up to his elbows, dark jeans and climbing boots. His salt and pepper hair was plentiful and flowed over his ears and down the back of his head. Alex was unable to see his eyes behind a large pair of dark glasses, but the smile in his deeply-lined face betrayed strength and confidence. The wavering afternoon sunlight glinted from a large silver belt buckle. He wore a broad-brimmed western hat, grey in color.

"Oh, my god!" she blurted. Instinctively, she put her hand to her mouth.

"Take it easy." He raised a placating hand.

"Oh, gosh! How long have you been here? Did you—?"

"I didn't see anything incriminating, if that's what you're thinking." He lowered his hand.

"But you—"

"I startled you. Sorry." He looked around, peering at her vehicle near the road, then returned his gaze to her.

"How embarrassing!" She moved toward the willow thicket, then turned. "Who—?"

"I live right over there." He thumbed over his shoulder, but kept his eyes on her.

"Oh. I guess I'm trespassing. Sorry." She blushed.

"Technically. But you seem harmless enough. Anyone with you?" He looked toward her car again.

"No." She frowned.

"Okay. Not to worry." He grinned.

She awarded him another half-smiling frown, then turned and pushed the willow fronds aside. She ducked and made her way to the stream bank.

"Your camera." He picked it up and followed her.

She looked back. "Oh—thank you." She crashed through the willows, leapt onto the first rock, lost her balance and fell into the icy water, bottom first. Both feet and legs followed, and she screeched. He was beside her in a flash, and hauled her out of the water from under her arms. He guided her to the opposite bank, stepping carefully but skillfully from rock to rock. She waded alongside as gingerly as a cat would when confronted with the same situation. She yelped with each step. With both on the bank, he backed away. She stood, wet, cold and shivering, her arms across her chest, teeth chattering.

"Got a blanket?"

She looked up at him sheepishly, hugging herself. She pointed from her folded arms. "No."

"Better come to the house and dry off."

She looked at him as though he were crazy. "What?!" She shook her head. "It's okay. I'll be fine." She waved him away.

He spread his arms out in a questioning gesture. "What're you gonna' do? Drive wet?" His eyes went wide.

"Yes. I'll be fine."

"There's nothing around here but the village store. Ten miles away. No facilities."

"I'll dry out in the car. But thanks." She started in that direction in her soaked shoes.

"Okay, but the offer still stands. Dry towels. Respectful, considerate man." He stuck both his hands in his rear pants pockets. "Up to you." He was talking to her back.

She turned to look at him out of the corner of her eye as she moved. "Yeah, sure."

He nodded sideways. "Absolutely. Scout's honor. Besides, my sister's there."

She stopped and looked down at her sodden dress, then back at him. "Really?" She hesitated. "Guess it was dumb to dress like this."

"Especially if you planned to go swimming."

She laughed, then was silent for a few seconds as she squinted and rubbed her nose. "Okay. I'll take you up on your offer." She looked at him squarely and pointed her finger at the sky. "But no funny business, or I'll scream to high heaven."

"Lot 'o good that'll do you around here." He waved his arms, indicating their remote surroundings.

She smiled ruefully, then, "Oh! My camera!"

"Right there." He pointed to the log where it rested.

After stripping, the big, fluffy bath towel he had provided felt wonderful. He had driven her car the short distance to the house as she shivered in the passenger seat, and had led her, shoeless, to a second-story bathroom. Then he retrieved her bag from the SUV. A short time later, he tapped on the door, announced himself, then opened it far enough to hand her traveling bag around the edge, then closed it.

She emerged from the bathroom dressed in jeans and a jersey top. She crossed the four-foot wide balcony to the railing and looked down into the large living room. It featured an open-beam, cathedral ceiling above a polished, dark wood floor. She saw a big, heavy door that opened to the front porch on the left. To her right was a south-facing kitchen with a series of half-windows which allowed sunlight to fill the room. Across the big space, with its sunken living area, was a rock fireplace. On the floor in front of it lay a large, red-dominated Navajo rug. Complementing it were two more Navajo weavings on the walls. In addition were paintings, etchings and drawings. Tasteful furniture, most of it leather, was strategically placed. An antique desk stood in one corner near the fireplace. She noticed her camera which rested on a small, old-fashioned marble-topped table next to the front door.

She looked down to her right. The kitchen floor and counter tops were tiled, and a dark wood trestle table with parallel benches stood in the far corner. Alex turned at the sound of a door opening beneath her bare feet. It was to her right, under her, at the bottom of the stairs.

He came into the open and peered up at her. "Dry?"

"Yes, thanks so much. Really."

Their eyes locked for a moment, then they both broke away.

"You can put your clothes in the dryer. Shouldn't take long." He pointed.

"It's fine, really. They're already packed."

"Okay. Come on down. Got something hot to drink on the stove." He moved into the kitchen.

When she arrived behind him, he was busy stirring a saucepan with a big wooden spoon. The vapors rising from it reached her nostrils, betraying the contents as milk chocolate. She stopped at the end of the island counter, her feet still bare.

"I guess my shoes are still in the car."

"I can get 'em for you."

"Don't bother. I have a pair of sandals. I'll put 'em on when I leave."

He put the spoon down and faced her. She saw his face clearly, and studied his eyes. They were grey-green, warm, intelligent, and sage, with laugh and age lines radiating onto smooth, sun-drenched skin. His mouth was firm, betraying kindness, strength and a wealth of experience.

He pointed to the pan on the stove. "Hot chocolate. Hope that suits."

"Yes, I love it." She glanced around. "Nice place."

"Thank you." He followed her gaze, then picked up the spoon.

"I should introduce myself. I'm Alex. Short for Alessandra. Petersen. With an "E.""

"We did forget the formalities, didn't we. I'm Mark Cassidy."

She took a step toward him, and they shook hands awkwardly.

"You said your sister was here." She studied his face.

He gestured casually. "Outside. Constitutional. Likes to wander about."

"I see." She nodded, her mouth pursed.

"She'll be in soon." He looked past her toward the rear of the house. "I hope."

They sat across from each other at the trestle table, sipping the hot brew and passing small talk. The afternoon sunlight beamed in through the range of windows, adding to the effect. She felt he was anxious when she noticed he was sneaking glances at his watch. He said little about himself, other than that he was retired and did some writing. She prattled about her home in Texas, family, friends, and her desire to be a photographer.

"I have a question," she said.

"Yes?"

"When I was sitting on the log, a woman in a truck came by."

"Yes?"

Alex shook her head. "Who was she?"

"Green truck? Uniform?"

"Yes."

"Forest Service. This is actually National Forest land. They patrol. They're friendly."

Alex smiled. "She was. But—"

"You want to know how I can be here. This house."

"Well—"

"Some of these places were here before the Forest Service. We were grand-fathered in. My grandfather, in fact, homesteaded this piece. We're allowed to live here under special agreement with the Service."

"Okay." Alex nodded. After an ensuing silence, she said, "Well, I better be going."

He looked at her, nodded, then rose. "Of course. Getting late, and you have some traveling ahead of you."

"Santa Fé. Visiting a friend. She. Woman friend." She wasn't sure why she had to add the last part. She waved her hand as though to brush aside a gaffe.

"Ah." He raised his eyebrows and nodded, then turned. "I better get your things. Upstairs."

"Sorry. I left my suitcase up there." She pointed,

"Okay. Be right down."

While Cassidy went upstairs, Alex strolled down into the living area and to the old roll-top desk. Idly, she tried to open it, but was frustrated because it was locked. It was then she noticed what looked like a phone line leading to it and through a small hole in the side. Between it and the rock fireplace, a tripod with a telescope leaned against the wall. She had noticed a portable telephone sitting on the ceramic tile-covered kitchen counter. She turned at the sound of his feet as he came back down the stairs.

"Here we are." He set her bag on the flagstone walkway that led to the front door, stepped down into the living area and went up to her.

Still next to the roll-top, she looked around at the walls. "I love your art."

He stopped and looked around, following her gaze. "Thanks. I didn't select it all. Just the Navajo pieces." He smiled down at her.

"They're gorgeous."

"Yes. Thanks. Unique."

He carried her bag to the car, set it on the floor behind her seat, then closed the rear and driver's doors. She settled in and strung her seat belt across her chest and lap.

She started the engine, then lowered her window. "Thanks again. Sorry to cause such a fuss."

He handed her a calling card. "I enjoyed it. Fall in my creek any time." He grinned and slapped the roof of the big Ford.

She held the little pasteboard up and read the legend. She looked at him. "Is that an invitation?"

"Of course." He pointed to the card. "Treat you to dinner in town." He slapped the Expedition roof, turned and walked back to the porch.

Alex put the transmission into reverse, then looked up before pressing the accelerator pedal. He was on the porch, leaning forward, both hands on the wood rail, watching her. Her attention was then drawn to her right. Beyond the corner of the house, she saw a figure walking toward it, seemingly oblivious to her presence. The clothes were those of a man, yet the stride and movements those of a woman. She shifted her eyes to the porch, but Mark Cassidy had disappeared. When she turned her head again, so had the figure.

# 2

Alex made her way slowly down the mountain, following the Pecos River canyon to the village of Pecos. From there, she turned west onto two-lane Highway Fifty. She was reluctant to leave the verdant valley, and stopped three times to take pictures. By the time she joined the Interstate, the sun was below the western escarpment of Glorieta Mesa, creating finger-like shafts of orange-white light that fanned out across the sky. Past the steep cut of Apache Canyon, she watched the purple and gold sunset against the horizon dominated by the Ortiz and Sandia mountains to the south. To the north, her right, the majestic Sangre de Cristo range was bathed in golden light on dark green.

Although the temperature inside the vehicle belied her, she felt cold, as though she had fallen into Holy Ghost Creek again. After her change of clothes in Mark Cassidy's bathroom, she was warm, and in more than one way. There was something about the man. What was the matter with her? Didn't she love her husband? Wasn't she supposed to love him after a quarter century? She had a home, family, friends, and children, although the latter were now essentially independent. She sighed as she realized she was only now admitting just how unhappy she really was. There was such a big world out there; so much she yearned for, to see and to feel; to experience. Yet her past tugged at her, beckoning her to remain, something of which Ted reminded her often. Was she required to remain in a failed marriage? She thought of their church pastor, with whom she had consulted this past week. She shuddered at the realization that at the same time he admonished her to stay bound by her matrimonial oath, he was insinuating himself on her. The idea, the possibility alone, of his touching her, made her ill. Then there was this beautiful, rugged country, with which she had fallen in love. Mark Cassidy, in some way, represented this place to her. She didn't know him, nor he her, and she had been in his presence for less than three hours. She shook her head.

She was in sight of Santa Fé when the cellular phone clipped to the center console chirped.

"Hello?"

"Mom?"

"Yes. Jackie?"

"Yeah. Hi. Where are you?"

"Just outside Santa Fé. Is anything wrong?"

"I thought dad was supposed to be back today. We were going to meet for lunch, and he didn't show up."

"Oh? Did you call the office?"

"Yes, but Maria hasn't seen him, and he hasn't called."

"Strange."

"Do you know if he was supposed to be in the office today?"

"I thought so, yes."

"Well, hm . . ."

"He probably got tied up and had to stay over, honey."

"Sure."

"Don't worry."

"Okay, mom. Where you headed?"

"Betty's."

"Oh, yeah. Well, see you later. Have fun."

"Thanks. Love ya'. Bye."

"Love ya', mom. Bye"


Alex parked in the lot as near as she could to the main supermarket door. She entered, grabbed a basket and wheeled through the store. She bought two bottles of local red wine, cheese, sour dough bread, high-grain breakfast cereal, milk, juice, fruit, pasta, eggs, and a small beef steak.

Betty had been a family friend for more than fifteen years. She and her husband partied with Ted and her, joined them for dinner, helped with the kids as they had with theirs. They had partnered with them at church functions. Betty had moved to Santa Fé more than four years ago, after her divorce.

It was totally dark as Alex turned the last corner onto Betty's street. The house was the third from the corner. She thought about how it was one of those "Santa Fé style" houses; a pseudo-Pueblo, frame stucco, designed to resemble an adobe structure, with fake *vigas* protruding from two of the exterior walls. She knew that in reality it was a neat, three-bedroom tract house, most likely built by a contractor from California. Betty traveled often, and she, Alex and the family had an open invitation to use the place when they were in town, whether she was home or not. In the spur of the moment she had not checked, but knew Betty was supposed to be traveling.

She parked in front of the double car garage, grabbed the groceries from the passenger seat, and headed for the front door. Odd, she thought; the porch light was out. Betty normally left it burning, regardless. There were perishables in the sacks that needed to go into the refrigerator. She'd return for her personal things in a few minutes. Alex put the sacks down on the porch floor, fished in the blackness of her purse for the key, and opened the door. She found the switch to the hall light, then made her way to the kitchen. She put the groceries on the counter before returning for her purse and bags, and locking the car. She made sure the porch light was on.

After putting the groceries away and parking her luggage in a corner of the kitchen, she headed for the guest bathroom. She flicked the hall light on as she went. The master bedroom door was open, and as she passed, she saw something in the shadows from the corner of her eye which caught her attention. She saw in the half-light that the king-size bed was unmade, the covers draped to the floor. Her heart racing, she stopped, took a step into the dark room, then reached for the light switch. A lamp on the far side of the bed came on. The opposite, matching table fixture lay on the floor, shade bent, bulb dark. On the carpeted floor, protruding from the edge of the shadow cast by the bed, was a leg and a bare foot. Before she budged from her frozen position, she knew whose foot it was. Nearly panicked and dizzy, she backed up to the doorframe and supported her weight with her right hand while her left covered her heaving chest. Her breathing coming fast, eyes wide, she peered around the edge of the door, then stepped fearfully into the room.

As she moved closer, she saw that a man lay on his back, his head in a small patch of dried blood. It ran down the front and side of his face and had caked on the light-colored carpet. His eyes and mouth were half open, his body at a crazy, unnatural angle. His right hand was on his bare chest, his left arm stretched out under the bed. The only article of clothing he wore were the bottoms to a pair of pajamas that she also recognized. It was her husband, Ted.

Close to fainting, and nauseous, Alex stepped back, and, about to leave, looked to her right and through the open door to the large bathroom. Even in the subdued light, she made out a dark patch on the tiled floor. She froze again, sure of what she would find. Moving slowly and furtively, she went to the half-open bathroom door and flicked the light on. Betty lay on the cold floor, her naked body in a fetal position, her head covered by a turbaned towel. She also lay in a small pool of blood. A white bath towel was clutched in her dead right hand.

She turned and hurried from the bedroom with the wild thought that if she didn't, one or both of the deceased would rise and threaten her, or that the killer, lurking in a closet, would chase her down and kill her as well. She stumbled down the hall, almost blind with shock and fear, rounded the corner, raced for the front door and threw it open. Unable to control herself, she leaned past the edge of the porch, and holding her midriff, retched, then lost her lunch into the bushes that paralleled the path to the porch.

She stood, wiped her mouth with the back of her hand, looked around at the silent, dark neighborhood, then staggered onto the concrete drive. Her breath coming in gasps, she closed, then opened, her eyes several times as though doing so might change the outcome; take her back in time as she teetered in an aimless circle. She leaned against her car for what seemed an eternity, then backed away and looked around through filmy, tear-filled eyes. There were no more than a half-dozen cars parked along the length of the street. Several, including a pickup truck, were parked in driveways up and down the street partially lit by a pair of widely-spaced bluish street lights. Several houses showed porch lights and windows gold from interior lights.

It was then she realized she needed the bathroom, and urgently. Her skin crawling, she rushed back into the house, down the hall past the master bedroom and to the hall bath. As she sat on the toilet in the dark, she began to sob fitfully.

Panting hard, but collecting herself, she went to her purse, then moved outside again at a fast walk. With the front door wide open, she keyed herself into the driver's seat of her car. For some reason, she felt safe there. She could drive away should danger appear. Calmer, but still fighting off panic and hyperventilation, she picked up the cell phone which had remained on the dash. Trembling, she entered 911.

Less than ten minutes later, two uniformed officers from the Santa Fé Police Department arrived in a patrol car, without lights or siren. The car pulled up into the drive and stopped at a crazy angle. The driver emerged cautiously, leaving his door open, and approached the house in a defensive posture, his .40 caliber semiautomatic pistol drawn and pointed as an extension of his out-stretched arm. He disappeared into the house.

Alex sat against the seat back, oblivious, her head to one side, eyes closed, face wet and streaked. The other officer tapped on her driver-side window, and she jerked forward in surprise. She recovered and lowered the glass.

"Ma'am," he said. He had his right hand on the butt of his holstered side-arm, a long, black, metal flashlight, held near the bulb end, in his left. He played its beam across her face.

Alex winced, mouth agape.

"You the one that called?"

"Yes." She blinked her red eyes at him as he lowered the sharp light.

"Please step out." He backed away, still in a defensive pose, watching her carefully.

Alex opened her door and eased out slowly as the patrolman looked her over, routinely watching for a weapon.

"Please move to the front of the police vehicle. Over there, in the light. Next to the vehicle. Thank you." He gestured.

Dazed and confused, Alex hesitated for a second, then did as she was asked. Behind her, the cop shone his light inside her vehicle, playing the light shaft over and under the seats, dash and floor in a quick, well-studied routine. He then turned, closed the door and went to her at the same time the first officer emerged from the house.

Although still panicky, Alex had the presence of mind to read the name on the second officer's badge. It was Sandoval.

Sandoval tucked his flashlight under his arm and removed a notebook from his black shirt pocket. "Your name, please?"

The first officer, who had searched the house, stopped several paces away and signaled to Sandoval, who broke off his interview and joined him. At the same time, he pressed the button on the radio mike pinned to his shirt and spoke into it. Finished, he turned, faced Sandoval and spoke in a low tone. Sandoval nodded and turned back to Alex.

"I'd like you to sit in the car." He gestured with his flashlight, then inserted it into its leather loop holster at his belt.

Sandoval opened the rear door of the patrol car and Alex got in, confusion and fear masking her features. The officer closed the door, taking care not to injure her in the process.

A second police cruiser arrived, driven by a woman officer. The passenger was a black man. Ten seconds later, a plain, brown sedan rolled up and parked behind both cruisers. A man in civilian clothes emerged and walked to the four uniformed officers, who were engaged in a conference.

"Hey, Manny." Officer Cohen, Sandoval's partner, spoke.

"Guys. Sharon. What we got?" Manny Griego stopped and put both hands on his belt, to which was attached a gold badge. He wore a beige windbreaker.

"Two deceased," Cohen said. "Man and a woman." He jerked his head toward the house.

Griego turned to glance at Alessandra Petersen who sat in the rear of the first patrol car. "And her?"

"Called it in," Sandoval said. "Pretty shook up."

"Nance'll be here in a few. Guess I'm primary." Griego scanned the faces of his fellow policemen. "Anyone call O.M.I.?"

"Not yet," Cohen said. "Waiting for you."

"Good." Griego turned fully to look at Alex, then glanced at the female officer. "Stay with her for now, okay, Sharon?"

Sharon nodded assent.

"'Kay, guys, let's have a look-see." Griego started toward the house, followed by the other three.

The black officer slowed, scouring the ground and the surroundings carefully as he moved.

Griego squatted next to the body of the woman, latex gloves covering his hands, his arms resting on his knees. Sandoval, Cohen and Deering, the black officer, circled him immediately inside the bathroom door.

He looked up. "I assume someone looked for a weapon." His eyes moved from man to man.

"I was first in," Cohen said. "Nothing so far."

"Nothing in the woman's car," Sandoval said.

"Stands to reason." Griego stood up. "But—" He waved his hand, pointing first at the body on the cold, tile floor, then into the bedroom where the dead man lay. "Something's not right." He shook his head and rolled his eyes around, ever vigilant.

The other three nodded and glanced at each other.

"No passion," Cohen said.

"Clean," Sandoval said.

"Yep," Griego added. "Targets." He jabbed his finger at both men in turn, signaling agreement.

"Targets?" Deering asked.

Griego cocked his head. "Targets. They were targeted. It's too clean. Professional stench about it. Look at the wounds. Both in the head. Small caliber. No exit wounds I can see. No sign of struggle. Surprise. Bang, bang and out."

At that moment, they were joined by a smaller, older man with a slight paunch. He wore civilian clothes. He walked up to the four officers, his hands in his pants pockets, his demeanor nonchalant. He wore a badge on his belt.

Deering was first to notice him. "Hey, Nance."

"Gentlemen. Thanks for the invite." Nance acknowledged each

man in turn, then peered with almost disdainful curiosity at the bodies, rising up on one foot as he did. He looked at Griego. "You case agent?"

"That's me," Griego answered. He both nodded and shook his head simultaneously, compressing his lips as he did.

Nance pointed at Griego, then himself. "You primary, me co-pilot. What can I do fer ye?"

"Woman out there in the cruiser called it in." Griego held his arms out at this sides, fingers splayed, as though the gloves he wore were contaminated. "Apparently this guy's her husband, and the gal here her friend." He gestured at the deceased. "I kinda' doubt she's the perp, but we need to get as much outa' her as we can. If you'd take her back to the ranch and talk to her. Take Sharon."

"Yassah, boss," Nance said, saluting. "Mind if I spend a few looking around before I do the deed?"

"Be my guest." Griego swept his arm around. "Sandoval, maybe you and Cohen better see if any of the neighbors saw or heard anything." He looked at his watch. "From the looks of the victims, I think we're talking around four or five hours."

Nance approached the patrol car where Alex languished, said something to Sharon, who he found leaning against the patrol car, her arms folded. He peered into the rear of the vehicle, then opened the door to look closely at Alex. His hands went back into his pockets. "I'm detective Nance. Mrs. Petersen, is it?"

Alex looked up at him, her eyes wide and red, her face pale. "Yes."

"Sorry about your loss, Mrs. Petersen. I know you'd like to get out of here, but we need to get some information from you."

"Okay. Now?"

Nance cocked his head in an apologetic gesture. "Really best. Memory fades, you know, and in cases such as this, time is of the essence."

"Okay."

"Anyone you'd like to call? Lawyer, friend, family?"

Alex thought a moment. "Yes."

"You have means?"

"Means?"

"Cell?"

"Yes."

Nance righted himself and arched his back to rid himself of the tightness developed from stooping. "Okay. Why don't you call, then we'll go to headquarters."

"Headquarters?"

"More comfortable there." He crinkled his face in a friendly half-wink, his hands still sunk into his pockets. He turned to Sharon, who had moved to stand next to him to watch Alex. "Transport her, okay?"

"Sure." She lowered her head to look into the car.

Nance started to walk away, then returned. He ducked to look at Alex. "Mrs. Petersen, if you don't mind, I'd like you to ride with officer Pettibone here. We'll bring you back for your vehicle. Okay?"

She looked up at him. "Okay. Yes." She nodded.

Alex had her cell phone in one hand and the business card Mark Cassidy had given her in the other. She keyed the number. Four rings later, she heard his voice.

"Hello?"

"Mark? Mark Cassidy?"

"Yes?"

"This is Alex. We met—"

"Yes. I recognize your voice. You sound stressed. Problem?"

She began to choke, but forced her words. "Yes. Serious. Very serious. I need help, and you're the only one I know around here."

"Where are you?"

She started to cry, then caught herself. "They're taking me to headquarters."

"Who?!"

"Police."

"What?! Why?!"

She choked again. "I can't talk. Can you please come?"

"Where?!"

"I don't—here, talk to the police." She handed the little phone to Sharon, then bent over until her hands covered her face and her head was on her knees.

# *3*

I t was close to nine o'clock when Mark Cassidy slowed his Jeep and turned into the Abiquiu Lodge parking lot. He sat for thirty seconds, first with his head still, looking into the internal rearview mirror, then swinging his head to look in all directions. The lot was occupied with less than a dozen cars, pickups and SUVs lined up outside the room doors. He felt for the butt of the semi-automatic pistol in the special holster under his seat, then removed his hand. Although he was required under New Mexico law to keep it exposed, he knew the chances of being caught and charged with a misdemeanor were minor. Just checking, he thought.

He got out, a white sack in his hand, set the alarm with the remote key fob, and went to the door of the room in front of his car. He stood with his back to the opening for ten seconds, still watching the lot, his ear close to its surface, listening. He heard nothing, then turned and rapped. Alex opened the door as far as the safety chain would allow and peered out, half of her face exposed. Despite the narrow opening, he saw that she was ravaged. She closed the door, removed the chain, then swung it open with such abandon that it banged against the knob-stop. Cassidy, his eyes on her, grabbed the door, closed and secured it.

She backed up with her head down, hair streaming across her face. Her breath was coming in deep gulps. She wore the same garb he had seen her in earlier in the day, then that which she wore to the police station. It consisted of a light-colored blouse and well-fitting blue jeans. Her feet were bare. Behind her and throughout, the room and bed were a shambles, despite her meager belongings in a rented room.

She looked up at him, then turned away. "Oh, God!"

He advanced on her and put his arm around her shoulder.

She shook her head. "I'm sorry." Her voice was tepid.

"What are friends for?" He patted her back, the sack still dangling from his hand. "Got some food here. You need to eat. Drink something."

He guided her to the side of the bed, where she sat, her unruly tresses still hiding her face. He then turned and set the sack on the window-side table. He stood two paces away and faced her.

She looked up. "The police want to talk to me again. I had to tell them where I am."

"Again? I thought they'd grilled you pretty well. When?" He frowned.

"He called. Said they were coming over. That it wouldn't take long." She shook her head again, pushed her hair away from her face, and tried to regain her composure. "Oh, God! I can't believe this! Ted and Betty!" She swallowed hard, coughed and nearly choked. She cleared her throat, then somewhat settled, continued, "Why would anyone—?!" She coughed again.

"Did you know, Alex?" He cocked his head. "About your husband and—?"

"Know?" She looked up, then down at the floor. "No! I had no idea. We've known each other—Jesus!" Her mouth curled again as silent tears flowed. Her head bobbed with her sobs.

Cassidy pulled a chair close to the bed and sat. She lay on her side, one foot on the floor. He rose, lifted her legs and straightened her so her entire body was on the bed. He pulled a pillow from under the covers and put it under her head. It was then they heard a knock on the door. Cassidy frowned, glanced at Alex, who was oblivious, then at the door. He figured he would be greeting the police, but wished he were armed in case he were wrong. He peered through the peep hole, then opened the door.

Detective Sergeant Manny Griego stood in the doorway. His badge was pinned to his belt, and he still wore the beige windbreaker. Behind him were two uniformed police officers. One was Sharon Pettibone. She was half a head shorter than her partners.

"Alessandra Petersen?" The man peered past Cassidy. "Griego.

Detective. Santa Fé P.D. homicide." He looked at Cassidy with a question in his eyes.

"She's here. What's this about? She was questioned earlier by—what's his name?"

"Nance."

"Right. Nance." Cassidy stepped aside and pointed to the bed. "Not in very good shape, I'm afraid."

"Who're you?"

"Cassidy. Her attorney. I accompanied her to the station. When she was with Nance."

"May we?" Griego moved past Cassidy into the room a few feet, turned and faced the other man.

The female officer followed, moved toward the bed, stood back and assumed a parade rest position, her hands clasped across her midriff, and stared down at Alex. The male officer assumed a stance outside, near the open door. He turned away and faced the lot.

"Is this really necessary?" Cassidy asked.

"Cassidy is it? Thing is, Mr. Cassidy, we've got a real hum-dinger on our hands here, and we'll be on this twenty-four seven until we ID the perp or reach the proverbial brick wall."

Cassidy raised his hand. "Okay. I understand, but take it easy, okay?"

"She pretty broken up?" Griego asked.

"As you can see." Cassidy nodded toward the woman on the bed.

Griego spent several seconds studying Alex, then turned back to Cassidy. "Give us five, okay?"

"It can't wait?"

Griego shook his head and raised his eyebrows. "Okay. One question, okay? But we may need more. In the morning." He raised his eyebrows.

"Questions."

"Sure." Griego shifted his weight and frowned.

Cassidy gestured for the detective to follow him away from the bed. He came close and lowered his voice. "Is it possible for me to see the scene? As her attorney?"

Griego pondered. "Not usual procedure under the circumstances, but I'll check to see where the forensic people are. Still being worked." Griego turned away, then back. "You'll have to sign a waver."

Cassidy nodded.

Griego gestured to the female officer, pulled her aside and spoke to her quietly.

As he did, Cassidy went to Alex, who had not moved a muscle. He leaned over and spoke into her ear. "The police are here. The detective has one question for you, then they'll go. I'm going with him, then I'll come back. Please eat."

She answered without opening her eyes, her words barely intelligible. "Not hungry."

"You need to eat. And drink. If nothing else, water."

"No."

Cassidy backed away, frustrated, eyed the detective and the uniformed officer, then looked at Alex again.

Griego bent over and spoke to Alex. "Mrs. Petersen. Mrs. Petersen?"

Alex shifted her weight, then looked up at the officer through barely open eyes. Her head was on the pillow, her right arm stretched out beneath it such that her hand extended to the edge of the bed. Griego looked closely at the back of her hand, then her face.

"Mrs. Petersen, when did you leave your house in Lubbock?"

"What?"

Griego licked his lips. "When—when did you leave Lubbock?"

"I don't know." Her voice was barely audible.

"You don't remember?" Griego lowered himself to a squat next to the bed, glanced at Cassidy, then touched Alex's hand. "Please try to remember."

Cassidy moved closer to Griego. "Nance asked her that. She was at my place around noon."

Griego looked up, hesitated, then straightened. "She was?"

"Yes."

"Your place? Where's that?"

Cassidy jerked his thumb. "Out near Pecos."

Griego looked at him closely. "Yeah? Why didn't we know this ear-lier?"

Cassidy shook his head. "I wasn't asked."

Griego made a face and put his hands on his hips. "Can you prove that?"

"Not easily. But I do know she stopped in the village on the way to my place and bought food."

"Really?" Griego squinted.

"Really."

Griego made a short, jerking nod. "Okay. We'll check it out."

Cassidy shook his head and frowned. "You don't really suspect her."

"No, but we have to—"

"Yeah, I know. Do your job. I respect that."

"This is a hard one. Okay, let's go." He stopped and looked at Alex. "We're going to need a DNA sample, Mrs. Petersen. Any objections?"

Alex stared at Griego, her eyes now open wide. She shook her head slowly. "No."

"May I ask why?" Cassidy asked.

"You may," Griego answered. "Routine." He shrugged, raised his eyebrows, then turned for the door. As he moved, he spoke again to Cassidy. "If it's sensitive at the crime scene, I may not be able to get you in. Okay?"

"Okay," Cassidy said.

"Let's go." Griego spoke without turning his head.

Griego's car left first, followed by Cassidy in his Jeep, then the cruiser with the uniformed officers rolled into the street. Behind them, in the motel room, Alex Petersen dozed off in a fetal position.

The front of the house was ringed by yellow "crime scene" tape. Police and forensic team vehicles, a District Attorney's car, and a medical investigator's van were scattered about, blocking the street. Red and blue strobe lights flashed atop the cop cars, and a small clot of sloppily-dressed neighbors stood chatting and speculating with each other. Another plain clothes detective talked to two of the civilians, notebook in hand. As Griego wedged his car between two other vehicles, a uniformed policeman recognized him and waved at him. At the same time, a TV news van arrived and parked as badly as the rest. Cassidy was forced to park a half block away, beyond the crazy-quilt of official and unofficial vehicles.

Griego Talked briefly to the officer, then beckoned to Cassidy after he spotted him walking toward him along the sidewalk. He immediately turned away to engage with three other officials. Cassidy came up, then stopped and stood back several respectful paces. Griego looked in his direction and pointed, explaining his presence. A moment later, the detective sergeant gestured for him to approach.

The house was crowded with forensics people looking, probing, dusting and photographing. Cassidy followed Griego, elbowing through the crowded hall to the door to the master bedroom. Griego stopped, held up his hand to stop Cassidy, nodded to someone in the room, then waved him on.

In the room, tape over the thick carpet traced the outline of the male victim next to the big bed. A female medical investigator knelt over the body, her gloved hands working carefully and slowly. A male photographer snapped shots where she directed. Another detective stood by, watching, while a forensics man dusted here and there behind him. Griego stopped and looked at the team next to the body for a few seconds, then glanced at Cassidy before moving on to the bathroom. There, he halted in the doorway and looked down. Cassidy came up behind him and peered over his shoulder.

Cassidy rebounded. "Jesus Christ!?" His voice was just above a whisper.

Griego wheeled and looked at him, frowning. "What?! What's going on?!"

Cassidy was silent for several seconds as he shook his head with a jerking motion. "Unbelievable! I—!"

Griego took Cassidy's arm and pushed him back into the bedroom away from the others. "What's going on?! If you're gonna—"

Cassidy dipped his head, then looked up. "No, no. It's not that. She just—"

"What, man?!" Griego peered hard into the other man's eyes.

Cassidy put his hand to his creased forehead, looked down, then up at the detective as he took in a deep breath. "It just that she—she looks like—"

"Like who?!"

Cassidy had calmed. "Like someone I know."

Griego stretched his arm to point toward the bathroom. "You know this woman?!"

Cassidy shook his head. "No, no. No, I don't. But she resembles someone I know."

"Who?" Griego pressed close to Cassidy again.

"Just someone I know. That's all. Sorry."

Griego was silent for five seconds, eyes feral. "Okay. But if you're holding back—"

"I'm not. It was a shock. That's all." He heaved a deep sigh, keeping his gaze directly on Griego.

Griego searched Cassidy's face, his mouth a thin line of doubt, then turned to enter the bathroom, said something Cassidy couldn't hear, and returned. "Okay, let's go."

"After seeing this, I don't see how you could suspect Mrs. Petersen." Cassidy looked at Griego as he and the detective walked out onto the driveway.

"Hey, listen, you've seen the crap on TV. Movies. Everyone's a suspect until proven otherwise. Especially family. My take? No, but I got my job. You know." He watched the street, busy with news reporters, officials and on-lookers.

"Of course." Cassidy swung his head back and forth, his eyes roving over everything in sight.

Griego noticed. "Problem?"

Cassidy responded by looking directly at the detective. "No. No. Everything's fine."

"You seem concerned." Griego squinted at Cassidy, his head at an angle.

"Not at all. Just never seen so many people gathered like this."

"Well, you know how that goes."

"Sure."

"You know you're under strict need-to-know, court doctrine and all that, Cassidy."

"Right."

Griego pointed his finger at Cassidy's chest. "So I'll tell you my take. On the Petersen woman."

"Appreciate it."

"Her demeanor, time frame, fact she called it in, all that." He hesitated. "The forensics. No wild stuff. No apparent struggle. Doesn't look like a crime of passion."

"Right."

"The wounds. Both shot in the head. Twice. Small caliber. Probably .22 or .25."

Cassidy nodded as Griego eyed him briefly.

"Has all the earmarks of a professional hit. Someone who knew what they were doing. No nerves. Take your time, take aim, squeeze the trigger. Walk away. And no brass. And no one heard a thing." Griego make a gun with his hand, squinted and pulled an imaginary trigger.

"No brass?"

"No casings. No brass."

"But if it's .22?"

"State police lab's pretty good at ballistic forensics."

"Hm."

"But the gun's history."

"I suppose. Any idea what kind of pistol? No brass; a revolver?"

Griego looked at him. "Hey, pretty good. Could be. But we think not."

"Yeah?"

"Yeah. May not seem like much, but wound patterns suggest a quick succession of shots. And, as you know, it's next to impossible to quiet a revolver. True, casings stay with a revolver cylinder, but if you're a 'pro,' you're gonna use a semi-auto with a suppressor. Silencer to you."

"I know the difference." Cassidy nodded.

"And it's easier to get off more than one shot, fast, with an automatic. Plus, a heavy silencer on the front end tends to steady the weapon. You count your shots and retrieve the brass."

"Right."

"And another thing. No autopsy yet, but it appears the slugs didn't penetrate real deep. No exits. That can mean sub-sonic. What you need for a silenced gun."

"Mm.

"Smells like a hit."

Cassidy cocked his head with a frown. "I don't mean to insinuate anything, but how often does the Santa Fé police department solve 'hit' cases?"

"Fair enough. We don't, but I did attend the police academy, and I go to cop seminars. I also read."

"My apologies. No offense, okay?"

"None taken, Mr. Cassidy."

"Good." He smiled.

"So, get my drift?"

"I do." Cassidy sobered, then said, "So, we have a double murder that looks like a professional hit. Drugs?"

Griego shrugged. "Again, I doubt it. Dealer conflicts can get mighty messy. Fight, struggle, multiple shots, high caliber, like that. This one has the stink of something else. Far too neat." He was silent, then said, "Too clean." Griego paused reflectively and looked toward the house. "Look, I gotta' go. Take care o' her, okay?" He pointed at Cassidy.

"You got it."

Cassidy watched his back all the way to the motel. He tapped on the motel room door.

Alex let him in, unable to speak since her mouth was full. She smiled, pointed to her mouth, then returned to the little table next to the large, curtained window that faced the motel parking lot. She sat at the table. The white sack, empty, lay on its side. Two tall, paper cups, a lump of something in aluminum foil and a crinkled ball of the thin metal accompanied it. She smiled up at him as she continued to masticate slowly.

Cassidy returned Alex's unspoken greeting. "Well, you look better."

She swallowed and made an apologetic gesture by touching her hand to her throat. "Yes. Thanks. Again."

"Alex, I'm not comfortable with you here by yourself." He pulled the chair opposite hers out and sat.

"I'll be okay." Her face pleaded.

"Come with me."

She cocked her head at him. "To your place?"

"Yes. You'll be safe there."

"I'm safe here." She peered at him with a question.

"We don't know what happened at that house, Alex. It's possible—"

"What's possible?"

"Look, we don't know what happened. We don't know—and the police sure don't know."

"Was that really your sister?"

"Yes."

"Why didn't she come in?"

He shrugged. "I don't know. You'll meet her."

Alex nodded, smiling.

# 4

Alex awoke suddenly, raised her head and looked around, confused, her eyes foggy and unfocused. Then it dawned on her where she was; in a spare bedroom in Mark Cassidy's house, half-way up Holy Ghost Canyon. On the one hand, she felt she should to get up; on the other, she was fatigued, and wanted sleep—lots of it. Slumber had not come easily, and what little she experienced was mixed with periods of wakefulness alternated with fitful, nonsensical dreams. She wiped moisture from her eyes, yawned stiffly and stirred, letting her feet slip from under the thick covers to the carpeted floor. She rested on her elbow for another minute, then sat up.

She turned to look out the window behind her and across the room. The curtains were open, and she saw the golden, morning-bright tops of the ponderosa trees, and was moderately cheered. A robe she found at the foot of the bed wrapped about her, her movements unstable, she stepped out into the hall. Only silence came from the floor below as she looked about. Strong beams of sunlight shown through the east-side windows that flanked the big stone fireplace in the immense living room.

Below, and to her right, a female figure emerged, moving toward the kitchen. As though operating with a sixth sense, the woman stopped, turned and looked up. Although she had not seen the woman before, and though she couldn't make out her features, Alex knew she had to be the wraith-like person she had seen moving toward the house as she sat in her car, engine running, ready to leave, the day before.

"There's coffee and Juice." The woman gestured with her head, then without waiting for a response, disappeared into the kitchen.

Alex had smelled the strong, fresh aroma of coffee as she left the bedroom, and enticed by the invitation and the growling in her stomach, first went to the hall bathroom, then made her way gingerly down the open stairway in her bare feet.

The woman sat on a padded bench that ran the length of a long, narrow set of windows that terminated at the far corner of the kitchen-dining area. She wore blue denim pants and a button-down shirt of a darker blue, untucked. Her feet were covered with a pair of running shoes. Her legs were drawn up under herself as she leaned against the padded back, her right arm stretched along its top. Her left forearm lay on the table, her hand clutching a cup of coffee. Her back was to Alex as she stared out the window into the morning sun that streaked through the branches, mottling the light in the room while warming it.

She turned at the sound of Alex's entrance. "Help yourself. Cups next to the pot."

"Oh my god!" Alex bent forward and threw both hands to her mouth, her eyes saucer-like.

The woman turned her body to face Alex fully, bringing her feet to the floor. "What?! What's wrong?!" She lost control of her cup, causing some of its contents to slosh onto the table.

Alex, frozen in the posture she had assumed, stared. "My god! You! You look just like her!"

"Who?! Who do I look like?!"

Alex dropped her hands slowly. She shook her head in disbelief, causing her hair to go wild. "You do! You look just like Betty! My friend!"

"The one who was killed?"

"Yes! Oh my God!"

The woman slid out and moved toward Alex, her arms outstretched at waist level. She stopped short. Her faced was screwed up in concern. "Are you alright?!"

Alex, staring, backed up a pace, still bent. "I can't believe it!" She covered her mouth with her hand again.

"It's okay! Take it easy." She dropped her arms. "Come on, sit down. I'll get you some coffee. I'm Evelyn. Mark's sister. Sit. Please." She gestured as she moved for the island counter.

Alex straightened, in part with relief at Evelyn's announcement of her relationship to Mark Cassidy. Then, moving as though under attack, she crept to the trestle bench that served the side of the long table opposite the windows. Evelyn turned, poured a cup, then set it down in front of Alex, who began to calm.

"Cream, sugar—all that—right there. Have some juice." Evelyn stood and looked down at the visitor. "Hungry?" She felt helpless in the face of Alex' distress.

"Thanks. No, not yet," Alex heard her own voice as rusty and cleared her throat. She sipped at the coffee, then reached for the little crockery creamer. The miniature pitcher shared the center of the rustic table with a container of orange juice, glasses for same, sugar, utensils, a paper napkin holder, and a wooden bowl with bananas.

As she stirred her coffee, Alex took Evelyn in. She stood no more than five feet seven inches tall, with a slender build, and a pretty, intelligent face draped in dark brown hair that reached her shoulders. Alex reckoned the woman exercised regularly. She glanced toward the rear of the house, hoping to see Evelyn's brother, Mark Cassidy, but resolved that she would not.

Evelyn caught Alex' eye movement. "He's out right now. Should be back soon." She moved back to the table with a dish towel, resumed her seat, and mopped up her coffee spill.

"I'm sorry. I'm Alex. Alessandra. Petersen. Mark—"

"I know. Mark's helping you. He's good at that. Helping." She looked away, then back, with a matter-of-fact face.

"I'm sorry about the outburst."

"No harm. Tell me, your husband? And a friend?" Evelyn crinkled her brow.

Alex nodded as tears began to well. She choked and coughed once; a bark.

Evelyn nodded and looked down. "Sorry. That's awful."

"I have to tell my son and daughter. I don't know how." She shook her bowed head.

"Of course. Won't be easy." Evelyn hesitated and drank slowly from the small amount of coffee that remained in her cup. "Any idea why?"

"Why?"

"Your husband and friend. Why them." She sipped again, watching Alex from under her eyebrows.

Alex straightened her back, shook her head dramatically and swallowed hard. "I have no idea! It's just crazy!" Her face was streaked with tears, both drying and fresh. "Why would anyone want to kill either of them?! I just don't understand!" She drooped, her back bowed, chin on her chest. She swept her hand through her unruly hair.

Evelyn looked down at the table, her cup encircled with both hands, lips pursed. She raised her head. "He's back." She moved her eyes about as though watching something no one else could see.

Alex recovered and sat up as she also heard the sound of a vehicle, first in front of the house, then as it moved slowly into the garage on the west side under the bedroom story. She stared at Evelyn, who was looking away, then looked around the room with a feeling of unease.

The engine sound stopped as the two women waited. Ten seconds after they heard doors opening and closing, Mark Cassidy entered the hall and came into the kitchen. He stood in silence, glanced at his sister, then looked at Alex. He wore a Levi's jacket over his trademark plaid shirt, and black denim pants over seasoned black western boots. His pants were held up with a broad leather belt whose buckle Alex reckoned was a turquoise-and-silver product of Navajo origin. He removed his well-worn, broad-brimmed western hat and laid it on the counter, crown down.

"Good morning," he said.

Evelyn cocked her head at him, then cast her eyes on Alex.

"Morning," Alex said, her voice a near whisper.

He turned to the counter, took a cup and poured coffee. "Sleep well?" He glanced at the woman from Texas.

Alex nodded, then, "Not real well, but okay for now." She managed a weak smile.

Cassidy brought his cup to the table and slid in along the padded seating, on his sister's side, beneath the windows. He reached for cream and a spoon. His brow crinkled up. "I guess you know the cops would like you to stick around for a couple of days." He sipped his coffee.

"Mark, I can't get over how much Evelyn looks like Betty!" She glanced at his sister.

Cassidy nodded emphatically. "Yes, quite true. An amazing coinci-dence."

He and Evelyn traded glances.

"I can't get over it," Alex said.

Cassidy nodded silently. "Listen—we need—you need—to advise your family. Two kids, right?"

"Yes." Alex nodded and sniffed.

"Mark, this lady needs something to eat. We all do," Evelyn slid out the end opposite the counter and rounded the table. In the kitchen area, she turned. "It's eggs and bacon, all. Tortillas or toast. Red or green. Fried 'taters. Papitas, as the locals call 'em. Or whatever." She spoke without looking as she moved toward the island counter.

"I don't know if I can eat," Alex said.

"Yes, you can. You need to," Evelyn said, reaching for a hanging, copper-clad frying pan. She pointed the pan at the other woman.

Her brother nodded assent. "She's right. You need to eat." He kept his eyes on her.

Alex nodded.

"So," Cassidy continued, "I have some contacts in Lubbock. I sug-gest we let them meet with your kids. Daughter and son, is it?" He slurped his coffee, then, without waiting for an answer, "At the same time you're on the phone with them. Might help ease the shock and all. Make sense?"

"Jackie's at home, but Jason's at school. University of Texas."

Undeterred, Cassidy went on. "Okay, well, we can work this out, but I have two points. One, they—the police—want you around, and I have guaranteed your presence, and second, you should not be traveling alone right now. So—" He tipped his cup high against his lips to drain the last of the brown liquid.

The two sitting at the table detected the aroma of bacon and turned their heads simultaneously to look at the source.

Alex ate almost as much as Cassidy; two eggs, bacon and diced, fried potatoes piled on a wheat tortilla slathered with red chile, while Evelyn consumed two slices of the fatty meat rolled into a tortilla with green chile. They all had juice and more coffee. Then Alex excused herself and went upstairs to bathe and dress.

Cassidy removed the used dishes and flat wear, then sat again. Evelyn positioned herself on the trestle bench and looked at her brother. "A mighty convenient coincidence, Mark." Her head bobbed as she turned to look at the stairs, then back.

"Yeah. I know. But I don't think—"

"Mark, this woman just happens to stumble onto this property in the middle of God-knows-where, then, miraculously, bumps into two bodies, one of which just happens to look a lot like me!" She pointed her finger at him, holding it there for a full five seconds.

Cassidy lowered and shook his head, took in a deep breath and blew it out. "I've those guys I told her about taking a look into her situation down there." He looked up. "Stop and think. Her husband was one of the victims. I understand fully your suspicions, but this whole thing has got to be nothing more than a fantastic coincidence." He leaned in, waved his hand and lowered his voice. "Look, I'm staying on top of it with the police. There's bound to be a simple answer that'll point away from what you're thinking." He sat back.

Evelyn stared hard at her brother. "They're coming for me, Mark. They're coming for me, goddamnit!" Her voiced had dropped to a whisper.

"We don't know that for sure, Evelyn!" He shook his head, eyes closed. "Not for sure."

"And you bring her back here!" She pointed toward the upper story.

"The better to watch her!" His voice carried a defensive modulation.

"Are you certain you weren't followed?"

"Certain."

"Jesus." She looked away.

They both went silent and turned their heads toward the stairs as they heard first one, then a second door close on the mezzanine.

Evelyn looked down at the table's surface, both arms on it, her hands folded. "I need to go. They're too close."

Cassidy leaned in again. "Ev, you don't know that. But if it's true, it's not safe to travel. This place is defensible!" He paused, stabbing his finger into the table top. "And if you're right, you know full well they have friends everywhere. The airports, the bus terminals, ports of entry—" He waved his arm. "Hell, the state police." He looked away and moderated his voice. "Jesus, Ev! Listen to me! I'm sounding paranoid." His voice was a decibel above a whisper.

She took in, then released a deep breath. "I know you're right, but it's instinctive for me to move."

"I know, I know. Natural instinct." He reached across the table and clutched her hand.

She looked up at him. "You know how brutal they can be." She squeezed his fingers in response.

"I know. Let me stay close to this thing in Santa Fé. And my people in Texas. Give it a couple of days, okay?" He leaned back and blew his breath out through pursed lips.

She nodded soberly. "Okay."

"I'll check the perimeter system."

"I'm gonna' take a look at the monitor tapes for the last twenty-four," she said.

"Right."

It was at that moment that Alex came off the stairs and into the kitchen. She wore a skirt, blouse and low-heeled shoes. Her hair was brushed, but she wore no makeup.

Cassidy looked at her critically, as a man, for the first time. She was a few pounds overweight, but maintained a good figure, which offset the fact. Shorter than his sister by an inch, and a "natural" blonde, he considered her pretty. He wondered why she and her husband had grown apart. He and his sister both smiled at her as she entered.

"Well, you're all spiffed up!" Cassidy said.

"I feel better, but honestly, I'm still tired. Kinda' drained, you know?" She looked first at Cassidy, then Evelyn.

"Hey, we understand, Alex," Evelyn said. She shot a glance at her brother.

Alex looked at Mark, both her hands fidgeting with each other at her waist. "Could we talk about telling my kids?"

Cassidy slid out and stood. "Absolutely."

## 5

W hile her brother, Mark, sat with Alex Petersen, plotting how they would handle telling the bad news to Alex' children, Evelyn Cassidy left them in the kitchen and went to the hallway that led to the garage. She stopped next to a door on the right, just short of the entrance to the garage, and looked back toward the hall that ran from the main part of the house to the west-side exterior. She heard the muted voices coming from the dining table.

She used a key that shared a ring with other two other keys in a rear pants pocket, unlocked the door, entered, then shut and locked it. She flicked the wall switch, and a lamp on a desk across the room brightened. The footprint of the room was the same as the bedroom above, but offset, and because it was situated between the living room and hall walls, was windowless. On one side was a desk with a computer screen, keyboard, mouse and other office paraphernalia. The screen was dark. Above it, mounted on the wall, was a flat TV screen with black-and-white scenes of the house exterior which changed to four different views every five seconds. She stared up at the security monitor and waited for the scenes of the narrow road taken by two cameras, one to the left, the other to the right. Both lacked traffic.

She went to the desk, used a key to unlock and open a file drawer, and removed a 9 mm semi-automatic Walther P99 A/S. She pulled the slide back, checked the breach, set the safety "on," then inserted it into a small hip holster and clipped it to her waist band. She pulled her hair together, wound it up and over her head, preventing it from cascading onto her shoulders, and pinned it into place. From a shelf over the desk, she removed a pair of dark glasses and shoved them into her blouse pocket.

She tugged her blouse out and away from her waist, making sure its material covered the weapon, then retraced her route to the living area end of the hall. She looked toward the dining area. Her brother and their sad visitor sat across from each other at the table, each with a portable phone to their ear. She then took a dark blue windbreaker and a Harvard hat from a row of wall pegs and donned them both. She put the sun glasses on and went to the outside door, where she emerged into the sunny morning for her coveted solitary nature and safety inspection tour.

The following morning, Cassidy, in his Jeep, followed Alex in her Ford SUV at a safe distance south through Pecos until she reached the north-bound on ramp to the Interstate which would lead her to secondary highways and the Texas panhandle. In his heightened state of awareness, he studied his rearview all the way; even scrutinizing the only vehicle to pass when an impatient local in a pickup, its bed empty, roared around both as they made their way through the National Monument grounds.

He had argued that she needed company on her trip; or at least a caravan car, but she declined. Anxious to return to her family, she insisted on leaving. He asked her to let him know the instant she arrived. She agreed to do so.

They waved at each other, arms high, as he peeled off onto the south-bound ramp, headed back toward Glorieta, El Dorado and Santa Fé, then got off at the Glorieta-Pecos exit. As he entered the Interstate, he keyed the number for the Santa Fé Police Department into his cell phone. He'd have to do it here, since the little communication device was useless at his house in the canyon. He asked for Sergeant Griego, but was told the detective would have to call him back.

Near the four-way junction of New Mexico 50 and 63, he turned right, and pulled into the paved, but unmarked, parking lot of the Pecos Country Store. There, he bought a copy of *The Santa Fé New Mexican*, the *Las Vegas Optic*, and picked up two more free local papers. He looked around, nodded to a clerk and a man and a woman whom he didn't know, but who recognized him as a sometime patron, and exited.

As he walked to his Jeep, a man in his sixties passed. The man nodded and said, "Mornin' Mr. Carmichael."

"Morning, Jake," Cassidy answered.

As he got back into his car, his cell phone chirped.

"Hello?"

"Mr. Cassidy? Sergeant Griego. You called?"

"Yes. Thanks for getting back to me."

"What can I do for you, Mr. Cassidy?"

"I'm calling regarding the murder the other night. Mrs. Petersen?" He framed it as a question.

"Right. What would you like to know?"

"Well, I'd like to know where you are with the case, but the main reason I called was to inform you that Mrs. Petersen has headed home to be with her children and start clearing up some problems that have arisen as a result of her husband's death. I'm sure you can understand."

"Well, Mr. Cassidy, I sure do understand, but I thought we had an agreement that she'd stick around until we're finished with her. We left her in your care; your recognizance. We agreed she'd be your responsibility."

"I'm fully aware, sergeant, but she's really a mess. I wasn't wild about letting her go, but she's shouldering a real burden right now. She'll return. Now—"

"Thing is, Mr. Cassidy, we were counting on you. It's an unofficial request, but—"

"Sergeant, look, two things. One, she'll be back. Two, I have two operatives in Lubbock who'er helping me with this, and I've charged them with not only watching over her, but ensuring she returns. But, you know, I'm not quite sure how much more help she could be."

There was a three second pause, then, "Okay, Cassidy, you're right, but we have procedure to follow. I hope I don't have to go to a judge and get a warrant."

"I doubt seriously that will be necessary. Alex—Mrs. Petersen—wants to know as much as you all do, and she'll be back. She also has some personal things at the Nolan residence she needs to recover." Cassidy knew Griego was bluffing, but didn't want to antagonize the man, so let the remark pass. He also knew that Alex Petersen had next to nothing to recover at the Nolan house.

"Yeah, okay. You stay in touch, okay?"

"I'm offering any help I can as well, Sergeant. Anything new?"

"Nada. As I told you, odd as it seems, it looks more and more like a 'hit.' I can't reveal any more than that, but I can say we've got an FBI profiler and the State Police in on this. Advisory roles. So far, they come up with the same conclusion. Look, that's more than I should say, but for some reason I trust you, even if you are a lawyer" He laughed, then sobered. "Don't disappoint me."

"Thanks for your trust, sergeant. I won't."

"'Kay. Hey—when's she due back? Mrs. Petersen."

"Within the week. Couple 'a days. Have a good one, sergeant."

"Okay. Let me know. Bye."

Cassidy sat for a few seconds, scanning the parking lot and thinking over his conversation. He picked up first the *New Mexican*, then the *Optic*, looked at the headlines, read the first two paragraphs of a story about a corrupt politician in the *Optic*, then started the engine.

# 6

Despite her mid-morning departure from Pecos and then Mark Cassidy, who had seen her off from the Rowe exit, Alessandra—Alex—Peterson entered the Lubbock ring road with the sun to her right and ten degrees above the horizon. She had stopped in a Santa Rosa truck stop for lunch. Although hungry, she could take on nothing more than a milk shake, and only half of that. The nausea that came shortly after held her captive in the truck stop lady's rest room for half an hour. The remainder of the trip was slow going, since she barely drove the speed limit, and much of the time under it.

The ring road was packed with fast traffic as usual, and despite her life-long residency in the west Texas town, nearly missed her off ramp, almost causing an accident as she veered across two lanes of traffic amid the cacophony of angry horns responding to her misdeed.

Even if she had been alert as she rocked her big, red Ford up the shallow concrete ramp onto her driveway, she would not have noticed the innocuous, light blue sedan parked half a block away and on the opposite side of the street. Two men in their thirties, one white, the other black, sat patiently, watching her house. With paper coffee cups in hand, they had seen the small General Motors car belonging to Alex' daughter, Jackie, arrive and park on one side of the wide apron that fronted the two-car garage of the big house. They had watched, wordlessly, as the young woman emerged and went inside not more than two hours before. Now they watched as her mother came home.

"What now?" the black man in the driver's seat, asked.

His partner shrugged. "We're being paid to watch and wait. Guess we watch and wait."

The driver made a face of resignation, peered into his empty paste board container, then tossed it into the rear of the car. "Let's call the guy."

"Right." The white man reached for the cell phone that rested on the dash, flipped it open and keyed in a series of numbers. He waited, then, with the little instrument to his ear, spoke into it. "Yeah, hi. Mama just got in. Looks like the girl's there, too. Right, the daughter. She was carrying books. You know, like college. We're across the street. Don't think we've been spotted, but sitting here makes us nervous. We think we oughta' move. What's next?"

Mark Cassidy had entered the kitchen from the garage when he heard the muffled ring. It took him a second to react, then made for the mantel over the fireplace, where he grabbed a small key and opened the roll-top desk. He picked up the receiver. "Yes?" He listened, then said, "I agree. Leave the area. I expect you to watch your backs. Get back tomorrow morning with a different operative and in a different car if you can. Stay with her to her office. You guys came highly recommended, and you're supposed to know the town, so do your best. I think she's clean, so in a day or two, I'll want your boss to contact her and offer assistance. Okay? Okay. And let me know if you think you're being followed." He hung up, cradled the phone and locked the desk. Then he stood staring at the floor for half a minute.

"So?" It was his sister, who stood behind him on the flagstone walkway from the front door to the rear of the house.

He turned. "The people in Lubbock. Detectives I hired."

"And?" Her arms were folded across her midriff.

"And, so far, so good. That is to say, nothing unusual." He walked toward her, waving his hand as though to brush the question aside.

She nodded and studied her shoes. "I hope you're right, Mark."

He stopped shortly before the walkway whose level was six inches higher than the hardwood covered living area and looked at her. After a five second hesitation, he said, "Evelyn, what we have here is an odd coincidence. Nothing more."

She shook her head. Her voice was low and controlled. "This woman, out of the blue, shows up here, just happens to fall in the creek. She's inside this house—which is supposed to be safe and secure—then stumbles onto a double murder. One of the deceased is a woman who just happens to strongly resemble me. How do we know—?" She wagged her finger at him.

"Evelyn, listen to me. I know. I know. Don't you think all this has occurred to me? But think. The time line doesn't work. I checked with the police. The murders went down while she was here. She had no means of communication. She didn't know you. And how would she have tracked you down? No. She's an ordinary woman from an ordinary town, who just got in the middle of something. She's clueless." He pursed his lips and held his palms out at waist level. "And," he added, "one of the victims was her husband."

She looked away, down, then up. "You're sure of that?"

"Cops checked it out. ID'd through Lubbock police." He shrugged in exasperation.

"Okay. Sorry. You're right."

"Plus, we don't know if there's a connection with you. The murders. We just don't know."

She nodded.

"I'm staying on it, Ev."

"I know you are. Thanks." She moved to him, her head now the same level as his, leaned over and hugged him, then backed away and sighed heavily.

"Hey, it's scary. I can't know how you feel, but I can imagine."

She faced him again and nodded. "I am scared, Mark. Those bastards are good at their jobs."

"Yeah? Then why so many fuck-ups?"

She smiled wryly and nodded quickly. "Mm. True. And one of the reasons they want me." She pointed at herself.

"Yes." He was silent, then said, "The investigators down there are staying on her. They're going to contact her and make sure she gets back here before Griego—the detective—gets antsy. I promised him she'd be back."

"She gonna' stay here?"

"Problem for you if she does?"

"Under the circumstances, no, but how do we know she won't lead someone here we don't want?" She furrowed her brow and squinted.

"I've thought of that. Number one, I can't believe anyone connected with her would be connected to your old buddies. Two, the police don't know where we live. Once she's here, we'll control her movements." He paused. "When she comes back, I'll convoy her in from Romeroville. She'll stay in town for a bit first."

Evelyn dropped down onto the main floor, went to one of the leather over-stuffed chairs and plopped into it. She ran her hand through her hair. "I'm sorry. I must seem like an ingrate. You've put your own business and career on hold just to help me. It's not fair. You must be losing big time." She looked across the room at nothing.

He followed her down and walked to one of the windows that fronted the house-long porch. He peered out, moving his head. "Not really. I've told the partners I needed time to write a book. I have investments."

"But for how long?"

He shrugged, his back to her.

"We've been here, what? Eight months?"

"Close to nine, and you're recovering from cancer."

"Jesus Christ! This could take forever!" She pounded the arm of the chair with her fist.

He turned and drew in a deep breath. "Yeah, I know. But I don't think so."

"Oh? You think they're gonna give up? That they have a red 'X' on a calendar that says 'We don't need to find her now'?"

He shook his head with a crooked smile. "No."

"Then what?!"

He moved to the long sofa across from her and sat forward, on the front edge. "You wait out the hearings. Didn't you tell me there were at least two others in your same situation?"

"Yeah, yeah." She looked away, then back. "But I don't know if they're alive or not. And I sure as hell can't contact them. Even if I knew their whereabouts." She paused. "They're afraid I'll show up at the hearings, Mark. Last thing they want."

"Granted. So we wait it out." He looked at her hard. "You still want to testify?"

She uttered a mocking laugh. "Still? Wanting to and doing it are two different things." She paused. "Yes and no. What good would it do? They're going to get away with murder. You know that. The way this country has gone. Shit!"

He nodded assent, and moved back.

"Bucket of goddamn worms."

"Yep." He waited, then, "How you feeling? Really."

"Okay. Not bad." She raised an eyebrow.

"How much longer?"

"The meds?"

"Yes."

She sighed. "Two more months on these, then they change 'em."

"Well, you're gonna beat it."

"Hope so." She sat back with an air of resignation.

# 7

J eremy Radcliff stood looking out his studio window into the sunny back yard, shadowed, in part, by the house in the late afternoon sun. He watched as Mandy, his two-year old calico cat, stalked an insect, creeping along, her stomach fur brushing the tall, unkempt grass of the lawn in dire need of mowing. He moved to his left so he could see where she was going, tilting his head to look past one of the wood mullions of the old window, deep-set into the thick adobe wall of the house. Mandy made a leap and disappeared behind a hollyhock just short of the dilapidated garden wall of stripped cedar—a so-called "coyote fence"—which leaned precariously from years of neglect. Beyond and high above the fence, the stark blue sky was divided sharply from the green-pocked hills south of Santa Fé.

He stepped back, looked up with pursed lips to consider the dark ceiling of hand-adzed *vigas* and rough planks, then down at the postcard in his right hand. He peered at it, holding it out at arm's length as though it were contaminated. He re-read the short message, then slapped his left palm with it, turned and moved slowly across the red brick floor of the studio, past the incomplete clay bust sculpture and to the hall door. In the kitchen, he fired up a front burner on the gas stove, lit the card and let it burn to ash in the sink before flushing it with the garbage disposal running. As the last of the blackened paper swirled into the drain, he looked through the window above the sink. The long graveled drive that led down to the old road to Pecos and the interstate beyond was clear. Above that he saw the late sun glint off the distant Ortiz and the Sandia Mountains farther to the south. He leaned forward, looked first to his left, then to his right, scouring his front yard. Nothing but his pickup truck.

He looked at his wrist watch, an instinct he had tried, but failed, to eradicate from his life, so deeply ingrained from the years within corporate, then government, environments. He reckoned the time to be half past three in the afternoon. The news would be on soon, but he had time to do one more thing. If nothing else, the one thing he had had drilled into his psyche, both from training and experience, was to have the tools of his old trade ready and in top condition, even now.

The bedroom he had converted to an office was in the rear corner of the house, farthest from the front. It was dim without the high-intensity lamps on the desk burning. Its one window was the cause, curtained as it was with dark cloth, mainly so he could more easily see the computer monitor screen. But that, too, was a part of him; a tendency toward secretiveness. Today, he was glad it was that way; not that it was remotely likely anyone would observe what he was about to do.

He closed the door to the hall and set the privacy lock, then went to the three-drawer filing cabinet next to the computer desk. He tapped the locking mechanism at the base with his booted toe, releasing the wheel brake, then rolled the tall steel box out and away from the thick wall behind it. In the open space created by his effort, a steel plate approximating the dimensions of the filing cabinet and the color of the brick that surrounded it was revealed. This he tilted up and leaned against the wall. Under that was a steel door with crinkled grey paint and a combination lock. He moved his lips silently as he twisted the dial back and forth, quoting the numbers, then pulled the heavy lid open after twisting the T-bar handle. Inside the safe was a blue steel box with a chromed handle which he removed and took to the table across the room.

With a key on a chain around his neck, he unlocked the box and opened it. He pulled a heavy, red cloth-covered bundle out, laid it on the table, and unwrapped it. The .22 caliber Walther semiautomatic pistol that lay there glistened with gun oil that coated its blue-black surface. Using a second cloth, he picked it up, pulled the slide back, inspected the empty breach, barrel and magazine chamber, then let the slide snap home. He inserted a full magazine and pulled the trigger as he eased the hammer down against the safety-protected firing pin. A drop of perspiration fell onto the weapon. He removed his steel-rimmed glasses, pulled a handkerchief from his pants pocket, and wiped his forehead. He shook his head, craned his neck to reduce the stiffness that had grown there, and frowned. This should not be happening, he thought.

He picked up a second loaded magazine, looked it over, laid it down, then wiped away the film of oil from the pistol. Next, he pulled a small, black, leather-covered voice recorder from the box, opened a tiny door that covered half the back side, and looked inside. He would install batteries later. He reached into the box and removed a second object wrapped in thick cotton cloth. This he unwrapped to reveal a four-inch long suppressor. He picked it up with one hand while lifting the pistol with the other, then fitted the two together. He thought for a moment, separated the two pieces, and returned the cylinder to its cloth wrapping and the box along with the extra magazine.

He pulled a small, black leather holster with a blue steel belt clip from the box, returned the box to the safe and covered the pit in the concrete underfloor. He then wheeled the cabinet into place over the cache. He took the gun and holster, went to his bedroom and slipped them under his bed pillow. In the kitchen, he removed two "AA" batteries from the refrigerator and went to the living room, where he turned the television set on. He sat, put the batteries in the hand-size tape recorder, and tested it while waiting for the picture to come up.

At six-thirty in the morning, Radcliff was up, alternately sipping coffee and orange juice while still in his underwear. He placed food and water for Mandy, then ate a breakfast of fried eggs, Canadian bacon, green chile and buttered wheat toast. After a shower and dressing, he spent an hour working on the sculpture. He stood back to look it over, then covered the big piece of clay with a wet cloth.

In his bedroom, he fitted the holster to his belt near the base of his spine. He pulled the Walther's slide back and released it, forcing a cartridge into the breach, let the hammer down carefully and checked the safety before inserting the semiautomatic into the belt holster. He grabbed a nylon windbreaker from the closet, put it on and zipped up the front half so the billowing back covered the lump at his belt line. After ensuring the recorder was working and in his jacket pocket, he walked through the house, checked all the openings, set the alarm and went out through the front door. He stood for thirty seconds, getting used to the bright morning sun under a broad-brimmed, tan fedora which protected a full head of dark, but greying hair. A pair of large sun glasses covered the eyes of his narrow face. His reading glasses rested in his shirt pocket. He was five feet, nine inches tall, trim, and wore khaki pants. The cotton shirt under his tan windbreaker was dark blue. He heard the thumping of a boom-box to his right, beyond the piñon and sage that covered his property to the road. The sound moved as he watched the Perez teenager pass slowly by the opening to the main road in his lowered Chevy, windows down so all could enjoy the latest rap tune. He studied his own vehicle, a dark blue Ford 150 pickup, from front to rear, then got down on his knees and looked under it. Nothing unusual. Realizing his heart rate was up, he resolved to calm himself; to stop thinking in the old ways. Those were over—or were supposed to be.

He pulled into the west end of the De Vargas mall and parked at the end of an empty row, near the exit. He sat for a moment, studying the lot through each window and the rearview mirrors, outside and inside. The place was empty but for a delivery truck negotiating a turn around the west end of a building behind him. He emerged, locked the truck, adjusted the bulky firearm and made his way to the mall with its thick pine posts holding up a traditional pueblo-style porch. He walked past the main south entrance, moved on to the newspaper racks outside the drug store and bought a copy of the daily *Santa Fé New Mexican*.

He stood for a moment, opened the paper, then turned so he could see the parking lot and people who came and went. Pretending to read, he moved slowly back toward the mall entrance. There, he stopped and leaned against the west side support post. Five minutes passed before he noticed a gray GMC pickup truck move slowly from the Paseo into the lot, turn right and park carefully between a set of lines. A man emerged, put on a light grey cowboy hat and walked to Starbuck's.

Radcliff watched the man disappear inside, then continued to stand and scour the lot. He folded the paper, pushed away from the post, crossed to the parking lot and walked by the truck. He looked inside without stopping, moved on to the Paseo sidewalk, then turned and strolled back toward Starbuck's. As he approached, the man in the western hat came out with a paper cup in one hand and a bulky napkin in the other. The man sat at one of the umbrella-protected tables and opened the napkin as Radcliff entered the coffee shop.

He paid for coffee and went out onto the patio, the paper still under his arm. He stood at the low, stuccoed perimeter wall, looking first to the clear western sky, then at the spring-green mountains to his left, still covered in white on the upper reaches. He turned toward the man in the grey hat, who had begun to read a newspaper. He waited another half minute before strolling to the man's table. As he did, he slid the power button on the voice recorder in his jacket to the "on" position.

"Nice hat," he said.

The man looked up. "Thanks." His accent was flat; eastern.

"Stetson?"

The man took a moment, then replied, "Resistol."

"I've heard they're good." Radcliff looked him over. The man wore blue jeans, a checked shirt under a Levi's jacket and black street shoes.

"I like it." The man peered up through dark clip-ons that covered his glasses.

"Expensive?" Radcliff sipped his coffee, raising his eyebrows.

"Have a seat," the man said, jerking his chin. "This one was not as much as I could have spent. Twenty X."

Radcliff nodded, pulled a plastic chair out and sat. He put his vapor-emitting coffee on the table next to the unread paper. "No boots." He nodded toward the man's feet.

He smiled. "Can't find any that fit."

"I could make some suggestions."

"Live around here?" The man asked, ignoring Radcliff's offer.

Radcliff was barely able to see the man's eyes as they flicked from his face to his immediate surroundings, as though he were expecting someone. "Santa Fé, yes."

"Nice weather. Dry, though, no?"

"I prefer it. The sun." Radcliff gestured skyward with his chin.

The man tapped the table unconsciously with his finger, turned his head around to look at the parking lot, then back at the café door before returning his gaze to Radcliff. "I take it you received your mail?"

Radcliff picked up his coffee, took a long drink and set it down. "I don't know you. Who are you?"

The man cracked a thin, knowing smile and looked down briefly, then up. "For the sake of what I'm about to say, and our relationship, you can call me Beakman."

"We don't have a relationship, Mr. Beakman." Radcliff's voice was low, but sharp. He sipped at the coffee again, giving himself time. "How the hell did you know to find me?! And a Pocatello postmark? Who do you know there?"

Beakman tapped the table again, then wiped away imaginary dirt with all four fingers and thumb. He shook his head almost imperceptibly, lifted his chin, looked down imperiously and raised one eyebrow. "*Vee heff our vays!*" He smiled, then sobered. "You should know better than that, Jeremy."

Radcliff shifted in his chair. He felt like jumping up, pulling the Walther, stuffing it into Beakman's mouth and pulling the trigger. He looked away, then down, forced a smile, then stared at the man in the cowboy hat. "We? We. Yeah, we. And you know my full name. I'll wager I'm looking at a company man."

Beakman remained silent as he continued to clean the table idly and stare at Radcliff.

"Right," Radcliff sighed. "A company man." He paused, looking away in reserved anger, then back. "So, to what do I owe this visit? Got a check for me? Some back pay for all the goddamn shit that went down? A long overdue medal for meritorious service?"

Beakman leaned forward, took a bite of the roll he had carried in the napkin, carefully dusted the sugar from his hands, then sipped his cooling latté. "Not precisely. Fact is, the company requires your services."

"Services?!" Radcliff lowered his head and looked at the other man from under his eyebrows. He turned his head hard left to glance at a woman who had taken the table a few feet away, but who was engrossed with her coffee and a paperback book. He lowered his voice to a stage whisper.

"Requires?! I'm retired! I have the IRA deposits to prove it! Go peddle you papers!" He stood, took a last draft from his paper cup, grabbed his newspaper and turned to leave.

"Morning Glory," Beakman said without rising.

Radcliff stopped but didn't turn around. His face clouded into a deep frown.

Beakman stood, took a last bite from the roll, wiped his hands with a flourish, adjusted his Resistol, then moved past Radcliff. "Let's take a stroll."

Radcliff stared after the man as he walked away without turning, then followed. He pulled up alongside as they walked westward along the mall front. "What about Morning Glory, Beakman?"

Beakman continued to face forward. "I've read the file."

"Goddamnit, Beakman, that action was righteous! The company knows it and you know it!" His breath was coming fast. "Who the fuck are you, anyway?! How the hell do I know you're with the company?" He jerked his head around, fearful his voice was carrying, and that someone would overhear.

Beakman continued his pace. "RASCON? Operation Hollow Breath? Frances Vizzigotti? Familiar?"

"Yeah, sure, but you could have picked those up from—"

Both men stopped as Beakman turned to face Radcliff. "How? How could I have? Those were all code blue ops. Deep cover. Strict need-to-know. Thing is, Radcliff, you may have been a company man for eighteen years, but I've been there for nearly ten, now, and I ain't exactly your junior G-man. I run with the alpha dogs." He bored in with his dark-covered eyes.

Radcliff nodded, looked away, then back. "Yeah, I guess so."

Beakman reached into his jacket pocket, pulled out a coin and handed it to Radcliff.

Radcliff looked at it, walked a few feet away, then came back. "Where'd you get this?"

"Charlie said I'd need it. With his compliments."

Radcliff turned the coin over in his hand. He sighed. "So, what do you want?"

"Charlie doesn't want to open a can of worms. None of us do, but one will be opened unless you help us."

"Why me? There're younger guys." He pointed away at nothing.

"It's here. And you're the best. You are the best, right?"

"What? What's here?!"

"The job." Beakman shifted his weight and checked the empty lot where they now stood. He tilted his head. "The job is here. Santa Fé, maybe. Close for sure."

Radcliff squinted at the other man. "Here? Who?" What?! Gimme, Beakman—or whatever your name is!" He waggled his fingers in the come-on gesture.

Beakman took in a deep breath and let it out. "Problem. We don't know for sure. Only thing we do know is it's a woman. She lives somewhere in northern New Mexico."

"A woman?! And you want me to—"

Beakman pursed his lips, eyes closed.

"Jesus."

"This is serious shit, Radcliff. Serious. Could take us all down. You, too." Beakman lowered his head, looking at Radcliff from under his eyebrows.

"Bullshit." He looked away, disgust marking his features.

Beakman shook his head in a single side jerk. "Morning Glory."

"You can't hold that over me!"

"That's part of it. You know how easy it is to make stuff up." He hesitated. "Got access to the internet?"

"Yeah, sure."

"Go to this site. Use these passwords." He held out a business card.

Radcliff took it without looking. "Do I know this person? This woman?"

Beakman shook his head. "Nope. Good thing, too. Don't want her spotting you."

"And you? Where will you be?"

"I understand there're some nice hotels here."

Radcliff looked over Beakman's shoulder toward the parking lot.

"The truck. Where'd you get it?"

"Rental."

"Goes with the hat, I suppose." Radcliff nodded, a wry smile momentarily creasing his face.

"I suppose."

"You live here now?" Radcliff squinted with his question.

"No. Beltway rat." Beakman paused. "We need to move quickly, Radcliff. Get on the net. Today. I'll be in touch."

Radcliff stared as the other man looked at him squarely, then turned and walked away. When Beakman was half-way to his vehicle, Radcliff pulled the little recorder out of his jacket pocket, switched it from record to rewind, waited for the tape to stop, then set it to play. The voices, although muffled by the jacket cloth, were intelligible.

Beakman turned left at the light on the Paseo and made his way up and out of the city proper, onto Hyde Park Road. He pulled over onto a wide swath of dirt shoulder on the right after the road flattened out before its ascent into the mountains beyond. He parked and shut the engine off. He studied the images in the rearview mirrors, then craned his head around. From his vantage point, he saw the Sangre de Cristo in front of him, the city below and to his right, the plain and the mountain ranges farther to the south. The sun was mid-morning high and intense in a cloudless, dense-blue sky.

Satisfied he had not been followed, he removed the cellular phone from his belt, shoved his dark glasses up onto his forehead, and keyed a number. When he heard the ringing, he lowered his sun glasses over his eyes, resumed his watch out the windshield and waited.

"Jerico corporation," a female voice said.

"Customer service, please," Beakman said. He watched a pickup truck, loaded with lumber, pass on the asphalt road.

Four seconds later, a male voice came on the line. "Customer service. Your customer number, please."

Beakman quoted it.

"One moment, please."

After another five second wait, two clicks and a hum, another male voice. "How may I help you?"

"Yes, the first merchandise was the wrong size, but I received the replacement. It came today. This morning, in fact."

"Very good. Anything else?"

"No. Payment will be in the mail."

"Thank you, sir. Goodbye."

"Bye." Beakman, folded the cellular phone closed, returned it to his belt and started the engine. It was then that he emitted a long sigh.

# 8

Radcliff stood for several seconds and watched Beakman leave the Vargas parking lot and turn left, east, onto the Paseo. He walked quickly to the boulevard and watched the grey pickup go through the intersection and continue toward the mountains. Only after the truck had disappeared from view did he go to his own vehicle. He got in, closed the door, and removed the uncomfortable Walther from his rear waistband and laid it on the seat, an act that made his possession of the firearm legal. He pulled the card Beakman had given him from his shirt pocket, opened his window and sat for two minutes, absorbing the encounter. The little piece of pasteboard contained the address of an Internet site and a series of alphanumeric access codes and passwords.

It was late morning by the time he had stopped for groceries, cold Mexican beer and a bottle of Australian red wine. The latter was purchased with the promise of female company later. He sat for a few seconds in front of his house, concentrating on the four, deep-set, twelve-light windows ranged along the front of the building that seemed to peer at him as though alive. He felt invaded and vulnerable and shook his head in disgust. His initial feeling was depression, but it quickly changed to a flash of controlled anger.

He slammed out of his truck, gathered the groceries from the bed and entered the house as Mandy appeared from nowhere and raced inside along with him. He put everything away as the cat whipped her tail, whined and cajoled him by rubbing against his pant legs. He spooned a large dollop of her favorite food into her dish, freshened her water, then headed for the back room and the computer. He locked the door and clicked on the high-intensity lamp next to the machine, the sole light in the room.

The Internet site looked like many others, with nothing about it that would suggest a government connection. It was built as a "dot com" site offering a line of high-tech electronic communications gear. After navigating through several layers of pages which would have been obscure and unusable to the uninitiated, he was asked for his sign-on name and password. Three pages later, he was required to enter another password, which resulted in the down-loading of yet another program, this one encrypted. Two minutes later, a warning appeared, telling him the new software resident on his hard drive would self-delete after five minutes. The image of a clock popped up in the upper right corner, and began to count down. It was accompanied by a ticking sound. He was then required to provide a third set of IDs.

Without preamble, a dossier appeared on the screen. It was of a woman, and began with well-focused head shots. They included a frontal, two side views and three of her in casual encounters with others, each of which covered the entire screen. It then reduced until half the monitor was filled with biographical information.

Her code name was "Wraith," real name Evelyn Thomas Cassidy. It revealed elements of her history such as birthplace, education and career, starting with her first job with the Company. Secretary, then code clerk, followed by desk analyst for South and Central America, then Europe, the Middle East, and finally covert field operative. Her assignments had been in European capitols, South America, and a short stint in Beirut. She had been under one or two control agents known to Radcliff, including one who had served as interim Director for a time. Under duress, and not because of any action that would have landed her in prison, but rather because of internal pressures, and after nearly a quarter century of service, she was retired with a full pension. She had disappeared soon after selling her house in suburban Alexandria. Possibilities were Canada, Kansas, Mexico, the south of France, the Netherlands and Denmark. Last confirmed sighting: Vancouver, Washington. Contact Requirement Level: Urgent. Need: Completion of "Q" secure files, Director level. It was believed she had secure, discreet connections in New Mexico.

A warning banner crawled across the center of the screen. Radcliff had two minutes left and counting, and he would not be able to access the account again for at least twenty-four hours. He wondered if they could worm out his multi-digit ISP address. Silly thought; of course they could. They were probably logging it then and there. Good thing he had no web cam, he thought. Someone behind Beakman was most likely watching his every keystroke and mouse click. Did he have help—local or otherwise?

Classified "Q" level encrypted files, Director access. Cute. He knew perfectly well the Director knew nothing of this. Or did he? "Q" files? A baboon's ass. Someone inside knew—or thought he or she knew—that the Wraith knew something that could end careers. Possibly send people to jail or scurrying to the far corners. Ruin profitable businesses. Beneficial scams. Maybe she did, and maybe she didn't, but that didn't matter. In the Company, cleaning house was the rule, no matter who got hurt—or terminated. Right. Clean house.

The dossier evaporated and the screen returned to the "home page" as he heard the hard drive scrambling to delete and wash the download, under direction of the embedded, clock-driven shred and wash—with "bleach"—command.

He killed the power to the computer, clicked off the lamp, then sat in the dark. Where was he supposed to begin? And why should he? What could they do to him if he refused? Would he have to disappear? He knew someone in Cuernavaca. And so did the Company and their friends in the Federales. He was dragged into Morning Glory, not knowing what it was for, but deeply involved before he could protest or resign. Was that what it was all about? Someone in the agency had framed all of them. Two were dead. Natural causes, it says here next to the asterisk. The others were somehow nowhere to be found. And where did the Wraith—Evelyn Cassidy—figure in? He'd never heard of her until now. Had she been watching the store? Did she stumble across something she wasn't supposed to see? See something ex-pat? Hear something? None of the above?

You're the appointed—and anointed—janitor, Radcliff, he thought. Clean house. Shit.

He sighed.

In the dark, with the only sound his own slow breathing, something began to bother him. There, in the back of his mind. Yes. But what? The dossier photo. Something about it triggered a memory. But what?

He stood abruptly, opened the door onto the hall washed in bright sun from the skylight he had installed in the flat roof. He strode to the door which led to the garage. The crowded external room was dominated by an old Volvo sedan. The periphery of the room featured the typical cast-off-but-don't-throw-away-stuff, narrow work bench, peg board tool wall and various outside tools. There was one thing more: a pile of discarded newspapers. He bent down and riffled through the neat stack of *Santa Fé New Mexicans;* more than two weeks worth. They were in "chron order," another of his subconscious bows to his regulated past. Four days. There it was. Front page. Double murder in the "city different." Man and woman found murdered. No witnesses. Police baffled, in part because there was no apparent break-in, no drugs found, no weapon, etc.

He studied the photos. One Theodore "Ted" Petersen and one Betty Nolan; he of Texas, she of here.

He sucked in his breath, then blew it out through tightened lips. "Jesus Christ!" he said under his breath. "Jesus fucking Christ!"

The sun was setting over the rolling hills between his place and the plateau that swept southwest to the Rio Grande when the little red sedan rolled into the drive. He was drawn to the kitchen window with the crunching sound of pea gravel under slow-moving tires. His hands were red and sticky from working Chimayó red chile powder, raw egg, garlic powder and chopped onions into fresh, ground bison. He wore an apron tied around his waist that he felt made him look silly on his male frame. He leaned over the sink and peered out. Behind him was an island work counter with an integrated cutting board at one end. It was cluttered with pans, bowls, plates, onions, red chile powder, cheese, eggs, tomatoes, garlic, sesame seed buns and assorted condiments. A glass of dark beer, half full, graced the wet counter.

Patsy Romero was all of five foot three, and moved in a manner Radcliff liked to describe as similar to a humming bird with the same boundless energy. Her dainty, bright smile that graced her smooth, olive skin that shone against her shiny, black hair pulled back against her head into a pair of braids had knocked him off his feet when he first laid eyes on her. No less happened as she bounced through the front door and into the kitchen.

She cocked her head at him as she thumped a large bag of citrus fruit up on the sink counter, then ran up to him, pressed against him and kissed him on the mouth. He wrapped his arms around her, careful not to touch her with his meat-stained hands as she moaned sexy sounds and wriggled against him.

She backed off and grinned, both her hands tugging on his belt. "Ooh, you handsome man!"

Radcliff merely shook his head and looked lovingly at her with a wide grin.

"So, what are you making?!" She circled the island. "Ooh, buffalo burgers! I love 'em!" She raised a triumphal fist.

"Don't let the fellows down at the museum hear you say that. Bison. No buffalo." He smiled, his red-stained hands dangling at his sides. "Only in zoos."

"Yes, right. Bison. I forget. But you forgive me, no?" She smiled coquettishly.

Radcliff resumed working the bowl of meat. "You are more than forgiven, *chiquita!*"

The thick bison burgers were great and filling, Radcliff and Patsy finished the wine, watched a movie on DVD, then went to bed and made love. Since she had to be at the hospital to begin her nursing shift in pre-natal early, she kissed him goodnight and left shortly after midnight.

He tried to sleep, but couldn't. He arose in the dark, left the lights off, and looked out his bedroom window, then padded into the living room in his bare feet and underwear and looked out there as well. He had the distinct feeling that Beakman or someone under his control might be watching him. He saw nothing. Paranoia. Stop it. Why would they watch him? He knew he could list a dozen reasons, but decided against it.

He went to the back room, closed the door before flicking the desk lamp on, grabbed the phone book and opened it on the desk to the "Cs." He knew looking for his quarry in the local phone directory would prove a waste of time, but realized if he didn't go through the motions, it would bother him from then on. Cassidys, yes; five. No Evelyns, or "Cassidy, E." If she were even anywhere near, and knew she was a target, would she be crazy enough to advertise? On the other hand, if she were nearby and circulated in public, she most likely would be unaware of the danger. How the hell was he supposed to find her?

He fired up the computer, connected to the Internet and navigated to the Google site. Thousands of Cassidys. Several Evelyns. Professor of Ancient Greek Architecture. Actress. Attorneys. Physicians. No Evelyn Cassidy, ex-spook, sought for secret crimes against whomever.

Sleep did not come easily, but it did, roiled with thoughts of what he was about to do. Or try to do.

# 9

Radcliff sat on the tall wooden stool he used while sculpting, his apron-covered legs splayed onto the floor, his hands resting on his thighs.

Mandy, the calico cat, purring after a fine breakfast of Iams' best, thanked her owner—not her master—by weaving in and out of his legs in a figure eight pattern, tail high, before exiting to an important mission in another part of the house.

He studied the clay bust upon which he had been working lo, these many weeks, but did not really see it. What he saw instead was Evelyn Cassidy's digital photo and a newspaper half-tone image of the woman whose body had been discovered recently in a Santa Fé residence not far from him.

He looked at his watch. Beakman had signaled a need for a meeting with an encrypted Email, and he was due in little less than an hour. Radcliff seriously entertained the idea of eliminating this madman, but he also realized that Beakman was the proverbial "tip of the iceberg." Other shadowy figures stood behind him, and the best he could expect would be to be arrested on a charge of murder if he were to carry out his true wish. With an assignment of this priority, there could be a team in the area, and layered, as usual, with Beakman his only direct contact. He would be very surprised if he himself were not under surveillance. It was an open question, and he might be wrong. A team, if present, might be uncovered. It was one thing for them to operate with near impunity in Beirut, Baghdad or Moscow—even London. But the streets of the U.S.? Very, very illegal.

He also knew if he did find the Cassidy woman and terminate her "with prejudice," that a black ops team could clean up for him and he could go Scott free. On the other hand, he reasoned, maybe not. Maybe they planned for him to take the fall for them; that there would be no clean up; that they—or Beakman alone—would simply disappear, leaving him to face justice alone after fingering him. He wondered how they—or he, Beakman—had found the woman mistaken for their real target, and how they—or he, Beakman—cleaned up afterward. More to the point, how was he to find Ms. E. Cassidy, if indeed she was in the area, and willing to stand still long enough for a couple of .22 sub-sonic hollow points to penetrate her scull. He mused about the ridiculous sight of stern-faced "company" operatives standing at the entrances to the local food markets, dark aviator glasses over their steely eyes, holding a photograph up to compare with every woman who vaguely fit the description. Maybe. Maybe not.

But someone had to have identified—mistakenly—the woman and tracked her to her middle-American lair. But who? Did they have moles in Whole Foods' produce department?

Would he be truly free after the deed was done? He wondered. He'd have to watch his back.

Radcliff collected Beakman from a strip mall along Cerrillos Road in his pickup truck. Beakman had wanted to drive, but Radcliff had sent a message saying absolutely not; that he knew the area better. To himself he said, I insist on control.

Beakman was outfitted more "western" than the first time he had seen him, something Radcliff believed made the man more conspicuous than if he were to wear a dark Saville Row suit, red silk tie and patent leather shoes. Beakman said nothing as he got in, and continued in silence for several blocks as he gawked at the wild collection of eclectic businesses that lined the long, busy street.

"So, what's up, Beakman?" Radcliff asked, breaking the silence. He didn't look at his passenger.

"Oh, not much. Just bored and needed some company." Beakman spoke to his side window.

"Well, 'ole buddy, if this trip is just to fill out your day at my expense, I got better things to do, in which case I'll take you back to where I picked you up. Maybe not. Maybe I'll just dump you here, and you can figure it out all by your lonesome." Radcliff wrenched the wheel violently to change lanes, eyeing the rearview as he did.

Beakman looked down, a smirk on his face, then looked over at Radcliff. "You're a very funny man, Radcliff. Very funny." He paused and sobered. "There is a reason for this trip."

"Which is?" Radcliff cranked the wheel and turned a corner, forcing Beakman to brace himself against his door.

"To see how you're doing. How the project is coming along." Beakman stared forward.

"Did you off that woman yourself? Or did you contract that out?"

"What woman?" Beakman didn't move a muscle, continuing his scrutiny of the road ahead.

"Don't play games, Beakman. The Nolan woman. And the guy they found with her. Petersen." Beakman threw Radcliff a glance.

"I checked it out," Radcliff said. "She's the spitting image of your target."

"Our target."

"Okay, fine; our target. But I repeat—"

"I admit a mistake was made, which we would prefer not to repeat. That's where you come in. You have currency here. Know your way around and all that."

"To an extent, Beakman, but nothing on the scale of the long-time locals."

"True, but you have a background; known for your bloodhound nose. It's not the first time." He awarded Radcliff a long look before returning his gaze to the street.

"Yeah, right."

"So, what's your plan?"

"No way, Beakman. I'm not telling you so you or one of the others you've got squirreled away here can get in on the act. Maybe fuck things up."

"Fair enough."

"Another question. What's my drop-dead; my time frame? What

if this woman's not anywhere near here? And what do I use as proof I've tried?" Radcliff took his eye off the road to look directly at Beakman.

"It could take six months. Or only three. A year. I don't know. But if she's here—and we think she is—she's bound to make a mistake."

"Mistake?"

"If she knows we're after her, she'll be lying very, very low. On the other hand—"

"The other hand?"

"If she thinks she's in the clear, then she's bound to be seen in the open."

"And that's what you or one of the other goons thought in the case of your 'mistake'."

"We jumped the gun. Maybe we didn't. There's no proof."

"That's putting it mildly. Two innocent people are dead because you guys—or you—'jumped the gun'. And you just proved it."

"Enough with the lecture, Radcliff. Your hands aren't exactly clean."

"And I'm not getting into a pissing contest with you, either. Those were sanctioned. National security. Outside the country. Not the same."

Beakman remained silent.

"So, do you have an arrangement with the cops here?"

Beakman shook his head. "Nope."

"How'd you sanitize the scene?"

"Clean operation. In and out. Victims were sloppy. Didn't even lock the front door, although we didn't use it."

"You were there?"

"Kept my distance. I'm oversight."

"Get this straight, Beakman; if and when I find Cassidy, and I take care of the Company's little problem, I go in alone. Alone. Understand?"

"And how do we know you've taken care of the problem?"

"You'll know. You'll have DNA. Maybe photos. If."

"Wow. Professional."

"Now, I want to end this conversation."

"What, no dinner invitation?"

"I'm picky when it comes to dinner guests."

"As you wish."

"You have someone watching my house?"

"Now, why in the world would I do a thing like that, Jeremy?" Beakman squinted at him.

"You can't shit an old turd like me, Beakman! Either you do or you don't! But I'll tell you this, pal: if you do, there's a very good possibility my neighbors would eventually smell him—or her—and call the cops. Where I live, everybody knows everybody and everything. So, a word to the wise."

"Not to worry."

"Oh, but I do." Radcliff glowered at his passenger.

Beakman nodded in silence, then reached into his inner jacket pocket and withdrew a thick, white, business-size envelope and held it out to Radcliff.

"What's this?" He glanced at Beakman, then back at the road. He was driving under the speed limit.

"Walking around money. There's also the route to an encrypted site letting you know where the rest of it is. More after. For now, let me know if you need more here."

"I see. What are we talking?

"Ten up front in the bank. Another ninety K at the end."

"Offshore?"

"Is there any other way?"

"What's the source? Usual drug score?"

Beakman sniffed a low chuckle and shook his head.

Radcliff let Beakman off a block from where he had picked him up, then sat and watched for two minutes before leaving. He did not detect a tail.

Radcliff pulled into the yard in front of his house, switched the engine off and sat. He let his hands fall into his lap, leaving the ignition key to dangle. He caught sight of a small jackrabbit as it poked its nose out from under a sage to his right. It went up on its hind legs, sniffed the air, then darted across the pea gravel to the opposite side and disappeared through a gap in the coyote fence. He knew full well Cassidy's pursuers had tracked her here, otherwise why the effort? But how? And if they were correct, where was she? Santa Fé was one thing; but it was ringed by possibilities. Española and Tesuque to the north. El Dorado, Cerrillos and La Cienega to the south. Pecos, Glorieta, La Cueva and Rowe to the east. Had she been using a credit card in her name? Was she traveling under an assumed identity, and they knew what it was? Had they tracked her cell phone? Had she been using the Internet, and they wormed tracking software onto her computer? Had someone close to her betrayed her, but also lost her? There had been talk of planting GPS tracking chips under people's skin, but that was not likely. If they had, and had it worked, he would be sculpting instead of thinking about how to find an assassination target.

He suspected that what actually happened was that Evelyn Cassidy was followed to within a few clicks of the surrounding area, and that either she detected her tail and shook it, or the tail simply lost her. Then they got crude, dumped the usual finesse, and blundered. No matter; he had his work cut out for him.

He longed to see Patsy Romero, but decided he'd have to stave off that hunger until he made a modicum of progress.

He sat in the dark of his secret office, still as a rock, thinking. Then, with slow deliberation, he turned the desk lamp on, reached for a five by eight legal tablet and a pen, and wrote, "Wraith, danger lurks. Contact benefactor."

He folded the yellow, lined paper and slid it into his pants pocket. Then he picked up the desk phone handset and keyed Patsy's number.

The following morning, he fixed a breakfast of coffee, juice, scrambled eggs, diced potatoes, onions, green chile, the latter served on a tortilla, for Ms. Romero and himself. After kissing her goodbye and watching her drive away, he checked on Mandy's victuals and left for downtown.

His route was indirect. He took Old Pecos to Old Santa Fe, turned on to the Paseo, then swung past the capital complex across from the Gann Gallery. Three blocks past the last four-way stop, he pulled over and waited for thirty seconds, watching his rearview mirror. He then pulled out, turned right at the next stop, and made his way up Marcy Street until he found an empty parking place. He emerged, locked the truck, and walked casually toward the Plaza. He went past the entrance to *The Santa Fé New Mexican* offices, turned left at the next corner, then stopped, turned and waited a full minute. He then back-tracked, entered the newspaper building and asked for the ad-taker.

# 10

Radcliff performed his morning ablutions, attended to the demanding Mandy, then drove away in his pickup.

His first stop was at the Office Depot store on Cerrillos. He purchased a good, black vinyl, one-inch wide, three-ring binder with clear plastic insert protector sheets. Added to that was a Cross brand gold and black pen and pencil set. Then a zipper-closure yearly calendar, complete with current inserts. Finally, a ream of white, 20-pound printer paper, a half-ream of glossy digital photo print paper, and a package of do-it-yourself business card blanks. He also splurged on a high-grade full-color digital photo printer and appropriate software. Next, he visited a luggage shop on San Francisco street. There, he spent another portion of the two thousand in cash Beakman had given him on a good, mid-range briefcase and a bright metal business card holder.

In his office, he spent most of the rest of the day down-loading pictures of people from various sites. They were mostly middle-aged, and both sexes. He re-formatted and organized them into special folders on his computer. He then printed them in full color with false names—surname first, given second—with fake, large dollar amounts under each one. The photographs with money legends he arranged neatly into the new three-ring binder between the protective plastic sheets. One of them was of the elusive Evelyn Cassidy, with her name the sole correct one. Each page held four, reasonably clear photos; nine pages total. Next, using the new software package, he created business cards with the title of a non-existent company, naming himself as the local manager. Of these, he printed one hundred, then placed as many as he could in the new metal card holder, with a like amount in the card section of the brief case.

From a lower drawer of the file cabinet, whose job, in part, included hiding the underfloor cavity, he found an old, but serviceable pair of horn-rimmed glasses. The lenses had no amplification power, but they could fool the average optician at a reasonable distance. These he removed to his bedroom closet, where he placed them in the left breast pocket of a dark suit he had not worn for several years. He thought for a moment, and recalled it had been to his mother's funeral. He retrieved a brush from a dresser drawer and proceeded to remove months of dust from the suit fabric.

He looked at his watch. It was late in the day, but he had one more task before he could relax and contact Patsy Romero. He drove to the Santa Fé municipal airport, parked as far away from the lobby as he could, then rented a late-model U.S.-made sedan, and headed for home.

Later, over an Italian-style dinner, he explained to Patsy that the clutch in the truck "went out," and it was in for repairs. Parts were on order. Could be a week, maybe two, he explained. She wanted to know why he had rented "that ugly hulk." Had to do with money and availability, he replied. They smiled at each other, kissed, and sipped their wine.

Beakman had checked out of his room at the Camel Rock Motel before racking up another day, turned in his rental truck, and took a taxi to the Santa Fé mall, where he spent the afternoon watching two movies. Late in the day, he walked to the Red Lobster, ate a fish dinner, then took a taxi to the airport. He sat in the lounge, alternatively reading a paperback novel and watching the few people the place serviced come and go. Around eight, he sauntered into the bar and ordered a draft beer of local origin. Around eight-thirty, he looked at his watch, then walked to the big, west-facing window and looked out.

At the same time, the co-pilot of a six-passenger, two-engine jet airplane made contact with the Santa Fé control tower, identified the aircraft, and asked for permission to land and instructions for same.

Twenty minutes later, Beakman was on the aircraft as it taxied to the end of the runway in preparation for take-off. He sat next to a man fifteen years his senior. His name was Powell. They were the only passengers.

"So, what's the status, Beakman?" Powell, in his late fifties, whose hair was nearly all white, kept his eyes on the pages of a golfing magazine as he asked the question.

"Got our man busy."

"You trust him?"

"Yes."

"Why?"

"He's on the list. He has a history with the Company."

Powell glanced at Beakman, then raised his head as he perused an ad for clubs through the reading portion of his tri-focals. "Better be."

"He is."

"If we can find the Wraith, so can the FBI or DNA. Not sure MI-6 isn't interested in our target, given the nature of the problem."

"I know." Beakman sipped at the martini the lone attendant had served him.

"These goddamn Congressional watchdogs, as they call themselves; these pansy, liberal asshole bastards. They're taking this country down the tubes. We do our job, and what do we get?"

"Yessir." Beakman tipped his glass again and tried to concentrate on the next martini. He'd need it.

"You clean up after yourself, Beakman?" Powell still didn't pay his seating partner the courtesy of a straight-on look.

"They'll never find a thing."

"Better not. You go down, we don't know you."

"I get that." He drank again, frowning, while instantaneously entertaining a mental picture of himself being guided by the police to a patrol car, his hands restrained behind his back.

"How'd you make that dumb-ass mistake, anyway?"

Beakman shook his head. "I thought I had her."

"Well, goddamnit, you didn't!" Powell spoke in a loud whisper as he finally glared directly at Beakman for a sustained three seconds.

They heard the twin engines spin up, then felt the craft lurch as the brakes were released, then the pull and surge of acceleration, as the jet rolled down the runway for rotation and take-off.

"Where we headed?" Beakman asked.

"Charlie wants a sit-down." The man flipped a page.

"DC?"

Powell shook his head. "Not this time. Away from prying eyes."

"Hm."

"Better have some answers, Beakman." Powell threw the golfing magazine aside. "You think this guy, Radcliff, can make it happen? You know him?"

"Not from the past, but yes. Charlie knows him." He looked at his empty martini glass as the plane tilted up at a thirty degree angle, climbing up and away from the Santa Fé airport, and forcing him backwards into his wide, comfortable seat. He felt mentally what he was feeling physically: trapped, and unable to extricate himself.

"Mm. I think you may need some help. And what about him? After?" The man brushed away an imaginary mote of dust from his pant leg.

Beakman paused. "He won't be able to tell the story."

"Keep a tail on 'im?"

"Not now." Beakman shot the man a glance. He didn't want to say that he had discovered that following people around northern New Mexico was nigh on to impossible.

"Of course. When you get back."

"Of course."

# 11

After kissing Patsy and seeing her out the door, Jeremy Radcliff donned a white shirt, an article of clothing he had not worn for several years. He selected a "conservative" tie from a paltry selection that dangled in a darkened corner of his clothes closet, and struggled it around his collar after three tries with the knot. He then climbed into his suit pants and jacket, latched a narrow leather belt around his waist, and checked his grooming in the dresser mirror. From there, he went to the office, where he put the fake glasses on. He picked up the new briefcase, locked the door, and headed for the rental car parked where his beloved pickup should have been.

He reasoned he would have to look in a wide circle for his quarry. On the one hand, there were several enclaves where Evelyn Cassidy could hide, assuming she knew she should hide. On the other, they were, fortunately for him he reasoned, few and far between. If she were in "the Santa Fé area," would that include as far north as Taos? Probably not. Would she be as far south as Bernalillo? Probably not. Bernalillo and environs was too open and had become too "Middle-America." Taos was small and incestuous. But he had to start somewhere, and he decided that would be Española, despite the fact that he had serious doubts. Los Cerrillos, La Cienega, La Bajada, and Madrid to the south would be next, although he felt it would be wasted time. Then there was El Dorado, Cañoncito, Glorieta, Pecos and Rowe to the east. Even Las Vegas.

As a way to satisfy his innate sense of discipline, he began his search at the Ohkay Casino on the San Juan Pueblo Reservation a short distance north of the Española city boundary. He introduced himself to the young female clerk at the hotel registration desk, explaining that he represented the insurance company shown on his newly-minted business card. He went on to say that he was charged with finding the people pictured in his three-ring binder, but was focused on this one here. She glanced at the card, then scanned the four, neatly arranged photographs that lay underneath each of the clear plastic insert-covered pages. She shook her head slowly. The manager did the same when he moseyed over and craned his neck to have a peek at what was transpiring. Radcliff pointed to the picture of Evelyn Cassidy, saying he felt that she was the most likely to be found hereabouts. He left his fake card and suggested that if they saw this woman or any of the others, to please call; that there was a "finders' fee" involved. Both smiled tolerantly, and he headed for the exit.

The results experienced at the casino were mimicked along Riverside Drive at Walgreen's, Wal-Mart and Super-Save. The same occurred at the Big Rock Casino on the Santa Clara Reservation, part of which lay within the city boundary. No luck at the post office or at Wells Fargo or Valley National Bank. In each case, he detected doubts about the promise of a fee. A good choice, he thought, as he made his way toward Nambé.

He drove slowly along the winding, dry arroyo-centered valley. At each stop at a commercial establishment, he came away with nothing in the way of where a fugitive of the CIA or any other woman might visit and be remembered. There was only Al's Liquors along the main highway, and that proved futile as well.

Chic, dense and likewise verdant Tesuque he felt might be more promising. There was the House of Old Things, El Nido, where at one time, flamenco was the rage during dinner. Then the Market and Restaurant which bore the name of the area, where all heads shook in the negative. Dutifully, he stopped at the post office. Bishop's Lodge Road was beautiful, but likewise fruitless in terms of possible venues where E. T. Cassidy might hang out or whose face might be recalled.

He dreaded searching in Santa Fé. Certainly, the "City Different," not unlike New York City, Los Angeles or Chicago, was easier for the sought-after to "hide in plain sight," but for the seeker, the opposite was true. His doubts were compounded. Where should he start?

He began with the main post office, then tried, out of desperation and a degree of musing, a few of the shops on the Plaza. Albertson's three stores were no better, as were Office or Home Depot, Smith's groceries or the phony "organic food" groceries.

He kept the car for a week, when his truck was returned, better than ever, with a non-existent new clutch, throw-out bearing and main seal, "As long as we're in there," the mechanic had said. Or so he explained to Patsy, who looked at him as though she were imitating a deer staring into bright headlights.

Everywhere he had been, which included the areas surrounding Santa Fé he had deemed possibilities, had resulted in the same, sad expressions on the part of his contacts. At one point, toward the end of his fruitless mission, he was passed by an ambulance, its lights flashing and siren blaring. Was it possible that Evelyn Cassidy would need to see a doctor or go to the hospital?

Late at night when Patsy was not present, and with his office door secured, he logged onto the encrypted web site and surfed to the dossier for Cassidy, E. Toward the end of the multi-page history, he found a one-sentence passage that revealed the possibility that E. Cassidy might be leaving the "company" for "personal reasons" that might include "reasons of ill-health." Possible diagnosis: cancer. He swore under his breath at himself for not keying on that tidbit earlier.

St. Vincent's Hospital complex was perched on a prominence in the southeast sector of the city. He found a rare, tight parking spot, climbed the walkway to the main entrance, and made his way to the geriatric candy-striper-occupied information desk. Taking a chance, he showed his card and book, and parroted his spiel. He was warned, however, that hospital administration might not take kindly to him repeating his quest in the various departments. Taking the advice, he removed the Cassidy photo and asked if he could leave the binder for safe-keeping at the desk. Yes, he could.

On his first visit after the information booth, the Emergency Room, he was rewarded

Her name tag read "Sarah," surname Spanish, but she appeared very "Anglo." She sat behind a glassed-in partition with a sliding window, at a file-strewn desk. She looked up as Radcliff, neat and official in his suit and tie, walked up to the little shelf that protruded from her domain. "Can I help you?"

"Perhaps." He held the Cassidy photograph up against the plane of the glass, his phony card alongside it. "I'm—my company—is looking for this woman. She has some—"

Sarah reached for the picture. "May I see it?"

"Yes, please do." He handed the photograph and his card through the opening under the glass partition.

"Why are you looking for her?" She glanced at the business card, laid it aside, then studied the picture.

"We believe she has insurance money coming. My company—"

"Yes." Sarah nodded as she stared at the photo.

"Yes?"

"Yes. I've seen her." She looked up briefly, then at the photo.

"You have?" His jaw slackened at the news.

"Yes. It's been a while."

"A while? How long—?"

Sarah held the picture to one side as she rolled her eyes up to study empty space. "Oh, let me think. About two or three months ago." She looked at the image again. "Yes, I'd say about that long." She handed the photo back along with the business card.

Radcliff took the photo and laid it on the shelf with one hand as he reached for the note pad in his inside jacket pocket. "You say about two or three months? Do you know why she was here?"

She shook her head. "I'm not sure, but I think it had to do with cancer."

"Why do you feel you remember her?"

"Because of what happened to her."

"Oh?"

"Yes. She fainted, and the man with her had to grab her."

"There was a man with her?"

"Yes."

"Do you remember him? What he looked like?"

She shook her head. "No."

"I see." He hesitated. "Do you remember her name?"

"No, I don't. Sorry."

She looked around him, and he turned. A woman carrying a small child stood behind him. He stepped aside.

"I'm sorry, but I have to—"

"Of course. I'm sorry." He looked at the distraught mother and smiled meekly as she edged up to the window.

"Uh, just one more question."

"Please, sir!" Sarah's mood had changed.

"Where would someone with cancer go?"

She frowned at him. "Cancer Center." She looked at the woman. "What seems to be the trouble? Your child?"

The Cancer Center was on the lowest level of the hospital campus, and attached to it.

The woman behind the high counter was busy riffling through files. She looked up. "May I help you?"

"I hope so." As he spoke, he handed her his card, then held up the photograph. "I have reason to believe this woman may be taking treatments here. We're trying to locate her because she is due funds from an insurance policy." He watched her closely as she peered at Cassidy's image. She showed no outward reaction. "I'm sorry, sir, I can neither confirm nor deny that this woman is, or has been, a patient here."

Her reaction and words brought two thoughts to Radcliff: one, she had just confirmed that the Cassidy woman was, indeed, a patient, and two, that she would work well in government service.

"Of course. Confidentiality and all that."

"Yes." She handed the picture back with a strained smile. After a delay, she asked, "You say she has money coming?"

"Yes. A sizable amount. And there's a 'finder's fee' for anyone who can lead us to her."

After a pregnant pause, during which the woman's eyes roved, then returned, she shook her head, her lips pursed. "I'm sorry. I can't help you. Or her."

"Or yourself," Radcliff shot back. He smiled and turned away.

Outside, he stood in the shade cast by the portico that lead to the lower entrance hall. The automatic doors opened, and a medical technician in white, a stethoscope draped around his neck, emerged and moved briskly toward the street.

Radcliff approached him. "Excuse me!"

The tech stopped and looked at him, his head cocked.

"Sorry, but I've got a question maybe you can answer."

"Yes?"

"I just found out I may have cancer." He thumbed toward the Center.

"Mm. Sorry to hear that. You're in the right place, though." He raised an eyebrow.

"Yes, yes, I know. The best. But here's my question: if I do—have cancer, that is—I assume they keep records. You know, X-rays and all that."

"MRI."

"Yes. Right."

"Well, if I wanted to see those records—you know, for my family, peace of mind. Insurance and all that—where would I go?" He peered at the man, his face deadly serious.

"Radiology."

"Radiology?"

"Yes, Radiology."

"I thought that was for X-rays."

"It is, but they keep cancer records as well. X-rays and MRIs." He nodded.

"Sure. Makes sense. Okay. Thanks. Really appreciate it." He made a two-finger salute.

"Hey, no problem. Good luck."

"Thanks." Radiology, he thought, as he watched the tech walk away.

The young woman who sat behind the Radiology department desk seemed to more resemble a teenager to Radcliff than someone older and presumably more capable of the job at hand. He reckoned he was aging more than he realized. He repeated his routine, aware of the possibility that he would again be rebuffed. In this case, he was pleasantly surprised. Yes, she recognized the face in the picture; no, she didn't know her name, nor could she confirm the name if she were aware of it, despite the finder's fee. However, she said, patients or concerned parties could, with a properly executed Power of Attorney, acquire copies of patient records.

Power of Attorney. Evelyn Cassidy's signature on same. How would he come up with that? He thanked her and walked away.

# 12

Beakman was slightly woozy after two hard drinks and a couple of canapés at a pressurized cabin altitude of roughly ten thousand feet. He peered out the window of the small jet aircraft window into the pitch blackness of the night. Occasional wisps of clouds seemed to drift by despite the speed at which they traveled. He saw the occasional grid of lights below that marked towns and cities. He sensed they were not flying east, rather in a northerly direction, in part because of the lack of banking and turning effected by the pilot after lifting off from Santa Fé. He was correct, but not certain until he spotted the Canadian maple leaf fluttering over the airport hutment in the half-light of a safety lamp, did he realize he was no longer in the United States.

Two men in civilian clothes, hatless and dressed in wind breakers and jeans, stood, hands folded at belt level, at the bottom of the jet stairway, staring stoically at nothing. Two others, similarly outfitted, hustled them to a waiting car. They were whisked away a short distance to what appeared to be an unused, single-story military barracks. His room was neat, clean and bare, save for a single cot, chair and small dresser; no mirror. The wall switch controlled a single, low-wattage lamp on the bedside table. He was informed tersely that a bathroom was available at the end of the hall. Except for two men who sat at either end of the long hall, he was alone in the building. Powell remained in the car as it glided away. Beakman did not sleep well. He felt they were "playing" him.

A rap on the door awakened him at six. After showering and shaving in the grotty, cold, bare-bones bathroom with its unadorned raw concrete floor, he was escorted to another building on the drab, abandoned military base.

He was led into what he reckoned had once been the lair of a high-ranking officer. The two old, wood-frame windows that faced the now weed-crowded flight apron were shuttered to the outside world with dusty, barely serviceable, Venetian blinds. A long, brown, folding-leg table was more or less centered in the room along with four steel folding chairs. On the table were two carafes, one with water, the other orange juice. Next to it was a large vacuum bottle with what he figured was coffee, something he desperately needed. Cups and glasses were present as well. What appeared to be a stab at breakfast was rounded out by a tray of doughnuts and pastries.

Powell leaned back in one of the fundamental chairs, his arms folded across his chest, with what Beakman considered an appropriately stale look on his face. The other occupant of the room, a short, grey-haired man with a pleasant, intelligent face, rose, came around the table and put out his hand.

"Charlie," Beakman said. His smile was fleeting.

"Beakman. Thanks for coming." The older man smiled broadly. "Have a seat." He gestured to one of the chairs nearest Beakman as he moved to his across the table. "There's coffee. Juice. Pastries." He waved his hand again as he sat. In front of him was a paper plate covered with scattered crumbs alongside an empty cup.

They've been here a while, Beakman thought. He sat after scraping his chair against the old wood floor as he pulled it back. "Thanks. Coffee I could use." He reached for a cup and the vacuum bottle.

Across from him, Charlie and Powell watched him in silence. Charlie sobered, while Powell, who sat up and moved his chair forward, remained stoical.

Beakman went through the coffee-preparation ritual, then sipped at the hot liquid. He sat back in an attempt to calm his jangled, sleep-starved nerves. "So. Why am I here? And why this god-forsaken place? You isolated me. Why?" He looked from under his eyebrows as he sipped at the hot, strong brew.

Charlie Henshaw spoke. His voice was low, controlled and tense, but consoling. "You know why, Stanley. This place? The last thing we need is for anyone inside—or outside—the agency to see us together."

"Okay. But why now? The operation's not over." Beakman shook his head.

Charlie reached out to the vacuum bottle, poured coffee into his cup, added creamer, then sat back with cup in hand. "I'm fully aware, but Radcliff's had—how long? A couple of weeks—more—now, and you're the man on the scene. Nothing written, no phone, no emails. This is the best way."

"Why the guards? You think I was going to take a hike?" Beakman swung his head around in annoyance.

Charlie lowered and shook his head. "No, Stanley. What was I to do? Leave you all alone? Put you in a hotel and let nature take its course? We don't know who's out there. Even here. But this was far better than DC or any other place in the states. It wasn't mistrust of you." He gestured toward Powell without looking at him. "We came in separately, too. Too dicey."

"Okay. I understand, but it's early in the game. She's not going to be easy if she's gone to ground. And I think she has. I think she knows." He sipped his coffee while he looked at both men from under his eyebrows.

"Thing is," Charlie went on, "we could be in a heap of hurt if this thing blows open at the hearings. Thing is, too, Beakman, we thought we had sent the right man to do the job." He cocked his head to one side in a condescending gesture, his voice still controlled.

Beakman drank again and set his cup on the table. "We've been over that. You didn't get on my case when you sent the coin."

Charlie waved his hand. "We had to move ahead. What's done is done. Mistakes have been made all around."

"You got that right."

"So, what to do, Beakman? If this woman goes in front of the committee and testifies, well, it could spell our end as we know it. It's bad for the company, too. In every direction." Henshaw cocked his head.

"I know."

"You know!" Powell spoke for the first time. He sat forward, spitting his words as he pointed his shaking finger at Beakman.

Charlie looked at Powell, raised his hand and spoke in a near whisper. "Easy, easy."

Powell calmed, but his feral eyes remained fixed on Beakman. He looked away, disgusted.

Beakman jumped up, turned, and marched across the room, his shoes drumming on the old, dried wood of the floor. He spun around to face his accusers. "God damn it! Yes! I screwed up!" He came half-way back to the table, his arm out, finger pointed, dancing back and forth between the two men who faced him. "And how many failures has the company seen?! Huh?! How many?! Bay of Pigs, Castro, Columbia, Iran, Iraq! I tried, and I failed—for now! Fuck!" He glared at the two seated men whose eyes had gone wide. "That's why I'm involved in this! Because of fuck-ups you guys helped create!" He waited two beats. "So, don't go getting holier than thou on me!"

He went silent for several seconds, frozen in place by his outburst, then returned to the table, picked up his cup and swilled half of it. He grabbed a pastry and tore into it. A large ragged bite missing, with crumbs falling away, he used it to point at Charlie Henshaw as he chewed, then swallowed. Too large and dry, it hurt as it went down. "You sent the coin, Charlie. You sent the coin, and I showed it to Radcliff. You knew this would be difficult. So why are you on my case now?!"

Henshaw looked down at the table's surface. "Perhaps we came off a bit rough. Sorry. You don't deserve it."

"Don't—!" Powell cut in.

"Hold on, Dennis," Henshaw said, raising his hand again. He held Powell's eyes for several seconds in an effort to bring him under control.

Powell calmed and sat back, shaking his head, his chin on his chest, arms folded.

Beakman glared at Dennis Powell. He shouted, "Hey, Powell, I used the information I had! You guys have no idea how it is trying to find someone there. It's weird. Fucking weird." He shook his head, threw his arm out to point at Powell, then cleared his mouth of sugary crumbs with the back of his hand. "And you guys—we're not supposed to operate in the states! Federal fucking offense, for chrissakes! The FBI and local law and Justice would have us for breakfast! Jesus!"

The room went silent.

Charlie peered at him. "How *did* you decide on this woman?" He spoke in a low, controlled tone.

Beakman sat heavily, smiled wryly, shook his head and made a wide gesture with both hands. "Hey, everyone I talked to at Langley believed the Wraith—Evelyn Cassidy—was *not* hiding. That she felt secure. That she could just go about her business. I get to Santa Fé where she'd been traced to, and assumed I could spot her in the potato section of the local super. Tell me anyone else felt differently." He looked at his inquisitors in turn with an increased confidence as he arched his back.

Powell squirmed and frowned. His voice under control, he said, "But you offed a citizen. Two citizens."

Beakman sighed and ran his hand through his hair. "Yeah, I know." He looked down and away.

Charlie ignored Powell's remark. "Again, how did you find the wrong target?" His voice was low and calm; measured.

"With her picture. Took me six weeks. I prowled the markets, the Plaza, read the paper, looking for anything. Finally spotted her involved with a woman's club deal. Tracked her, found where she lived." He shrugged. "Christ, she looked just like her. In every way. It fit."

"The man. Didn't you know he was there?" This from Powell, who still strained to control his temper.

Beakman lowered his head and shook it. "No. That got past me. She had been alone. I researched her. Different name, but that fit, too. No men I could determine. This guy came out of nowhere. No car. She must have picked him up from a rendezvous spot. Papers said he was married. Guess he was keeping it under wraps."

Charlie asked, "And so when you went in, he was there?"

Beakman nodded. His hands rested in his lap as he turned sideways in his chair. Both Henshaw and Powell glanced at each other.

"And you left nothing behind to point to you?" Charlie asked.

"No. Picked up the brass. Wore gloves. Standard procedure. Gun's long gone."

"And the investigation?" Powell asked.

"Into the killing? Can't really say. Not much in the local rag. Little on TV. That's out of Albuquerque, and they had one story so far as I know." Beakman worked his jaw and reached for his cooling coffee. "Hell, there're murders every day in Albuquerque." He threw out his hand in exasperation and looked away.

Charlie leaned forward earnestly. "What's Radcliff's attitude?"

Beakman raised his eyebrows. "Didn't like it. Not a bit. He believed me when I showed him the coin. He knows he's vulnerable."

And you haven't followed him," Charlie said.

"As I told you—"

Charlie raised his hand to stop Beakman. "Right. Right. Hard to tail." He paused. "But you got to find a way. And after—"

"After." He jerked his jaw toward Powell. "As I've already been, shall we say, 'advised.'"

"We simply can't leave a trace. No loose ends, Beakman," Charlie said.

"And what about me?"

Charlie and Powell traded wry smiles.

"As I told you," Charlie said, "There's already a pile in your offshore. And more to come. We're in this together. Same instincts, same profiles, same drama."

"Who else?"

"Who else?" Charlie raised his eyebrow.

"Who else is involved. Besides me." Beakman pointed to himself.

"This group." He waved his finger at Powell, Beakman, then himself. "And now Radcliff." Charlie answered as he drew a circle in the air.

"So, I'm to handle this alone." He rocked back and forth, his mouth firm.

Charlie shook his head and looked down. "This simply cannot go any further than this group." He held up his finger pointed down and described another circle.

"And Radcliff," Beakman said.

"And Radcliff," Powell offered.

Beakman shook his head slowly, looked hard into Charlie's eyes, then Powell's. He nodded. "One more thing."

"Yes?" Charlie said.

Beakman sighed and lowered his head, but looked at both men in turn. "If something happens to me—"

"Yeah?" Powell cut in with sarcasm.

"You know," Beakman said.

"The letter to the press routine?" Charlie asked.

"Yep." Beakman's lips were pursed.

"We understand," Charlie said. He closed his eyes in sage understanding.

"Radcliff's no dummy," Beakman said.

"Oh, I know," Charlie said. "We go back."

"Better just pay 'im."

Charlie nodded, then looked at Powell, who looked away.

"Can I go now?"

"Not quite yet, if you please." Charlie rose as he spoke, stretched, and took two steps to the window nearest him and peeked through the blinds. "We think there may be a way to help your man—and you—find the target."

"Yeah?" Beakman frowned at Charlie's back, then glanced at Powell, who was studying his fingernails.

"Siblings," Charlie said.

"Siblings?"

Charlie turned. "Siblings. She has a brother and a sister."

"Yes?" Beakman moved to his chair and sat slowly, keeping his eyes glued to Charlie.

"Yes," Charlie said. "The brother."

Beakman, silent, looked around the room as though no one else were there.

"And we think—"

Beakman looked up at his mentor. "And you think he may lead us to her."

Charlie strolled away, his back to both other men. "Quite possible. And where you come in."

"You want me to track him down?"

Charlie returned to the table and stood next to it. "He's a lawyer. Head of his own firm. Seattle. You need to get up there. Pronto."

"What do we know?" Beakman asked.

Powell scraped his chair closer to the table. "Not much. Yet. You need to move on it."

"Why didn't I know this earlier? He scowled.

Charlie shrugged with his eyebrows and held out both hands in questioning gesture. Powell studied the floor.

Beakman shook his head. "Jesus."

"Okay, I admit we should have seen this opportunity before."

"You guys are flying by the seats of your pants." Beakman shook his head.

Charlie paced a small circle, then settled. "The whole operation was sudden. And we have to be careful in what assets we use. You know that." He peered at Beakman.

Beakman drew in a deep breath and sighed. "Yeah. I know. Plausible deniability or whatever." He paused. "The address?"

Charlie slid a letter-size manila envelope across the table to Beakman, then pointed at it. "No photo."

Beakman nodded and picked up the envelope. He looked at both men and stood. "I'll get back to you."

"Use the encrypted site." Charlie Henshaw threw his head toward Powell. "Get our man out of here." He looked at Beakman. "Take another pastry. I've found them rather good." He smiled wryly.

Powell stood and followed as Beakman ignored the offer of more food and turned toward the door.

Charlie, still next to the table, said, "Powell. A minute, okay? Got some paperwork for you to look over. He'll be right along, Beakman." He waved and smiled a send-off to Beakman, who had turned at Charlie's call to Powell.

Powell came back to the table as Charlie watched the door close.

Charlie looked at Powell closely. "What do you think?"

"About our friend there?"

"Uh-huh."

"Disappointed. Hope he doesn't fuck this up."

"Any more than we have?"

"Yeah."

"Short leash?"

"Maybe a choke chain."

"We shall see. Maybe he'll redeem himself. Remember his threat. Safe home."

"Thanks."

# 13

Radcliff had known Patsy Romero for less than a month before Beakman showed up to interfere with his increasingly idyllic retirement. He had been at the hospital for a routine, insurance-mandated procedure and gone to the cafeteria for lunch. Faced with choosing a place to take his tray in the crowded place, he had spotted an empty chair at a window-side table across from a pretty young Hispanic woman. She had looked up from her soup and sandwich and smiled at him, an unspoken, instantaneous approval and invitation for which he was surprised and grateful. They had made small talk, and she had finished before he did. She had risen, taken her tray and detritus to the trash bin and walked slowly away before he had gotten up the gumption to follow her. He had accosted her at the exit.

"Excuse me!" He had said as he approached her.

She had turned and looked at him, obviously pleased. He had blurted to her that he thought it a good idea for them to meet again, an idea to which she instantly agreed. In less than a week, after two dates, they had become close.

Now they both stood in his kitchen, doing something they both relished, fixing food and sipping an inexpensive, but good, wine.

"I want you to tell me something, Jeremy." She was grating cheddar into a bowl.

"Oh? What would you like to know? A fact about history? Let me see—"

"No, you silly man. A fact about this house."

"Well," he said as he continued arranging the table, "the house is said to have been built around—"

"Jeremy! Let me finish!" She smiled at him tolerantly.

"Okay. What?" He stopped what he was doing and turned to her, flat wear in his hand.

"That room. The one that's always locked. What's in there, and why is it locked all the time?" She didn't look at him, rather continued to study the little strings of yellow cheese as they fell into the bowl.

"The room down the hall?"

"Yes, Jeremy, my love. The room down the hall. Stop being such a *pendejo*!"

"I really like that word. *Pendejo. Pen-deh-ho*. It's got such a great Spanish ring to it."

"Jeremy!" She turned her head down and around to smile menacingly at him.

"The room down the hall. Right. It's where I keep the bodies of all the other beautiful gals I've loved and murdered." He returned to his job at the table.

"How do you keep the odor down?" She had decided to join in on the joke.

"Oh, well, you see, they're buried. Under the floor. And I used this special chemical—" He waved with a fork before putting it down on the left side of her plate.

She turned full around and glared at him with a smile short of a laugh.

"Right," he said as he made a wide-eyed face. "That room, my dear, is my office. As you know, the other bedroom is my studio, such as it is."

"Why is it locked? You don't want me to see? Secrets? Hm?" She turned back to the cheese, in part because she was afraid of what he might say, and not only with words, but with his eyes.

He sighed as he leaned against a tall kitchen stool. "No, not really."

"Then?" Finished, she turned to him as she wiped her hands on a towel.

He shook his head, searching for words. "Well, I—"

"Jeremy, it's okay, *mi amor*. But please be honest with me. You know I love you."

He nodded emphatically. "I know; and I love you."

"Jeremy, what did you do before you came here? You haven't been an artist all your life. What?" There was pleading in her eyes.

He sighed. "Wow." He hesitated. "If I tell you the truth, you might walk away. So, what'll it be, politics or honesty?"

"Is it bad?"

"Some might say so; others might not." He looked away, a new sobriety on his face.

"Tell me. I can take it."

He chuckled. "Here's the thing; I don't know right now if you knowing about my past would hurt you or not, but it's the last thing I want. I wouldn't want it for anyone, especially you."

"So, what is it, and what's it got to do with the room?" She leaned against the island, her arms folded across her middle, her heart rate up. The smile had been replaced with a frown.

"I worked for the CIA, Patsy. I was a government agent. CIA agent." He peered at her under his eyebrows.

She shook her head and frowned. "That's it?"

"Isn't that enough?" He awarded her a wry smile.

"Well—did you do anything bad?" She dropped her arms to her side, relieved.

"I did my job. I was asked to do things. Some good, some I didn't like doing. They were for the good of the nation. At least, that's the way we saw it."

"God!" She arched forward.

He pushed away from the stool, walked to the window over the sink and looked out. "Looking back, I believe some of what I did—we did—were not for the good of the country."

Patsy came to him, leaned against his back and put her arms around his waist, her cheek against his shoulder. "I've really fallen for you," she whispered.

They were both silent for a time, then he turned, took her in his arms and kissed her. He pulled away, patted her sleek hair, and said, "I'm hungry."

She looked up at him. "Then, the room, your office—what?"

He stroked her cheek and moved slowly away. "The fact is, Patsy, my dear, that when you leave the CIA, you don't really leave. It doesn't really leave you. There's stuff in there I should get rid of, I suppose, but haven't. But there's more to it."

"What?" The worry had returned to her countenance.

He shook his head in one, rapid jerking motion. "Patsy, I just can't tell you. You could be in danger if I did."

"Jeremy! What?!"

"Patsy, please don't ask. It doesn't involve you. It's okay." He looked at her from across the room and over the waiting table.

She shook her head as tears welled in her eyes. "Are you in danger?"

"No. I'm not in danger. Please; it's okay." He waved the thought off with both hands as he ducked his head.

"You're doing something else for them, aren't you?!"

He advanced on her. "Patsy, you must calm down. There's no danger." He came to her and put both his hands on her small shoulders. "Listen. Sometimes ex-agents are asked to perform small duties for the agency. Happens all the time. When they're in the right place at the right time, and they're short of help. This is one of those times. Please don't worry, but please let it go, and please—please—forget I have told you this about me. You must not tell anyone. No one. Okay?" He pulled back and looked her in the eye. He held her hands in his.

She nodded sadly. "I'm worried about you. I don't want anything to happen to you. To us. For the first time in my life, I—"

"I know. Me, too."

He pulled her in and kissed her on the forehead.

"Let me worry." She smiled wanly and wiped at a tear.

"Okay, but not excess. Now, let's eat!"

Radcliff had a new concern: confiding in Patsy Romero. If she knew the truth, he thought. If she knew the truth. What could he have done? It was stupid to close off the room he used as an office. But he hadn't planned on a Patsy. Nor had he planned on falling in love at this stage in his life. In his late forties, no less.

He sat alone in front of the computer, staring at the screen for a long time before invoking the series of encrypted sites that led him to the Wraith's CIA profile. There it was; her signature on one of the several IDs provided by the "company." Not every one read Evelyn Cassidy. Which one should he use? Was she now solely herself, E. Cassidy, or was she someone else? Would she use her true identity at the Cancer Center, or would she, because she knew she was a target for "extreme prejudice," use false identification? What about insurance? Would she pay cash? Had she established an entirely new identity with all the attendant features?

Each of the signatures had certain characteristics that resembled each of the others, but he saw that she had been skilled in making subtle changes even to those. Smart lady. Skilled lady. Soon to be killed lady.

If he walked into St. Vincent's Hospital with a POA signed by one Evelyn Cassidy, and she were using another name, what would he do then? Recruit Patsy or someone else to do the same using other aliases? That would surely raise suspicion. Inoperative, as they were wont to say at Langley. But he had no choice.

Using Google, he found and downloaded a POA form and printed several copies. He made an over-sized replica of her original signature, and practiced it many times before trying it on seven different copies of a fake Power of Attorney giving him, J. Radcliff, counselor-at-law, the right to her medical records.

The following day, he learned two things: one, according to St. Vincent's Hospital, Evelyn Cassidy had never used their facilities, and two, Evelyn Cassidy was in hiding.

At one point while crossing the hospital grounds, he felt a strange tingling sensation, as though he were being watched, and found himself instinctually turning to look behind himself. He sat for a time at the wheel of his recovered truck, his heart racing as he came close to hyperventilating. He was the hunter, yes; but he was chasing a feral animal, and the animal could smell his aroma; his rank fear.

# 14

Operatives hired by PPI, Panhandle Private Investigations, Inc., stayed close to Alessandra Petersen for three days. A middle-aged Hispanic woman, driving a small foreign car, followed her to the grocery store, through the aisles pushing an empty shopping cart, and to an appointment with her physician. An older man, wearing a white straw western-style hat, tailed her to her husband's office in an old pickup truck which had not experienced water on its surface, save for rain, for many months. He also sat and watched as well-wishers and relatives crowded into the Petersen's upper-middle class house on Oxford Avenue in the southwest section of the city on the day of her husband's funeral. The original team, consisting of the black man and his white partner, managed, with discretion, to take photographs at the cemetery. All reported that Alex had not demonstrated a single suspicious move that could have led Mark Cassidy or anyone else to believe she had sinister connections.

Two days after the funeral, Chuck Halstrom, the proprietor of PPI, the detective agency hired to verify Mrs. Petersen's status as an innocent citizen, rang the doorbell at her house. It was close to ten in the morning, and he knew she was home, because he had been advised so by his female operative with the Spanish name, who had been hovering close-by. Halstrom was of average height, but thick-bodied, with a neck and paunch to match. He had served in the Army as a military policeman during the Vietnam War, then as a sheriff, then a policeman.

After a wait of nearly two minutes, Alex' daughter, Jackie, a pretty girl with long, dark hair, in her early twenties, opened the heavy, dark-wood door. "Yes?" She wore a deep frown.

"Miss Petersen?"

"Who are you?"

"Sorry, Miss Petersen, name's Halstrom. I represent—"

"What do you want?!"

Halstrom took a step back, folded his hands across his belt line, and looked down with a tolerant half-smile. "To speak with your mother. Is she home?"

Jackie looked back toward the interior of the house, then at Halstrom. "She's very tired. She's upset. We all are. Who are you and what do you want?!"

Halstrom looked up. "Miss Petersen—Jackie, is it?—I understand full well your mother's situation, but I really need to speak to her. Concerns the Santa Fé police. Can't be helped."

"The police? Are you with the police? Them?" She softened her tone. "Do they know who killed my father?"

Halstrom shook his head. "No. I'm not. And far as I know, they don't."

"Then—?"

"Miss Petersen, I'm here to help your mom—your mother. I've been hired by a friend of hers. To help."

"Who?" Her frown returned.

"I think it best I talk to your mother." He nodded sagely, then turned his head to peer out of the corner of his eye at the little car with the woman at the wheel parked half a block down the street.

"Who's there?" The question came from inside the house, and from a woman.

Halstrom peered up and over Jackie at the sound.

Jackie turned. "It's a man to see you, mother." Her edgy voice betrayed impatience.

"Sure like to speak with you, Mrs. Petersen." Halstrom bent his head sideways, trying to see past Jackie. He projected his voice.

Jackie turned and looked at him. "Can't you come back later?!"

Halstrom sighed and shook his head. "Miss Petersen—"

At that moment, Alex appeared behind her daughter, and Jackie stepped aside far enough so Halstrom could see her. She was in a house dress and slippers, and to him she appeared haggard.

She looked at the detective with sad, blood-shot eyes. "What is it?" Her voice was weak.

"You don't have to do this, mother!" Jackie shook her angry head at Alex, then glared at Halstrom.

"It's okay, Jackie. What—who are you?" Alex looked up at Halstrom.

"Chuck Halstrom, Mrs. Petersen. Mr. Cassidy asked me to look after you and see if there's anything you need or we can do for you. And to assist when you go back to New Mexico."

"Oh, I see." Alex developed a tepid smile. "That was nice." She brushed at her tangled hair with her hand.

Jackie leaned into her mother. "Mother, what's this all about?!"

Alex looked at Jackie, then Halstrom. "Uh, Jackie—Mr. Halstrom—uh, would you like to come in for some coffee?"

"Oh, no, thank you, ma'am. I need to get on. I just wanted to contact you and let you know we're here to help."

"I see; well . . ."

"Now, I understand the police up there expect you back. That is true, right?"

"Yes. Yes. I have to go back."

"And soon, is that right?"

"Yes." Alex looked confused.

"Well, ma'am, I doubt there's anything wrong. You know how it is in a case like this is."

"Yes."

"Well, ma'am, can you be ready in another coupla' days? I know it's been tough an' all."

"Yes. I'll be ready."

"Great. Mr. Cassidy has asked us to make sure you're safe and sound. We can even offer transportation."

"Oh, that won't be necessary. I can drive."

"You're sure?"

"Yes."

"Well, okay, but we'll be there for you. All the way."

"Really? But I don't need—"

Halstrom interrupted. "Mr. Cassidy's orders, Mrs. Petersen." He smiled and gave her a reassuring side-nod of his head. "We don't want any harm to come to you. We'll be discreet."

"Well, okay. That's very nice of him."

"I'll check back later." He awarded her a two-finger salute.

Jackie, who had been watching and listening, turned to Halstrom. "Why did Cassidy hire you? What do you do?"

"I'm in the business of helping people, Miss Cassidy. G'day to you both." He turned and walked away before any more questions were asked.

When Halstrom was half way to his car, which he had parked three houses away and opposite from his operative's vehicle, he looked at the woman who sat in it and drew his hand across his throat. Seeing his gesture, she started the engine and drove away. He then pulled his cell phone from his pants pocket, flipped it open and keyed in a series of numbers.

It was mid-morning when Mark Cassidy was outside and heard the chirping of the remote phone sensor in his pocket. He rushed inside and answered the lock-down phone in his roll-top desk. He listened. "Okay, Halstrom. Don't push her, but have them stay with her all the way, and watch for any funny business. When they get within a couple of hours of here, have 'em call me. I'll pick 'er up at Romeroville. The Sixty-Six station. Can't miss it. Look for a wire transfer to your account."

He locked the desk, then turned toward the front door to resume his outside tasks. Evelyn entered the hall from his left.

"I don't suppose you've seen this little gem," she said. She stopped and held a folded newspaper up.

He stood still and looked at her. "What gem?"

"Better take a look, Mark." She thrust the paper toward him.

They met half-way, where she opened the paper and pointed. He looked up at her, then down at the place where she had circled in red.

"Mm," he mused.

"I told you," she said. She walked to the front windows and peered out, her arms folded across her chest.

Cassidy stood quietly, holding the paper at his side, studying the polished wood at his feet. "So you think this is you?"

"Yes. Who else?"

"Right."

"So, what's next?" She arched her back and moved her head back and forth as though working out a pain, but remained at the window.

Cassidy, also in place, shook his head in a short, jerking motion. "I don't know. I really don't know." He slapped his leg with the newspaper and moved toward the kitchen. "Yes, I do know."

"Oh?" She turned to eye him sarcastically.

He took in a deep breath and released it. "We do nothing. For now." He went to an overhead cabinet, removed a tumbler, filled it half-full with tap water, then drank. He set the glass down on the counter. "They're guessing. True, they've guessed right that you're here, but they don't know where."

Evelyn walked slowly toward the kitchen, her head down in concentration. "Why the 'danger' bit? A come-on?"

"Probably." He sat at the trestle table. "Who the hell is 'benefactor'?"

"Don't know. I'm gonna' have to skull on it."

"Think it's a trap?" He squinted up at her as she moved into the kitchen.

"What do you think? Of course!" She shook her head broadly.

"They think you're stupid enough to fall for it?"

"Why place the ad?" She looked at him squarely.

"Maybe someone trying to warn you?"

"Possible; not probable."

"Plan?"

"Hell, Mark, I don't know!"

He stood and walked past her, pacing in thought. "Okay. But who's 'benefactor'? No idea?"

"At this moment, no. I need to think about it." She had not turned to follow his march.

"Right." He turned to look at her back. "I don't think this changes the way we behave. Here, at least."

"Mm." Her mouth was firm.

He furrowed his brow and moved closer as she turned to face him. "Was there ever a time that we—you and I—were seen together around that group?"

"Company people?"

"Yes."

"Not that I can recall. Why?" She crossed the space between the island counter and the overhead cabinets to get a glass.

"Well, in case they've got my picture. Name."

She took the glass to the refrigerator, opened it and poured three ounces of fruit juice into it. "I never discussed you that I can remember. But you can be damn sure they know I have family. Siblings." She sipped, then went to the table and sat. "And if they know that, they know you exist." She drank again. "And if they know who you are, then they have damn sure tried to track you down. It follows that they know about Cassidy, Bergman and Sterns. If they know that, they have access to your photograph. So, my question to you is, did you tell your partners where you'd be?" She looked up at him over the rim of the glass as she took more of the cold juice.

Cassidy looked away, then at the ceiling, then the floor. "No. I was careful not to tell anyone. I'm trying to think how they might track me, though."

"Internet?" Her eyes went wide.

"Internet?" He made a face at her.

"Mark, my dear, ignorant brother, it's possible to track down a computer to within a few miles using ISP addresses." She gave him a motherly stare, then looked away.

Cassidy leaned against the island counter with a blank stare. "You think they're looking for me, too?"

"Count on it." Evelyn drained her juice glass and set it down carefully on the table.

# 15

The offices of Cassidy, Bergman and Sterns, P.A., occupied the second floor of a modest, solid, "fifties" style building on Seneca street, within three blocks of the seat of power in downtown Seattle. Three lawyers—one missing—two paralegals and one secretary/receptionist were present when Beakman got off the elevator and walked into the lobby.

The secretary-cum-receptionist looked up from her desk and smiled. She was a dark-haired woman in her fifties, trim and attractive, who appeared ten years younger to the visitor. She greeted him. "May I help you, sir?"

Beakman, dressed in gray slacks and dark blue windbreaker, nodded. "Yes, I wonder if I could speak with Mr. Cassidy." He pretended to read from a note pad, then looked up.

The secretary made an apologetic face. "Oh, I'm sorry, Mr. Cassidy is unavailable. May I ask your business, sir?"

Beakman put the note pad in his shirt pocket. "Yes, I was hoping to see Mr. Cassidy about a bit of a problem I have. Legal problem. Personal."

"Perhaps you'd like to see Mr. Sterns. Mr. Bergman is in conference at the moment, but I believe Mr. Sterns will be free soon."

"I see. Well, do you expect Mr. Cassidy to be available soon?"

"Mr. Cassidy is actually not in the office. He's on sabbatical. He's not expected back for a few weeks." She raised her eyebrows and nodded.

"A few weeks. Okay; well—" He scratched his head, glanced around the reception area, hoping to see a photograph of the partners, then returned his gaze to the receptionist. "Sure. If Mr. Sterns—did you say?—is not busy."

"Let me buzz him." She picked up the phone handset, pressed a button and waited. "Yes, Mr. Sterns, a gentleman to see you. No, he doesn't. Yes, of course." She looked up. "He'll be with you in a few minutes. If you'd have a seat." She nodded toward a thinly-padded couch across from her.

Five minutes later, Sterns appeared at the entrance to the hall on Beakman's right and walked over to him. He was a slight, short man, younger than Beakman expected, with a bright, intelligent face and clear, dark eyes. Beakman stood as the attorney extended his hand.

"Nathan Sterns. Mr.?"

"Forster. Jim Forster, Mr. Sterns. Thanks for seeing me."

Sterns turned and beckoned with his hand high. "C'mon in."

Beakman followed Sterns into his office, a spacious, well-appointed room with a large desk centered against a street-side window. Sterns indicated one of the two leather chairs that faced it, and Beakman sat.

Sterns went around to his high-backed desk chair and settled into it. "So, Mr. Forster, what can I do for you?"

"I guess your secretary told you I had hoped to see Mr. Cassidy—no offense." Beakman held up his hand, palm out.

Sterns moved in his chair. "None taken. Mr. Cassidy, as perhaps Nora may have told you, is on sabbatical." He donned a serious demeanor.

"Yes, right, well, I guess you can help me as well." He smiled wryly at Sterns.

"I'm curious. How did you learn of our firm and of Mr. Cassidy?" Sterns made a tent with his hands, finger tips touching, elbows on the arms of his chair.

"I saw your ad. In the book, then asked a friend. She said Mr. Cassidy was—how did she put it—really great for my kind of problem."

Sterns reached for a legal pad. "And what is the problem?" He looked up, pen poised.

"Inheritance."

"Inheritance?"

Beakman pulled at his ear. "I got a sister who's contesting our father's will."

Sterns scribbled. "I see." He looked up again, squinting. "And your sister is in conflict with you over a will, is it? How many siblings do you have?"

"Just the one. Sister, that is."

"Why is your sister contesting? What does she expect to gain by doing so?"

Beakman shrugged. "We've never really gotten along. She thinks I'm stealing from her. I'm not married—not any more—and she has kids."

Sterns wrote on the pad. "Do you have a copy of the will?"

"Yes."

"With you?"

"Sorry, no."

Sterns set his pen down. "I'll have to see it before I can advise you."

"Sure. I guess there's the matter of a fee."

"Our fees are two hundred." Sterns sat back.

"Per hour?"

"Yes, but that's clock time. I'm not going to post our visit, but I will need a retainer."

"Okay." Beakman reached inside his jacket pocket. "I don't have my checkbook with me. Is cash okay?"

"Of course. I'll have Nora get you a receipt." He picked up the phone handset and pushed a button. "Yes, Nora, would you please print a receipt for Mr. Forster?" He looked at Beakman. "How much? Whatever you can do today."

Beakman had his wallet out and spread open. "I got a hundred here."

"We normally require more, but that'll do for now." He smiled and closed his eyes for a second in confirmation. "One hundred, Nora." He put the receiver down.

Beakman held out the money, scratched his cheek and frowned. "So, just curious. Why is Mr. Cassidy gone? You said sabbatical?"

Sterns sat back again. "If you'd give that to Nora, please. He's writing a book."

Beakman pulled his cash-holding hand back. "Really?" Beakman feigned excitement.

"That's what he said."

"Does he just stay home to do that?" Beakman grinned.

"Mm, no, I got the impression he went somewhere else. Why?"

Beakman squirmed, pretending to be embarrassed. "Well, truth be known, I've done a bit of writing myself. Novel. Can't seem to get anywhere. I guess if I was serious, I'd hide out, as they say. Get away from distractions." He smiled and shook his head. "Sure like to ask him. You know, get some advice."

Sterns cocked his head. "Sorry. He's gone incognito. Doesn't want to be disturbed. Hasn't even told us. Afraid we'll call to get his advice." He chuckled.

"Too bad. Sure like to pick his brains. Maybe give me some pointers. I'm kinda' stuck."

Sterns slapped the arms of his chair with both hands and stood. "Nice to meet you Mr. Forster." He held his hand out across the desk.

Beakman shook his hand. "Jim."

"Right. Jim. Well, bring me the will, and we'll see how we can help resolve the issue between you and your sister."

Sterns followed him to the door.

Before turning the doorknob, Beakman stopped and turned. "Say, did I see a picture of Mr. Cassidy in your ad?" He waved the cash.

Sterns frowned and looked aside, then back. "No. Why?"

"Oh, nothing, but I thought I had, and that he looked like someone I knew from college."

"Where'd you go to college?" Sterns stepped aside and opened the door.

"Back east."

Sterns shook his head. "Mr. Cassify got his degrees here in Washington state."

Beakman followed Sterns to Nora's desk. "Then I was mistaken."

Nora, the receptionist, traded Beakman's cash for a receipt. He nodded in response.

Sterns turned to look down the opposite hallway, then looked at Beakman. "There's a shot of him down here."

"Oh, great."

The two men walked into the other hall, where Sterns stopped and nodded at one of several framed photographs.

"That's him," Sterns said.

"Ah," Beakman uttered. "Guess I was mistaken. No resemblance." He looked at Sterns. "You know, I may be able to get back with the will today. What time do you close?"

"Eh, we try to get out of here at five. "I've got a meeting at four, so I'll be gone, but you can leave it with Nora. She closes the office at five. Bergman is gone at noon today. Any time, and I'll review it. Be sure and leave your number if I'm not here."

"Yes, I'd like to get this out of the way. You know how it is with family sometimes."

"I certainly do," Sterns replied.

As Beakman left, he looked closely at the door hardware. He also looked for a security panel near the entrance, inside the office and in the hall, but saw none. Once in the corridor, he looked both ways, then walked its length, studying everything, until he came to a plain door on the opposite side of the hall from the law firm entrance. He checked his surroundings, tried the knob, and the door opened to a small room containing janitorial supplies. He closed it carefully, then went to the next door, ten feet away. Again, he was rewarded with an unlocked door. He found a smaller room, large enough for two people standing, one wall of which was covered with a telephone patch board and electrical distribution panels. He closed that door and headed for the elevator.

It was ten minutes before five in the afternoon when Beakman, wearing a Harvard hat, dark glasses and a different jacket, entered the same building and made for the stairs. He stopped at the second floor landing, cracked open the hallway door, and looked out. The hall was empty. He looked at his watch. It read seven minutes to five. He held the door open two inches and watched for movement in the corridor. Shortly after five, he saw Nora, the law firm receptionist, emerge, pull the hall door shut, check to see it secured, then head for the elevator.

He waited another five minutes. She had turned off the main lighting in the reception area, but Beakman reasoned that didn't mean there was no one left inside. With stealth, he made for the service closet and entered. He closed the door carefully, and left the light out. Then he slid to the floor, his back against the end wall, his knees up, and closed his eyes.

At nine o'clock, sleepy, hungry and thirsty, he forced himself awake, removed a penlight from a small tool pouch attached to his belt, clicked it on, and focused it on his watch. He stood, massaged his legs, arms and face, then opened the door a crack.

The hall was dimly lit, and the clear, decorative glass that surrounded the entrance to Cassidy, Bergman and Sterns, Attorneys at Law, shown only minimal light from inside. He opened the door all the way, closed and latched it carefully, and looked around. He instinctively felt for the cold, hard, black steel that would have been under his left armpit during an operation such as this, and wished it were there. Without it, he felt vulnerable.

His head bent forward as though he were being watched, he moved slowly along the corridor to the law firm entrance. There, he pulled a small leather packet from the tool kit at his middle, opened it, and under the subdued light that emitted from the reception area, selected two thin steel picks. With these, he worked the lock on the door. Twenty seconds later he opened the door, slipped in, and with great care, closed and locked it again.

In case a janitor, security guard, or worse, a member of the firm, should see him from the hall, Beakman moved quickly away from the entrance, and down the hall opposite the one he had used to visit Sterns. His guess was correct. The name on the door at the end was M. Cassidy. His skin crawled as he realized he might find something worthwhile inside. The threat of discovery and a possible jail term for breaking and entering did not cross his mind.

Remarkably, the door was unlocked. As he turned the knob without opening the door, he halted and pondered. Why? Why would Cassidy leave the door to his office unlocked, given that he might be away for some time? Had Nora or one of the other partners needed something and forgot to re-lock the door? Was Cassidy cunning enough to think that by leaving his office open to intrusion and inspection he was signaling that he had nothing to hide?

Beakman opened the door slowly to the large office. He snapped the penlight on and played it around the dark room, careful not to allow its beam to penetrate the window behind the desk. He turned the little light off, went to the opening, closed the blinds over it, then turned to survey the room with his light. One wall was occupied by the usual law books, federal registers and state rulings. There was a scarcity of photographs; certainly none he could see of his and Radcliff's target, the Wraith, his sister, Evelyn. There was no file cabinet. Of course; that, along with others, would be in another room, and it would be a futile gesture to paw through the files there.

The shallow center desk drawer revealed nothing, as did the drawer sets on either side of the desk. And none were locked. *None were locked*. How curious, Beakman thought. Was this man *inviting* a search; taunting his sister's pursuers? No; a fantastic thought. Nonsense. The man simply had nothing to hide. Beakman sat in the tall, leather chair behind the desk after shutting the penlight off, in the dark, thinking. Smart man. Smart woman. This was proving to be difficult. He had had easier assignments in foreign countries.

He rose, set the blinds to where he had found them, and left the room, closing the door behind himself. Wiping any prints away was unnecessary; no obvious crime had been committed. He went to the framed photograph he had seen earlier, lifted it off the wall, and moved under the periphery of light from the reception area. There, using the miniature camera from his kit, he took several shots of the image at different angles avoiding reflections from the protective glass. He then replaced the framed photograph to its spot on the wall where he had found it.

To exit the building, he used the stairs again, looking first up and down the shaft, then found his way outside through a one-way door into the dark alley behind. He stopped at the corner to inspect the deserted street before heading for his rental car. He would call the law firm in a couple of days, say that he and his sister had reached a compromise, and that the retainer was not a problem; there was lots of money to replace it. Always try to wipe away traces of your presence, they had taught him. No use alerting Cassidy, he reasoned.

# 16

Alex Petersen was aware of the tail conducted by two men, one black and one white between Lubbock and the junction of highway eighty-four and north-south Interstate Twenty-Five. She wondered why it was important, and why Mark Cassidy had arranged for it. She would surely ask him.

His Jeep was parked in the Phillips 66 parking lot near the Interstate off ramp. He stood next to it as she pulled up alongside. He had called her on her cell not half an hour earlier, advising her he would be there. He waved, looked around, then came over to her Ford. She lowered her window.

"Hi," he said. "How you doing?" He was wearing clothes that caused her to think he was making repairs of some sort.

"I'm fine. Bit tired. But Mark, what's this all about? Those guys?" She smiled, but her forehead was creased with a question as she waved her hand behind her head, meant to indicate her followers.

"Give me a minute, okay? I need to talk to them." He gestured toward the detective's car that rolled slowly up alongside her SUV on the passenger side. He slapped the window sill and moved around the front of the car.

She watched as he said something to the black man at the wheel, nodded, waved, and returned as they drove to the station gas bays.

Cassidy stood at the side of her car again. "I'll explain, but let's get to the house first, okay?"

"Did you think—do you think—I'm in some sort of danger, Mark?" She cocked her head at him.

He winced. "Not really, Alex." He looked up as a pickup truck rolled by, headed for the bays. "Let's go, please. We'll talk when we get to the house." He took two steps away.

"Your place?"

He stepped backward, frustration evident on his features. "We'd be happy to have you stay as long as you like. We have room. But we need to talk." He squinted at her.

She sighed. "I don't want to bother."

"No bother." He turned and headed for his vehicle, then stopped, turned, and faced her. "Follow me, okay?"

"Okay." She started her engine.

Beakman sat on one of the nineteenth century style steel and wood benches in the Plaza. He watched the tourists mingle with the small coterie of twenty-somethings dressed as though the "Hippy" styles of the 1960s had returned in a real way. Many of them lounged and cavorted self-consciously, anxious for all and sundry to watch and admire them for their studied, detached "coolness."

He was there no more than ten minutes when Radcliff strolled by, subtly scanning the area. Beakman watched him go to a vendor's stand, purchase an Italian Ice, then circle the square on the sidewalk and back to the bench, where he sat, casually finishing the confection.

Radcliff spoke to the trees. "So what's the occasion?" He looked away.

Beakman turned his head after scanning the area in front. "I have a picture of the brother."

"With you?" Radcliff pretended to dust his hands off after he tossed the remains of the ice into a nearby trash barrel.

"No. It's on the site." Beakman continued to look forward.

"So, why are we here?"

Beakman hesitated, smiling. "I've missed you."

Radcliff's face displayed mild disgust. "I'm sure you have. Been away, have we?"

"None of your concern, but yes."

"You don't have backup, do you." It was a statement, not a question.

Beakman took five seconds to respond. "Why have you come to that conclusion, my friend?"

"An educated hunch. I've been thinking—"

Beakman interrupted. "Dangerous, thinking is. Can get you into trouble."

"Despite that, I've been thinking, and it stands to reason that for the sake of safety for your tidy little group, you'd need to keep the numbers down. Am I right, or am I right?"

"You're entitled to your opinion."

"And, a reminder: I'm not your friend."

Beakman nodded and looked at the flagstone path at his feet. "Doesn't bother me. Just a job." He paused. "Anyway, we think—feel—the photo might be of use to you."

"Right."

"So, any progress?"

Radcliff rubbed the end of his nose with his finger. "Not much. Thought I had a lead, but it was a dead end."

"Willing to tell me?"

"No. I told you—"

"Okay. Don't get steamed."

"Question for you."

"Shoot."

"How do you know we're not being watched?" He looked squarely at Beakman, then away.

"I don't. But who would it be?"

Radcliff shook his head. "Don't play games. You know who. The opposition. The ones who want to see you—us—go down. That's who."

Beakman, speechless, looked forward, his face a blank stare. He looked up briefly as another of the myriad couples and groups strolled by.

"And if we are being watched, where are they now? Huh? That guy over there—" He pointed vaguely. "Is he it?"

Beakman turned his head toward his tormentor. "Hey, man, keep your voice down."

"Fuck you! I'm outa' here!" Radcliff jumped up and stalked away.

Beakman didn't watch him go, rather he stared at the path and the feet passing by.

Evelyn Cassidy sat in the monitor room, shifting her eyes between the computer screen and the security monitor over her head. Her naked, loaded Walther semi-automatic pistol lay to the right of the PC mouse, butt out.

Her attention was drawn to the monitor as it showed the side of the road leading out of the valley and to the Pecos River. The image of a vehicle appeared, then another, both moving at a normal pace along the wracked tarmac, toward the house. It required only two seconds for her to identify the lead car, that of her brother. The second she realized belonged to the Texas woman. It was no surprise.

She froze the monitor when it focused on the front of the garage. She watched the Jeep disappear inside and the SUV park behind.

Cassidy helped Alex in with her belongings, and took them up-stairs, while she stood, tired and confused, in the kitchen. She looked to her left as Evelyn entered from the hall.

"Safe trip?" Evelyn asked. She stopped and looked at Alex in the eye. Her manner was professional.

"Oh, hi. Yes, but I'm kinda' bushed. Three hundred miles. You know."

Evelyn walked past her into the kitchen, then spoke without turning. "I know. How 'bout something to drink? We're well stocked. Beer, wine, cocktail?"

Alex faced her. "Oh, no, thanks. Some water."

"We can oblige," Evelyn said. She opened an overhead cabinet, grabbed a tumbler and went to the refrigerator. "Ice?"

"No. Thanks."

Cassidy descended the stairs and stood behind Alex. He spoke past her. "Me, I'm gonna' suck a beer." He glanced at Alex as he edged past her. "Sure you won't join me? Hate to drink alone."

"No, really. Thanks."

"Evelyn?" he asked.

"Not now," she said as she filled Alex' glass.

"Hey, come on in an' set a spell." He smiled as he gestured to the trestle table. He opened the refrigerator and retrieved a bottle of beer.

Alex followed his invitation, went to the table and sat on the outside bench. Evelyn put the glass of water in front of Alex, then scooted in on the window side. Alex picked the glass up and sipped. Except for the hiss that came from the beer bottle as Cassidy opened it, there was silence in the room.

Alex looked up at him as he approached the table where the two women sat. "You said we would talk."

"Yes. I did." He sat across from her, on the same side as his sister. He looked at Evelyn, studied her features for two seconds, then, his hand wrapped around the cold, sweating bottle, he faced Alex. "Alex, we have a problem."

Alex went rigid and shook her head. "Have I caused a problem?"

Cassidy closed his eyes and raised his hand in a defensive gesture. "No, no, Alex. Not at all. I meant that *we* have a problem. Evelyn and I." He nodded his head toward Evelyn. "You have not caused a problem." He shook his head.

Evelyn sighed, moved her head around as though trying to stretch a muscle, then stared at the table's surface.

"Let me start by asking you a question, Alex."

"Okay," she replied.

"Am I correct when I assume you saw a distinct resemblance between your friend, Betty, and Evelyn?"

Alex looked at Evelyn wide-eyed, then at Cassidy. She answered slowly. "Yes . . ."

Cassidy nodded. "Well, Alex, so did I. And so did Evelyn."

Alex frowned and shook her head. "What is this all about?" She looked at the siblings across from her, first Evelyn, then Mark Cassidy.

"Alex, I'm going to cut to the chase. You asked me why I had you followed—no, guarded—between here and Lubbock." He quaffed his beer.

"Yes?"

"I didn't know but what you might be in danger. Because of what happened. To your husband." He shot a glance at his sister.

"Yes?" Alex frowned, curiosity rising.

"Well, it's more than that. And I—we—now don't believe you're in danger."

Alex merely shook her head and continued to frown.

"My sister is the one in danger."

Alex looked at Evelyn, then back at Cassidy. "Evelyn?"

"The resemblance, Alex." Cassidy peered at her.

Alex was silent, then her mouth went slack and her eyes widened as she looked back and forth at the people seated across from her. "Oh, my God! You mean—!"

Cassidy nodded and looked down.

"Oh, my God!" Alex stretched her words out, buried her head in her hands, then spread them out on both her cheeks as she looked at both again, her mouth still open. "How can that be?! Why? Why?!" Her voice raised in pitch.

Cassidy reached across the table, offering his hand to her, but she remained in her attitude of fear and questioning. He withdrew his hand, sipped at the beer, rose, paced away several steps and turned to face her.

Alex continued to stare forward, then turned slowly to look up at him. Tears brimmed in her eyes. "Why?" Her words were choked.

Cassidy tightened his lips, then spoke. "Alex, Evelyn and I have discussed this at length, and we have decided we have no choice but to bring you into our confidence. What you are about to learn must be kept secret between the three of us. Can we trust you to honor that?"

Alex shook her head in a short, tight burst, then nodded assent. "I guess so, yes." She looked at Evelyn, then Cassidy.

"It has to be firm, Alex. Yes or no." Cassidy cocked his head in a challenge pose, his eyes widened.

"Yes," she said. "Yes, I agree. I will keep the secret."

Evelyn moved sideways across the bench, reached for a napkin, and handed it to Alex, who dried her tears.

"This will make more sense to you when I tell you that it was Evelyn they were after when they shot and killed your friend. Your husband was in the wrong place at the wrong time." He turned, stopped, then turned to face her again. "We didn't know if they were after you as well, or if you were somehow involved."

"Me?!" Alex went rigid with a look of surprise and anguish.

"You showed up here—admittedly before the murders—but here nonetheless."

"Yes?"

"After that, and because of what happened in Santa Fé, we were somewhat suspicious."

"Suspicious? Of me?!" She pointed her finger at her chest.

"Sorry, but yes. That there might have been a connection. Bit of a stretch, but almost too much of a coincidence."

"But why?!"

Cassidy looked at Evelyn. "Perhaps my sister can help here. Ev?"

Evelyn hesitated. "You're the lawyer. You do the deed." She waved him away and looked down.

Cassidy nodded and planted both feet astride. "Okay. Here's the scoop." He pointed at Evelyn. "This woman, my sister, was an undercover agent for the CIA. The Central Intelligence Agency."

Alex' jaw dropped as she looked at Cassidy, then stared at Evelyn. Evelyn looked squarely at her, then raised and lowered her eyebrows in confirmation. Alex returned her stunned gaze to Cassidy.

"Yep. CIA." He massaged his jaw, then continued. "For quite some time. Saw a lot of stuff come down. Some of it not so good. I don't know all the facts, nor do I want to. Nor can she tell me. Fact is, she saw some things that went beyond the pale. Way beyond what the agency's mission was and is. And it's some of those things that could hurt certain people inside and outside of the agency. That's why she's in danger. And that's why we believe your friend—and your husband—ended up dead. By mistake."

Alex started to shake as though she were freezing. She hugged herself, began to make small noises as though in pain, and rocked back and forth on the bench. Cassidy hesitated a moment, then rushed to her side as Evelyn hurried out from her position and came around as well.

"She needs to lie down!" Evelyn said, keeping her voice under control. "Get her to the sofa!"

Cassidy helped Alex up and walked her down into the living room where he stretched her out on the long piece of furniture. Evelyn arrived with Alex' water, which she refused, so Evelyn put it on the sofa-side coffee table.

Evelyn looked at her brother. "I believe you now."

He kept his eyes on the prostrate woman. "Let's get her a blanket."

Alex sat on the kitchen table window-side bench, both hands wrapped around a cup of hot tea. Her face was pale, her eyes red from the deep emotions she had again experienced so soon after the shock of the murders. Evelyn sat next to her, both arms on the table, her hands folded. Mark Cassidy sat across from them. Only after a long silence did anyone utter a sound.

Mark Cassidy was first. "I think I speak for both of us, Alex, when I say you'd be within your rights to go to the police with what we've told you." His voice was low; close to a whisper.

Evelyn nodded quiet assent.

He continued, "I also repeat that I believe you are in no danger. The police may think you are, but I don't." He looked at his sister. "You agree, Ev?"

Again she nodded, glancing at Alex, who made a quarter turn of her head in acknowledgment.

"I doubt if the assailant—or assailants—are looking for you. That's because we're pretty sure they know now they made a mistake. A serious mistake. And you arrived after they had fled."

Alex looked up at Cassidy. "Are you going to tell the police? You know, what you think's happened?" She glanced at Evelyn.

Cassidy cleared his throat. "Alex, we don't dare. We don't know who we're dealing with. We think we know; have some ideas, but not really. Evelyn has some ideas. It could be wider now. There may be money involved, and—"

"Money?" Alex frowned.

"Payoff money. If these guys are as desperate to find Evelyn as we think they are, there could be people in the police and other government and state agencies willing to take bribes. It's not unheard of."

Alex shook her head. "God! That's awful! How could they?!"

Silence again ensued, then Cassidy continued. "I know." He hesitated. "You have to go to the house. And the police are expecting you to let them know you're back. We feel it might be best if you go on to Santa Fé, check into a motel, then let them know you're here. And you want to get to Betty's house for your personal items. Make sure the cops are there." He wagged his finger.

Alex nodded, her demeanor unchanged, then shook her head. "I don't think I left anything."

"I didn't think so." He waved his hand in an offhand gesture. "But if they want to talk to you again, I should be there. In Santa Fé." He took in and released a deep breath. "I've told them I'm your attorney. I am an attorney, but not licensed here. So, if it comes to a point where you need local representation, then I'll have to back away. I don't think it'll come to that."

"Okay," Alex said. She had bucked up, and sipped her cooling tea.

"If they want to talk, to interview you again, I want you to call me. I'm going to give you a special number. That has to be a part of the secret here. Please don't tell anyone else you have it. If they do, if they want to talk, you call me, and we'll meet half-way. You may not recognize me right away." He looked at Evelyn, then at Alex again. "We think it likely they have a photograph of me. The bad guys." He stopped for several seconds. "I'll ask you to drive."

Alex looked down, sat back and straightened. "Mark, why was I followed? Did you really suspect I was involved?" She shot Evelyn a glance.

Cassidy exhaled loudly and raised his finger. "Look at it this way. Let's say you had been an operative, a hired gun, working with them. You're part of a team. At the same time you find us, others find the wrong woman; your friend, Betty. It's too late to call them off, and the damage is done. You pretend to be Betty's friend, leave evidence, claim the man is your husband, and so on. We had to know. Yes, you were checked out." He made an open, apologetic face and held up his hands, palms out.

Alex nodded. "You can count on me, but it scares me."

Evelyn put her hand on Alex' shoulder without looking at her and nodded.

"Of course you are, Alex. So are we. Especially her." Cassidy cocked his head toward Evelyn. He looked at Alex again. "How are you feeling?"

"I'm okay."

"One more favor," Cassidy said.

Alex cocked her head at him. "Yes?"

Cassidy cleared his throat again. "Evelyn has been undergoing treatment for cancer."

Alex looked directly at Evelyn, concern on her face. "Oh, no! I'm sorry."

Evelyn smiled. "Thanks. I think I'm going to beat it. Treatments are going well."

"The treatments," Cassidy said. "The treatments she's taking are at the hospital in town. The cancer center."

Alex frowned in sympathy. "I see."

"I've been taking her. But because of the possibility of them knowing my face as well, we think we need a different plan."

Alex nodded. "And that's where I come in?"

"Yes. Exactly. If you're willing."

"Of course." She nodded emphatically.

"They don't know you. And it's easier to disguise a woman. Also, they don't know your vehicle. But we can even change that."

"So, you want me to take you in?" Alex addressed Evelyn.

"If that works for you."

"Sure."

The two women clasped their hands together and smiled directly. Alex looked at Cassidy, who had relaxed measurably.

"You haven't had anything to eat," Evelyn said.

"I'm not real hungry." She smiled ruefully at Cassidy's sister.

"It's getting dark," Cassidy said. "I think it'd be okay of you leave tomorrow. We can time it to appear as though you're coming straight from Lubbock."

Alex pondered, then, "I think I'll take you up on your offer." She looked at the two Cassidys.

"Good," Cassidy said.

"Let's have some chow and a couple'a drinks." Evelyn looked from Alex to her brother and back again.

"Sounds like a plan," Cassidy said. He knocked twice on the table with his knuckles.

# 17

The time was a few minutes before three in the afternoon the following day when Alessandra Petersen pulled into the motel parking lot in Santa Fé. She had called ahead for a room, and was assured of one. She also left a message for Sergeant Griego.

Her cell phone buzzed as she shut the engine down. Griego would arrange to meet her the following morning to retrieve anything she might have left at the residence of her deceased friend. He thanked her for checking in, and told her there was little new, but that they would talk on the morrow. Her response was silence, to which he asked if she were still there. She answered in the affirmative, and they rang off.

In the room, after using the toilet and unpacking her clothes, she wanted to call Mark Cassidy on the secret number he had given her, but she resisted. It was later, at Maria's café, as she began to tuck into a green chile chicken enchilada, that her cell phone beckoned. Yes, she would meet the Cassidys the following afternoon. She sipped at her margarita with the salted rim and looked around the room with unfounded fears that she was being watched. No one looked her way, so she forced herself to relax.

Sergeant Griego and the same female officer who had serviced the murder scene, Sharon Pettibone, met Alex two hours before noon at Betty's house. Alex looked throughout the house with Griego as the uniformed police woman trailed her respectfully.

In the door of the guest room where she was to stay, she turned to them and shrugged. "I didn't leave anything. I was in such a hurry. Sorry." She paused. "Just groceries."

"Do you want to take those?" Griego asked.

She shook her head with a pained expression. "No. Somebody else can have them."

"Okay. No problem," Griego said. "I'd like to spend a few minutes. Okay if I call you Alessandra?"

Alex frowned and cocked her head at him. "Yes." Her answer was more like a question. "And it's Alex."

Griego held out his hand, inviting her to go before. "Okay, Alex. Coupla' things we're trying to clear up."

They moved to the living room, where Griego invited Alex to sit. She sat nervously on the edge of the sofa, while he stood. Sharon stood in the doorway to the hall, her hands clasped across her front. Alex looked up expectantly, shot a glance at Sharon, then watched Griego.

"We've pretty much dried up any leads we had, Mrs. Petersen—Alex—but sometimes something new crops up. We don't give up easily. Want you to know that."

"Thank you. You have something new?"

"First, to be honest. We've investigated your situation." Griego moved for the sofa and sat a foot away from her on it.

She turned her body to face him and looked at him squarely. "My situation?"

"In Lubbock."

"Lubbock?"

"Yes. Understand that in any case where a spouse or family member is killed—murdered—another family member is often involved." He lowered his head, a gesture of sincerity, as he spoke. "It's routine." He watched her eyes.

"You suspected me?!" Alex pointed her finger at herself with a pained expression on her face.

"We're obliged to follow up. I'm being straight. We had people in Lubbock take a peek."

"Oh, my god!" She put her hand to her chest. "Who?!"

Griego shook his head. "Contacts. Means I'm not free to discuss. As well as in the police department. No need for alarm. You have so far—as does the rest of your family—a clean bill of health."

Alex shook her head as she began to tear up. "So far?!" She sat up straight.

The detective sergeant shook his head. "We believe your friend was the target, and your husband was in the wrong place at the wrong time." Griego pulled a notebook from his jacket pocket, then reached for a pen from his shirt pocket. He held the pen prominently so Alex could see it.

She glanced at his movements, the items he held, then watched his face.

He hesitated, studying her, then held the pen up. "Recognize this?"

"What, the pen?"

"Yes."

"No." She cocked her head at him. Then studied the writing instrument. "What's that on the end?

The pen was a gold-colored Cross brand with a small, circular device near the top.

Griego looked at it closely. "It's the Masonic symbol. The Masons."

"Oh."

"Was your husband a member? Of the Masons?"

She shook her head emphatically. "No."

Griego nodded, hesitating. "It was found later. But you don't recognize it?"

Alex shook her head slowly as she peered into Griego's eyes. "Is it important?"

Griego raised his eyebrows in a shrug. "Don't know. Could be. Do you know of anyone else—a man—who might belong to the Masons? A boy friend. Of Betty's?"

Alex frowned. She answered slowly, dragging her word out as though it were a question. "No." Griego began to speak, then she interrupted. "Do you think the killer—?"

"Could be." The detective waited a beat. "Know any of her men friends?"

Alex was silent for several seconds, then shook her head. "'Fraid not." She lowered her head. Her words were low and subdued. "Betty didn't have any secrets. I thought. Guess she did. Guess Ted was her secret." She looked up. Her mouth was turned down dramatically.

Griego nodded, looked at the floor, up at the female officer, then Alex. "What we can't get our arms around, Alex, is why and who would want to kill your friend, assuming they weren't targeting your husband."

"I know. I don't know."

Griego nodded, his lips tight in frustration. "If you ever think of anything."

Alex had been so bound up in her fears, frustrations and the interview that she had let Mark and his sister slip from her mind. Recalling what they had revealed to her, she experienced a nervous twitch which translated to her legs, at the same time causing her head to move abruptly to one side. A tiny yelp emitted from her mouth, which she covered with her hand.

Griego looked at her. "Something?"

Alex looked at him. "No. No. Just thinking. About things."

Griego looked up at Sharon, then at Alex. He squinted his eyes at her. "Sure? Thought of something? Don't hold back. Sometimes the smallest things."

Alex shook her head in a fast, jerking motion. "No. No. It's nothing. Really." She forced a weak smile and looked away.

Griego nodded, doubts clouding his thoughts. "Okay. Well. Guess we've taken up enough of your time." He stood and looked down at her. "Talked to—what's his name? The lawyer friend? Cassidy?"

Alex' mind reeled with what she felt was guilty knowledge. She was unable to put the pieces together and wanted to leave. She stood. "He's been very kind."

"Is he your attorney?" Griego looked at her squarely.

"Not really. Just a friend. I didn't know he was a lawyer." She grasped her purse closely to her middle and took a tentative step toward the hall.

"He let me know when you went home and assured me you'd return."

She turned. "He told me he would."

Griego smiled and spoke in a broad tone. "Okay, Alex. Thanks." He scratched his head. "How long you plan to stay? In Santa Fé?"

"I don't know. When I came up the first time, it was going to be for just a few days." Her face screwed up into a worried frown.

Griego smiled in recognition of her concern and shook his head. "You don't have to stick around on our account. Just let us know your whereabouts. In case we have anything new." He squinted at her pleasantly.

"Oh, I will. You can count on that."

Griego's partner had their shared car on another case, so he had asked uniformed officer Sharon Pettibone if she would accompany him to the crime scene in her squad car. Her partner had agreed, staying behind to complete paperwork. They drove away after watching Alex' SUV disappear at the next corner.

Griego, in the passenger seat, stared straight ahead. "What's your take?"

Sharon tilted her head, but kept her eyes on the task at hand as driver. "Probably innocent. Or she's one hell of an actress. Nothing outa' Lubbock?"

"Nope. But we'll keep digging."

"Have they looked at the house there? Searched?"

Griego drew in his breath and released it volubly. "No cause. Locals know them, and aren't comfy with the idea. We'd need a lot more to go on. Nothing with the family business. Jurisdictions and all that. And you know how Texans can be about us dumb Mexicans."

"Yeah." She smiled at the roadway.

"Thing that bugs me is the way it came down. If she—or anyone else connected—had bought a hit, why the 'pro' look to it?"

"Yeah. Right."

"Too damned clean. Amateurs we'd o' been on before breakfast."

"Mm." Sharon stopped at a red and white sign, looked both ways, then continued.

"No brass."

"Mm."

"The shooter was good. Head shots; no stippling. Did it from ten or more feet away. Probably used a silencer."

"Had to be good shot."

"Yep."

"The pen. Who's it belong to?"

"Yeah, the pen. Good question."

"No prints?"

"No prints. Smudge or two on the pen, but not clear enough to lift anything. We'll keep looking. Here and Texas." Griego looked out his passenger window at nothing.

"You gonna' stay on her?"

Griego cocked his head in frustration. "Trying to convince the captain to let us tail 'er. He's a hard sell. Figures the woman's genuine. The evidence package and forensics talk pro all the way. She'd need big bucks to hire that."

As Alex drove away, she strained to explain to herself why she should keep quiet about the Cassidy revelation. Perhaps telling the police what she knew would help solve the case. Was she breaking the law? Why should she keep what she had been told a secret? They had told her it was possible for the police to be on the wrong side. But what if the brother and sister team were lying? Why would they lie? She felt her heart rate go up.

Alex pulled into the broad dirt yard that fronted the abandoned commercial building at the junction of the interstate and the highway that led south to El Dorado and Cline's Corners. After stopping with the nose of her Ford pointed toward the controlled intersection, she shut the engine off and waited. Two minutes later, Cassidy's Jeep appeared, moved in a circle around her, then stopped close to the dilapidated building whose porch seemed ready to collapse. As instructed, she remained in her seat and watched the vehicle in her rearview mirror as the two people in the front seat, both wearing dark glasses, remained motionless. A minute later, what appeared to be a small, slim man wearing boots, tight jeans, a blue Levi's jacket and grey, broad-brimmed western hat emerged from the passenger side and moved quickly for Alex' car.

Evelyn jerked at the passenger door handle that Alex had forgotten to unlock. Alex made a sound, enabled the handle and Evelyn got in. "Let's go," she said. "Get on the Interstate."

Although Evelyn's face was forward, Alex could see she wore no makeup.

"You okay?" Alex asked.

Evelyn sighed. "Yeah." She hesitated. "No. I want this to be over. Both problems. Not sure they ever will be." She shot Alex a glance with a tepid smile, then faced forward. "Thanks for helping."

Jeremy Radcliff wheeled his pickup into the drive leading to the hospital entrance nearest the Cancer Center. Ahead of him with one car separation was a red Ford SUV with Texas plates. To his left, two cars waited to move from the crowded parking lot, forcing him to continue up the drive to the canopied entrance. A foreshortened bus awaiting the arrival of geriatric patients from the hospital was parked across from the entrance, blocking the second lane such that he had to stop behind the Texas vehicle.

He watched a man wearing western garb emerge from the passenger side and move toward the Cancer Center. He turned his head to look at the car stopped behind him, then watched the man who had left the Ford move toward the Cancer entrance. Something about him was bothersome. He was small, and seemed unsteady on his boots. Further, he seemed to have an oddly-shaped behind; more like a woman's; full, with flared hips. He also noticed the way the man's arms and legs moved. Rather than his lower arms angled toward his body, they oriented out, like a woman's. His heart rate rose as he realized he was looking at a woman, not a man. Walking toward the Cancer Center. Cancer. The Wraith was reported to have cancer. And she would very likely be in disguise.

The red SUV moved on, and he followed into the parking lot. As the Texas vehicle moved on, he spotted an opening near the southwest corner, pulled in, shut the engine down, grabbed his cell phone and pressed a speed dial key.

"Patsy? Hi. Yeah, it's me. Listen, I—" He listened, then said, "I'm gonna' be a little late. Okay?" He held the device to his ear another ten seconds, then, "Okay. Be there as soon as I can. Love you."

He flipped the phone closed, clipped it to his belt, and grabbed the morning newspaper. He donned his hat, exited and locked the truck, then moved at a quick pace toward the hospital. As he moved, he put his dark glasses on, then began scouring the lot for the Texas car. It was nowhere to be seen.

Radcliff sat on the covered bus bench pretending to read the paper, glancing now and then toward the Cancer Center entrance. City buses came and went, as did private cars, taxis and more than one geriatric transport. People entered and exited the Cancer Center for nearly an hour when the red Ford appeared and stopped close to the curb in front. He leaped up and walked rapidly for the Center, turned toward the hospital entrance, then spun around and moved for the Cancer Center. He burst through the door and into the foyer. Moving for the exit was the person he had seen leaving the SUV earlier, the little man. Through his dark glasses, pretending to be on a personal mission, he watched the man put on his sun shades, but not before he confirmed his suspicion that the "man" was not a man, but a woman. She also seemed familiar. He was certain. It was she; Evelyn Cassidy, the Wraith.

Perspiring and his heart pounding, he moved into the lobby, stopped, turned and followed. By the time he was on the sidewalk, his quarry had gotten into the Texas SUV, and the vehicle began to move. As he raced across the lot for his truck, cursing himself for not finding a spot closer to the hospital, he kept one eye on the Ford. He made his old truck by the time the big red vehicle came to a stop at the boulevard. Frantically starting the truck and backing, he lost track of the other car momentarily, then saw it as it turned left onto St. Michael's Drive. He made his way onto the street as the SUV went through the next intersection. He was forced to stop as the light turned red, but brought his speed beyond the legal limit so as to keep the big car in sight, watching the rearview intermittently. He was relieved when he realized it had entered the Interstate from the north-bound ramp.

He kept the Texas vehicle within sight and a half mile in front as they both moved at the speed limit. Finally, he saw it exit at the Cañoncito off ramp. He followed down the ramp, where he saw the Ford stop near a grey, four-door Jeep. Acting quickly, he continued through the ramp connector intersection onto a paved road that swept down into the canyon, out of sight of the two parked cars. He halted his pickup, burst out and ran up the embankment to where he could see the two cars from a crouch, leaving his door open. The person he had seen at the Cancer Center exited the Ford and made for the Jeep. The Jeep then sped away, up the north-bound ramp, while the Ford turned and made its way back under the overpass bridge in the direction from which it had come, back toward Santa Fé.

He half-ran, half stumbled down the embankment and into his truck, which he had left running. Panting furiously, he careened backward up the sloped road to the crude intersection, jammed the transmission into forward, cranked the wheel and raced up the on ramp to the north-bound lanes of the Interstate. He barely missed being struck by an eighteen-wheel truck as it veered into the passing lane, its loud horns blaring a well-deserved protest.

The grey Jeep was no longer in sight, so he pushed the pickup as hard as he could. He hoped the roar he heard from the old, re-built engine was not a sign of rapid decay in the form of action leading to a swallowed valve or a thrown rod. He next spotted the Jeep at the brow of Glorieta Hill before the highway swept down into the broad valley of the Pecos, and was able to slow. He held back, then watched as it took the off ramp to Pecos and Glorieta. At the stop sign, the grey car turned left, toward Pecos.

Radcliff was feeling triumphant, but with mixed emotions.

He stayed behind the Jeep, expecting it to leave the two-lane highway at any moment, but it traversed the entire east-west highway until it reached the north-south route through the village of Pecos. There, it turned left; north into the upper Pecos River Valley. He moved to the right lane when another car, a small, red foreign job, pulled alongside his left while he pondered his next move. His heart thudded. The driver was a young woman, and she drove straight across the intersection toward the river and East Pecos. He saw no other vehicle in the rearview. He decided he had pushed his luck, and turned right at the four-way stop. He reasoned that if he were to follow, he risked being spotted, especially by someone as savvy as Evelyn Cassidy, if indeed it were she in the grey Jeep. He had not had a look at the driver, but remembered the photograph Beakman had provided of her brother. He would have to retreat and think over his next move.

Then he thought of the woman driving the red Ford SUV. Who was she, and what was her connection? As he drove south through the National Monument grounds, he remembered the article about the double murder. The man had been from Texas. The dead woman had resembled the Wraith. Ridiculous. Too much of a coincidence. He shook his head and banged his fist on the steering wheel.

What would he tell Beakman?

Half panicked, he grabbed his cell phone and punched the speed dial key. Patsy would kill him. Worse, what was his excuse? He'd have to think fast.

Cassidy had waved to Alex as his sister got into his Jeep at the Cañoncito ramp, then left immediately for the highway. The appearance of the old, re-built Ford pickup truck that passed in front of them and made its way down the local access road had not piqued his interest to any degree; nor had it in Evelyn's mind. After he executed the left turn at the four-way junction in Pecos, he felt there was something bothering him. He frowned and squinted, trying to fathom what it might be. He went back over the period of time since he had met his sister. Then it occurred to him. The truck behind them at the stop. He thought he had seen it somewhere before. But where? No; there were dozens of such vehicles in the area. Besides, he saw it only from the front in his mirrors. He relaxed and let the thought drift away as Evelyn pointed out the amount of water flowing in the river.

Alex had not had the time nor the desire to reveal the facts of her meeting with Sergeant Griego of the Santa Fé Police Department, Homicide Division, to Evelyn. She had assured Mark Cassidy she would advise him of any such get-together, and invite him to attend. She also recalled that he and his sister had serious concerns not only about being spotted by the people purportedly out to get Evelyn, as well as their suspicions of authority figures subject to bribes. She decided her tete-a-tete with Griego had been benign. A wave of delicious independence and excitement wept over her, crowding out the underlying fear.

On the other hand, she felt empty and alone, and what she wanted now was to call Mark Cassidy. In her new-found self, she admitted she wanted to be in his presence. And more.

# 18

Radcliff parked his pickup truck in the crowded city parking lot on Water Street and walked through the two-story retail shop building across from it to reach the town square. The time was close to noon, and the tourists were out in force.

Since leaving the house, actually, since his sojourn to Pecos, he had been watching for red SUVs sporting Texas license plates, and no less so this morning. He somehow felt he might be able to find the vehicle and glue himself to the driver, whom he believed to be a woman. Although his enthusiasm for the dark mission foisted upon him by his unwelcome associate left him with a bitter taste in his mouth, he had become fascinated by developments of late. Who was this woman, and why Texas? Why the transfer at a lonely spot along the Interstate in Cañoncito? Odd. Suspicious. Who, if he had been correct about recognizing the Wraith, was the Jeep driver, and where was she hiding? Was the Jeep's turn up into the Pecos River canyon a ruse? Had he been spotted? Had they waited for him to follow, then executed a U-turn and headed south once the coast was clear? He didn't think so, and was anxious to investigate further.

He stood under the south portal along San Francisco Street amidst a stream of outlanders dressed for southern Arizona. They rushed from one over-priced curio shop to the next, or headed for restaurants with cute, up-scale names, there to consume a sub-standard portion of same-caliber food priced at ten times the value. He wished he clutched a brown paper sack containing a baloney and cheese white bread sandwich. He would eat it openly while seated on one of the park benches on the green across the traffic-free street. He was a few minutes early for his rendez-vous with Beakman, but he figured the bastard would be there, watching for him as well. Birds of a feather.

He pushed off, braved the human onslaught, and made a bee line for the military monument centered on the plaza. As he gained the surrounding sidewalk, Beakman came up alongside him on his left, but remained two feet away. Radcliff glanced at him, then faced forward. He slowed his pace, as did the active CIA agent.

"How goes it?" Beakman asked, his head down and toward Rad-cliff.

"How goes what, Beakman?" Radcliff purposely looked away in annoyance.

Beakman smiled, shaking his head and roving his head around as though clearing a crick in his neck or scouring the trees for pigeons. He wore his grey western hat. "Shit." This he said almost under his breath, but his companion heard nonetheless. "What's it gonna' take, Radcliff?"

Radcliff, who also wore a hat, a modified fedora, screwed his face up in a way he had seen Frenchmen who could not care less do. In reality, his mind was racing. "Doin' my best, Beakman."

They had reached the north edge of the plaza green, across from the Pueblo Indian purveyors ranged along the front of the ancient Gov-ernor's Palace. When they stopped, they both instinctively scanned for curious eyes. They did not face each other, rather they stood and looked around as though they were two tourists trying to figure out where they were and where the nearest restroom might be.

"Looks like you've got some extra time," Beakman said.

"What're you saying?" He frowned.

"It means our favorite congressional committee, in their infinite wisdom, has pushed the hearing back. That means we've got extra time." Beakman studied his footwear for a few seconds before looking up. He subconsciously doubled his fists at his sides in an attempt to hide his an-noyance.

"Peachy," Radcliff said.

Beakman, choosing not to rise to Radcliff's obviously negative demeanor, went on. "But please, tell me if you have anything of value to report."

Radcliff shook his head rapidly, barely moving it from side to side. He sniffed. "Nada. Nyet. Nothing." He looked away, then back. "But I'm trying." He raised his eyebrows and smiled momentarily.

Beakman was silent as he studied Radcliff's face. "Okay; well, I sure hope we can solve this little problem. Soon."

"Little problem. Right." Radcliff chuckled. "So, Beakman, what are you doing to contribute?" He peered into the agent's face.

"You may recall, Jeremy, that I got you the brother's picture. Not too shabby, huh?"

"Point. My compliments."

"Thanks."

"Are we through here?" Radcliff asked.

"For the time being."

"Okay. *Hasta luego*, pal." Radcliff turned and crossed the street where he walked slowly along the Palace porch, pretending to be interested in the turquoise and silver jewelry displayed on the walkway.

Beakman stood stock still and watched Radcliff's back as he moved off. His instincts told him the man was lying.

What neither of them knew was that Alessandra Petersen, aka Alex, was also studying the Amerind crafts laid out along the front of the old, thick-walled adobe building under the porch. She was no more than fifty feet from Radcliff.

Ten minutes later, Radcliff made his way circuitously back to his pickup, glancing back occasionally. He knew Beakman had retreated shortly after their visit, but he was not sure of late that he was not being followed by someone else. He walked between the clot of tightly-parked vehicles, most of which were from New Mexico. He noted the plates on other vehicles. The next greatest number were from Texas, a fact he had learned to accept over time. Next, from his moving vantage were Arizona, California, one or two from Colorado, and an eastern state here and there. If he had looked carefully, he would have seen the red Ford in the southeast corner, but he got into his truck ignorant of that essential fact, keyed the engine on, and drove away. As Radcliff moved out onto Water Street after paying the parking toll, Alex Petersen entered the parking lot and went to her vehicle. Two minutes later, he waited behind three cars on narrow, crowded Shelby Street who were, in turn, waiting to enter the high-traffic, west-bound lane of Alameda. Motion in his interior rearview mirror drew his attention to a monstrous vehicle behind him. As it came closer and slowed to a stop, his heart rate rose. The automobile was a red SUV, and a woman was at the wheel.

First one, then all of the cars in front found openings on Alameda, and it was his turn. To his left, the traffic light at the intersection with Old Santa Fé Trail had gone green and allowed another group of slow-moving cars through. His chance came, and he pulled onto the wider Alameda as the red car behind him assumed his former position, to wait. He had to move, but was in a quandary: if the car behind him was his target, where would it go next? The intersection with Don Gaspar, then Ortiz, then two controlled intersections followed. He could lose it soon. His palms were sweaty against the steering wheel as his mind raced. He was pinned be-tween cars, and there were no parking spots on his right. He decided to gamble, and stayed in line. As he passed Don Gaspar and moved along the first of The Inn of The Governors, he saw the red SUV enter the traf-fic on Alameda in his mirror. The motel's entry drive was clear, so in a sudden maneuver, he swung the pickup into the drive, cranked the wheel left, backed right, wheeled left, then punched the accelerator, bringing the nose of the old truck to the curb on Alameda. The red Ford was only then clearing the intersection with Don Gaspar, so he nosed out into traffic. The driver of a small Japanese car leaned on his horn switch in annoyance and fear of an accident. Radcliff ignored him, focused on the SUV and its now obviously female driver. He pulled out behind it, forcing another car to brake violently as its horn sounded. He straightened the wheel, came up to the speed of the target vehicle, then backed off enough so he could read the plate. Texas. He pinched up his mouth in triumph and banged the wheel with his fist.

He allowed the distance between his truck and the red car to widen between Guadalupe and St. Francis, where the Texas car turned left, then eased to the right lane. Careful not to allow other vehicles to come between him and his target, he followed it to the four-lane, divided Cerrillos, where it made a right turn onto the south-bound lanes. More than a mile of travel later, and after having stayed behind the woman's vehicle, he watched as it entered a motel parking lot on the southeast side of the street. He drove on, made a U-turn and returned to the motel, where he drove slowly into the parking lot. He found the red SUV parked near the rear on the east side, but it was empty. He stopped in the traffic lane, the engine running, and pondered his next move.

If Alex had looked out the curtained window of her motel room, she could have seen the old, but shiny, re-built Ford pickup truck with a man at the wheel, stopped a few feet beyond her car. She did not, though; she had gone immediately to the bathroom and relieved herself. She sat on the edge of one of the two double beds, sipping water from a plastic cup, thoughtfully provided by the motel management, pondering her situation in the semi-darkness of the curtained room. Her impression was that the police were finished with her, and that she should return home; but to what? The thought depressed her. Her somewhat overbearing daughter was there; her son had returned to school. The house was cared for meticulously by their long-time, faithful housekeeper, Lorenza, who, in her typical Mexican fashion, had assumed a motherly attitude toward them all as well as her own family. She looked around at the clothes scattered across the bed and onto the floor that she had failed to put away in her frenetic state. Then, without actually thinking about what she was doing, she took the card Cassidy had given her from her purse, picked up the telephone handset and keyed the number.

Radcliff pulled slowly ahead, found an empty parking slot five cars along the way, and backed in. He got out, closed the door quietly, then looked around. He walked to the front of the motel. On Cerrillos, traffic streamed by noisily. Beyond the wood fence that bordered the motel property, was a sign announcing the location of a fast-food restaurant. He took another look around, then strode to the sidewalk and the restaurant.

He hurried into the men's room, came out and ordered two hamburgers, extra French fries and a large soft drink. He rushed back to his truck, put the viands on the seat, then walked along the east wall of the motel until he saw the red Texas SUV. Back in the truck, he tucked into one of the hamburgers as well as a sack of fries. He also sucked on the iced drink. After a few bites, he keyed the ignition to the accessory position, flipped the radio on to an FM music station and sat back. The ample remains of the first sandwich he wrapped and stuffed into the white paper sack from the fast food place along with his likely dinner. He would have to finish the drink so the cup could be used in lieu of a bathroom, but that could wait for the time being. He hoped the woman from Texas would move soon, and worried about his cat, Mandy. He might have to call Patsy Romero for assistance and hope she would not be upset with him.

He closed his eyes against the bright light streaming through the windshield and soon dozed off. Two minutes later, he was awakened by the sound of a car passing in the lot. It was a big, four-door sedan with a middle-aged man at the wheel and a woman of the same vintage beside him. Although his heart rate had risen, he shut his eyes again. Not fifteen minutes later, he became aware of another vehicle passing. This time, it was the red Texas car, the woman at the wheel.

Half asleep, he flailed, throwing his arms out to push himself up-right into driving position. In doing so, he knocked the soft drink in the waxy cardboard container to the floor, and it began to leak through the straw cap onto the rubber mat-covered floor on the passenger side. Ignoring the mishap, he cranked the engine to life, checked his surroundings, jammed the transmission into gear, and fell in behind the big red car. He detected the saccharine odor of the shallow, but spreading pool of dark cola down and to his right.

No more than two vehicles behind the Texas car through the crazy-quilt city, Radcliff stayed safely behind until it entered the Interstate at the Cerrillos on ramp. There, the SUV rocketed up to eighty miles per hour. He dropped the pickup back, thinking that if the mysterious woman were possessed of any professionalism, she would be watching her mirrors for any suspicious vehicles. He needn't have worried.

As before, she pulled off at the Cañoncito exit. Radcliff cursed silently, and made the decision to continue. Past the Apache Canyon cut, where the highway rose up the slope to Glorieta Pass, he swerved off the highway onto the broad dirt apron that fronted the shabby little makeshift Glorieta Battle Monument. He pulled to a stop, and faced the truck at a forty-five degree angle to the pavement so he could see the on-coming traffic, but left the engine running. He waited for five minutes, as one big-rig, two pickups, several passenger cars and a bus passed in his direction. Then, approaching from around the bend, he saw the brilliant red of a large vehicle. At that moment, he dropped the clutch, burned a pair of ruts into the dirt, and accelerated as hard as he could onto the Interstate. Although the SUV was coming fast, he was able to gain enough speed to match that of the Texas car and stay well ahead. He saw a vehicle not more than three lengths behind the red car. He was sure it was the Jeep he had followed into Pecos.

Sharing his attention between the road ahead and the vehicle images in his mirrors, Radcliff made the judgment to exit at the Glorieta-Pecos ramp. He would cross the Interstate bridge, and head east on the two-lane highway toward Pecos. He was correct. The red SUV and the Jeep were behind him. At the four-way junction in Pecos, he cranked the steering wheel left, and began the drive north into the upper Pecos River Canyon. The two large vehicles also turned north. He was careful to keep his followers in sight as they negotiated the winding road up into the southern Rockies. As he crossed the river bridge a quarter mile south of Terrero, he noticed that his quarry had slowed, and as he progressed more slowly himself, he saw first the SUV, then the Jeep, negotiate the turn onto a secondary road short of the old, abandoned trestle bridge.

He pulled into the broad parking lot at the Terrero store, turned back onto the highway and made his way to the narrow canyon entrance. He stopped the truck and read the small sign. It read, "Holy Ghost Canyon."

To follow now, he realized, would invite curiosity. Fearing he might be watched, he drove away, south, at a slow pace, thinking. He had spotted the Wraith. He had narrowed the search. Now what?

Alex had caved in to her desire to be with Mark Cassidy, resulting in her calling him. He had answered on her third try, and by that time, she had become anxious to the point of developing an aching stomach. It disappeared when she heard his voice at last. Her excuse for seeing him, as she put it, was to report on her visit with Sgt. Griego of the Santa Fé police department, and felt it would be better if it were in person. Her true reason she decided to keep to herself. Cassidy had told her it would be best if she not check out of the motel, and that she should inform Griego that she was still in the area, but without specifics. He told her to meet him in Cañoncito; that they should caravan so he could watch their backs. He suggested she bring her personal belongings

As Alex slowed to a stop at the canyon house, Cassidy, two lengths behind, kept his eyes on his rear. There had been nothing more than one or two locals behind them, both of whom had peeled off before they left the main mountain highway, but he could not be sure there was not someone who had sneaked in behind. He had noticed the pickup in front of them, but had discounted it, especially after seeing it continue past the turn-off. After parking alongside the red SUV, and before putting it into the garage, he walked out onto the crumbling tarmac and studied the road in. The way was devoid of traffic, and the sounds were nothing more than breeze-driven tree branches. He turned, drove the Jeep into the garage, and entered the house, where Alex had already gone, but not before collecting the large caliber, semi-automatic pistol which lay on the passenger seat.

Beakman sat in the semi-darkness of his motel room, staring at his laptop computer screen. Across its face was an arcane series of lines, each with latitude and longitude entries matched against dates and times. The latest for that day had been downloaded a few minutes earlier. He noticed that the input stopped, then started, with a gap of nearly an hour. He moved the computer mouse, pressed a switch on it, then made a few strokes on the keyboard. Another screen appeared; this one a map of the United States. He pointed and clicked again, and the map zoomed in on the southwest, then the southern Rockies. Two more steps, and it showed the area in and around Santa Fé, New Mexico. That included north-south Interstate Twenty-Five and the Pecos River Valley. Red dots showed here and there, accompanied by date and time data.

He stared at the screen for a full minute, rubbing his chin, around his mouth and across his cheeks. With a sudden move, he killed the connection, causing the map to evaporate, then invoked the encrypted e-mail software and began to type.

Radcliff arrived at the four-way junction in Pecos, stopped, then turned right and headed home. He picked up his cell phone and dialed Patsy's number. He would have to think, but couldn't do it now. One thing he did know: Beakman would not know of his find. Not now.

# 19

Alessandra "Alex" Petersen had left her motel room in a state of excitement which she had not felt in a very long time. She had heeded Mark Cassidy's advice to drive at the speed limit at all times—within reason, she felt—and to watch for "tails" as he had called them. She had noticed, but only momentarily, an old, but well-kept pickup truck enter the north-bound Interstate after she had done so, but it was well back, and she quickly lost interest. She certainly felt no threat. If she had been alert, she would have seen that although other vehicles passed her on the highway, the pickup stayed behind. She would also have noticed, if she had looked up at the Cañoncito off ramp, that the same little truck stayed on track and passed by.

Cassidy had asked her when she stopped by his Jeep if she had watched for a follower, to which she replied in the affirmative. He had been standing by his car when she stopped, then had pushed off and come to her window. She was reminded of the stop at the service station at Romeroville. He had leaned down as she opened her window. He had smiled in a friendly fashion, but she had hoped for more, resulting in her sobering for the time being. After giving her instructions as to how they were to proceed, she had driven on. If she had been looking for it, she would have seen the same pickup truck in front of her, but she had not.

Cassidy, behind her the entire distance to the house in Holy Ghost Canyon, had been unaware of the pickup truck until they had reached the old trestle river bridge at the junction. After their arrival at the house, he had stood in the road to inspect the way in, then put the Jeep away and entered the house. But something had bothered him, and he couldn't put his mental finger on it.

He shoved the semi-automatic pistol into the small, wall-mounted cupboard placed there for it in the hall, and walked into the living room. Alex and his sister sat across from each other, Evelyn holding a novel she had been reading. Both women looked up.

"How'd it go with Griego? I assume you spoke with him." He looked at Alex, then his sister, in an attempt to defuse what he considered to be growing tender feelings coming in his direction from the Texas woman.

Alex nodded, trading looks between the two Cassidys. "Yes, it was Griego. It went okay. I'm sorry. I know you wanted to be there, but he pushed me."

Cassidy waved her remark away. "Not a problem."

She told of her looking for non-existent belongings, the sit-down in the living room and the pen with what appeared to be the Masonic symbol, and the fact that it meant nothing to her.

Cassidy and Evelyn looked at each other, then Alex.

Cassidy addressed his sister. "Mean anything to you?"

Evelyn put her book aside and stared at the floor, shaking her head slowly. She spoke in a low monotone. "Masons. We were discouraged from joining any organizations unless it was for the company." She looked up. "That doesn't mean . . ."

Cassidy cut in. "That a company man wouldn't have been a member, or was assigned to be."

"Right," Evelyn said.

"Well, think about it, Ev," Cassidy said. He looked at Alex with a developing frown. "Alex, I was wondering. Did you happen to notice anyone driving in front of us up from Pecos?"

She looked up at him, her eyes wide. "From Pecos? In front?"

"Yes. In front."

She cocked her head at him. "I—I don't think so." She looked down, then up. "Wait. Yes. I think there was a truck."

He turned his head in a quizzical manner and looked down at her from the corners of his eyes. "A truck?"

"Yes. A pickup."

"A pickup."

"I think so."

"What are you thinking?" Evelyn asked.

"Not sure. But it bothers me."

"He didn't follow," Evelyn said.

"Oh, my God! Did I do something?!" Alex leaned forward, both hands outspread.

Cassidy moved to her side and touch her shoulder. He shook his head. "No. No. Don't worry. You did nothing wrong, Alex. It's probably nothing. We're just a bit nervous."

Evelyn stood, walked away, then turned. "Paranoid, you mean." She hesitated. "If there was a truck, and it was in front, where did it go? Lots of people in pickups up this way."

"Yeah," Cassidy said, "but it only takes one."

"Was anyone behind you on the way up the canyon?"

"No."

Evelyn went to the windows arrayed along the front and peered out. "Right."

Alex stood. "I feel—"

Cassidy took her hand. "Alex. It's okay. Nothing."

Alex looked at Cassidy's eyes with renewed interest.

Evelyn turned to look at her brother and the woman from Lubbock. She saw what she felt was something passing between them. If not from her brother, then certainly from Alex. She smiled and nodded to herself. The other two did not notice.

Cassidy broke away and walked to the upper part of the floor that led to the front door. He turned. "I'm going to have a look about."

"Where?" Evelyn asked.

"Think I'll take a ride. The two of you—have a drink. I won't be long."

Evelyn strode for the kitchen. "Sounds like a plan. With me, Alex?"

Cassidy started toward the interior hall, then stopped and turned. "Alex, the garage will hold two cars. Put yours in there, okay? Evelyn will get the door for you, right, Ev?"

Both women looked at Cassidy.

"Good idea, Mark," Evelyn said. "C'mon, Alex, let's do that now.

Mark Cassidy parked a few feet away from the Terrero store, exited and went inside.

A boy in his late teens, the sole person in the little store, was busy arranging fishing tackle on a wall behind one of the old, wood-and-glass counters. He turned at the sound of Cassidy's entrance. "Hi," he said.

"Hello." Cassidy approached the counter as the young man stood behind it.

"Can I help you?" The boy's face was blank, as was his voice.

"Yes. Been looking for a friend. He may have gotten lost. Pickup truck."

"Pickup?"

"Yes. Did you happen to notice one? About a half hour or so ago?"

The teenager screwed up his face and looked at the old ceiling. "There was a pickup that pulled into the yard." He pointed toward a window that fronted the porch. "But he spun around and took off."

"I see. Did you happen to remember the color? Of the truck?"

"Mm. Think it was blue. Kinda' sky blue, you know. Old. Looked rebuilt."

Cassidy smiled. "Old truck. Blue? That's him. Guess he got real lost."

"Sorry."

Cassidy pondered, then, "Did you happen to notice where he went after he left?"

"Naw. I just saw him turn, then lost sight. Been stockin' tackle." He turned and gestured at the wall. "Saw 'im outa' the corner of my eye through the window as he 'brodied'."

"'Brodied'?"

"Yeah. You know, when someone spins in a circle."

Cassidy nodded. "Sure. Yeah. Well, thanks for the help." He turned to leave.

"If he comes back, I'll tell 'im your lookin' for 'im. What's your name?"

Cassidy continued, raising his arm in thanks. "No problem. I think

I know where he went. I'll find him. Thanks."

He sat in the Jeep, the engine quiet, staring out the windshield for two minutes, concern written on his face. Then he cranked the power source to life, backed, and headed down the highway slowly, scouring every open space as he went. He drove the entire length of the two-lane paved road below the speed limit to the junction in Pecos. From there, he drove through the heart of the village and to the verge of the Historical Park, where he reversed direction. No old pickup with anything resembling a sky blue paint job. He thought of asking, but figured his quarry, if he or she were the enemy, would have left little or no trace.

He headed back to the canyon.

Jeremy Radcliff, his head spinning, wrestled with what his next move should be as he slowed to the approach to the off ramp to US 285 and the Old Pecos Highway. He was secure in the fact he had indeed found the Wraith. Now he had to pin-point her. But had he seen a classical company maneuver when the two vehicles disappeared up the mountain canyon road? He realized he should have waited, out of sight, to see if his quarry was merely shaking a tail. He would have to return.

As he pulled into his graveled yard, Mandy sat on the porch pad, watching his approach. He leaned down, grabbed the empty drink container and the bag with the half-eaten and complete hamburgers. The puddle of drying soda on the passenger-side floor mat would have to be cleaned up later. He exited. The calico arched her back and uttered a complaint as Radcliff keyed himself into the house, then she ran ahead of him to the kitchen, where she expected, as though by magic, her repast would be waiting for her.

First, he dumped the cold, greasy fast-food remains into the garbage can, then spooned food into Mandy's dish as she circled, thanking him with a sinuous hair transfer to his pant legs. After calling Patsy and arranging for a mutual supper to be held at his house that evening, he picked up the portable phone along with the local phone directory, walked into the living room, sat, and began to flip through the yellow pages. He keyed a number into the phone and listened.

At ten the following morning, as Radcliff walked to his pickup, he saw thunder heads developing over the western horizon. He figured they'd bring moisture by early afternoon, and that didn't augur well for what he was about to do. He couldn't stop now, though.

The trip to Albuquerque was uneventful, but he always found himself annoyed at the drivers who considered the left, or passing lane, private property, forming an ad-hoc convoy of entitlement. He maintained the speed limit, and watched occasionally for a possible tail. He was passed by all vehicles, and he made a point of performing a minor study of drivers and occupants. He felt sharp; alive, and actually enjoying himself.

Rain began to fall in earnest as he and another man at the rental agency loaded the Royal Enfield motorcycle onto the pickup bed and tied it down. After piling the leathers, boots and helmet onto the passenger seat, he headed north on Second Street. He stopped at the Mule Driver Inn for a lunch of their green chile stew with a white flour tortilla. Most of the storm had passed as he entered the Interstate north. Swaths of lightning-glorified dark clouds and angled sweeps of rain filled the horizon to the north, and the highway was wet in patches. He figured the storms would erase what remained of the white stuff on the Jemez and Sangre de Cristo mountains.

By late afternoon, after the storm from the west had dampened the area in and around Santa Fé and moved on, Radcliff arrived at his house off the Old Pecos Highway. He drove around to the back, over the seldom-used, weed-invaded, but wet, drive to the frame, board and batten storage shed some fifty feet from the main structure. He angled the truck so the tail gate was positioned closely to the wood edifice, then struggled the motorcycle down, using the single ramp the lender had provided. After creaking the door open on its old, dry hinges and clearing a space, he placed the machine, along with the helmet and riding gear, on the machine's seat and shut the door. He then moved the pickup back to the front of the house and went inside.

He was up early the next day, confusing Mandy, who had her own internal clock management system, and who let Radcliff know of her displeasure. After placating her with special breakfast food, and fortifying himself with two eggs, bacon and toast, he dressed minimally, then went to the shed for the Royal Enfield. He carried a sealed plastic container with two sandwiches, an apple and a bottle of water. There, he stuffed the plastic box into a saddlebag, donned the leathers, gloves, boots and helmet, pulled the shiny machine out, shut the shed door, and started the engine. He found it difficult to see clearly until he became accustomed to looking through the helmet visor. As a test of his rusty skills, he rode slowly out onto the frontage road, then up and down, near the house, before heading north. If he fell and scraped himself, he'd be near the house for first aid.

He did not notice, in the course of his self-training, a small, dark car parked a quarter mile away along the highway verge. Beakman was in the driver's seat, watching through a pair of sun glass-filtered binoculars.

Radcliff couldn't bring himself to brave the posted speed of seventy-five MPH on the Interstate at first; rather, he rode along at around fifty, then later, sixty. As he re-acquainted himself with motorcycle riding, he came close to the limit by the time he reached the Pecos-Glorieta off ramp. From there, it was all at the two-lane, unlimited access highway at the speed limit to Pecos. At the village crossroads, he turned north into the river canyon. He was careful on the sinuous two-lane blacktop as it rose into the southern Rockies. He re-learned how to lean into the left and right curves as the pavement followed the ancient river carved into the rock faces that lined the canyon. He resolved to do more of this. Perhaps he could persuade Patsy to ride behind him.

He slowed at the old trestle bridge, and glanced toward the road into Holy Ghost Canyon. The way was devoid of traffic, both vehicular and pedestrian. He rode on a few hundred yards before stopping. Several vehicles, principally pickups, were parked along the flat verge next to the Pecos River. People, including children, milled about. Two men stood in the flowing water, fishing.

He circled about, headed back to the road junction, and started into the verdant canyon. A quarter mile up the eroding road, a green Forest Service truck passed, headed for the main highway. The driver, a woman in uniform, waved. He held up his gloved right hand in response.

Radcliff rode the length of the old, narrow and badly-kept road to its end, passing a number of look-alike bungalows, but no sign of either of the vehicles he had tracked from Santa Fé, then Cañoncito. Was he tricked?

Or was one or more here, but garaged? Was he mistaken?

On his way back to the Pecos Valley and the main road, he rode slowly, pondering and watching. At the junction, he stopped, turned left, north, then stopped at the north end of the trestle bridge. He faced the machine south, shut the engine down, and pulled his helmet off. He angled the British motorcycle onto its stand, dismounted, put the helmet on the seat and strolled to the water's edge. After a minute of peering into the crystal-clear stream, he found a large rock, sat, looked around, then at the sky, then at his watch. He hoped there would be no rain.

Nearly an hour later, with boredom setting in, Radcliff heard a vehicle on the Holy Ghost road as it approached the junction, then stopped at the highway's edge. It was the Jeep. From his vantage point, he saw a man at the wheel, but no one else. He started to leap up, then thought better of it. If he did, he reasoned, the driver might see his action and become suspicious. He tried to see what the driver looked like; to see if it was the elusive brother. He was uncertain.

The Jeep turned right onto the main road, and Radcliff rose slowly, walked to the motorcycle, put his helmet and gloves on carefully, straddled the machine and cranked it to life. He was elated. He had struck pay-dirt.

He waited until the Jeep was out of sight around the next bend in the highway before he dropped the clutch and moved onto the tarmac. He sped up until he saw the large car in front, then stayed well back, allowing the Jeep to disappear from sight, then reappear alternately. As he came around the final bend in the highway before the four-way stop in Pecos, he saw the Jeep go through the junction, slow, and pull into the parking lot at the country store. He looked left, then right. To his left, the highway dropped down to the river, and was blind to the approach to the store. To his right, the highway to the Interstate and Santa Fé rose, with enough open space that he could observe the activities at the store and the nearby service station. He signaled a right turn, rode halfway up the hill, checked both directions, then circled back and parked on the verge. With his helmet on and the engine off, he watched the lot at the store with its scattering of vehicles. He was in time to see the man from the Jeep emerge, cross the street, disappear for several minutes, then reappear and enter the store.

He decided to chance the possibility his quarry would return to the canyon immediately. But if he didn't, Radcliff thought, he would eventually. He started the engine, moved to the four-way stop, turned left, and rode as fast as he could back to the trestle bridge, then up into Holy Ghost Canyon. As he entered the narrow trace, he slowed. Here, he was in the dark. He had no idea where the Jeep would go. Here, as well, his presence, if detected by the Jeep driver, would most likely set off an undesirable chain of events. If the driver was savvy, he would become suspicious, and the advantage he, Radcliff had, would be lost.

He reasoned that the driver must be quartered at one of the houses along the way. More than one seemed unoccupied, whereas others appeared to have people in and out. It would be at one of these places where the Jeep would be garaged. He noticed that not all the houses sported garages, thus narrowing the possibilities. Also, some of those that appeared to be occupied, were complete with cars, trucks or SUVs parked outside. They also tended to have evidence of vehicle traffic borne out by the presence of tire impressions. It made even more sense to him that he had indeed found the Wraith, given the fact that he had not been able to see the Jeep parked along the way. It would be kept out of sight.

He moved slowly up the canyon, keeping his eye on the rearview mirrors mounted on the handlebars. There was no traffic behind him, but if the Jeep were to return soon, he had to be ready. To do what, he wasn't sure.

Roughly a half mile along the canyon road, he spied a house to his left. Attached to it was what appeared to be a double garage. As he rode past, he started to wonder what it was about the place that bothered him. Then it struck him. The attachment looked newer than the rest of the place. All the structures he had seen seemed to be old, with dark, aging wood in every case. This place was different. The main part looked like the others, but the garage wood was definitely fresher. In addition, he saw not one, but two sets of tire tracks leading to the garage.

He slowed, circled and stopped. His heart rate up, he dismounted and pushed the machine, its engine still running, between high bushes alongside the road. He shut the engine off, pulled his helmet and gloves free, set them on the saddle, then moved cautiously onto the road verge and began to walk toward the house, now on the same side of the road. He didn't have to wait long. He pushed his way behind a pair of evergreen trees and some flowering bushes as the Jeep approached, turned into the drive and stopped in front of the garage. He watched as the male driver got out, opened the garage door, then disappeared the Jeep inside. Radcliff hadn't been able to see the man's face, but he had a good idea of who he was.

He stood up from the crouch position he had assumed and walked back to the bike. He removed the plastic lunch box from the saddlebag, opened it, removed the apple, and took a huge, crackling bite. It was then that he truly relaxed for the first time since arising that morning. He took in, then released a deep breath. Yet, there seemed to be a dark cloud developing in the back of his mind as he chewed on the crisp fruit. He frowned in response.

It was at that moment that the first big splat of rain hit his bare head.

Beakman was dumbfounded. He wondered why Radcliff had gone to Albuquerque, but saw nothing suspicious or untoward in the trip at the time. Now he knew why. He cursed under his breath as he watched Radcliff disappear. Following a motorcycle would be next to impossible, especially if the machine should move onto unpaved trails. But why had Radcliff taken this measure? What was he up to? Beakman was certain Jeremy Radcliff was less than truthful at their last meeting. On the other hand, Radcliff had warned him to let him handle the job by himself. He sighed and tried to relax.

In his room, Beakman looked again at the archived GPS data on his laptop computer. It showed clearly that the truck had gone to Albuquerque and returned. Present locator data showed it parked at Radcliff's place. Radcliff was somewhere else. On the damned two-wheeled machine. He invoked the special site, then wrote and fired off an encrypted e-mail. He wanted help. The mission was getting away from him, and he would be on the griddle if he failed. Or worse.

Radcliff suffered through an intense, five-minute rain storm which left him cold, wet, shivering and wondering why he had forgotten to bring a poncho.

After dark settled over the narrow valley, and having subsisted on the apple, sandwiches and water, he pushed the Royal Enfield out onto the road. He then steered the motorcycle across the trace to put as much distance as possible between himself and the target manse as he passed. A series of rectilinear windows across the front of the house under the porch roof revealed muted, yellowish interior light. As he trundled the cycle along, he saw what appeared to be a male figure move across one window to another, then disappear downward as though taking a seat. A moment later, another figure, a woman, flashed across one of the windows, but at such a distance that he was unable to get a good look.

Fearing detection, either from an electronic surveillance system or by someone in or near the house, he continued until the place was behind him by several hundred feet. He then mounted the bike, started it, and began the slow trip down to the main road, dodging pot holes, cracks, and one frightened, light-dodging rabbit. Once on the north-south riverside highway, and with his confidence returned, he picked up speed. He was home in less than forty-five minutes, albeit cold and wet, but none the worse for wear.

# *20*

Beakman stood in an alcove shop on the top floor of the Albuquerque airport, holding an open romance paperback novel close to his face, his peripheral vision vaguely on the huge lobby.

Ordinarily, he was self-assured and unflappable. He prided himself on his ability to confront the trickiest of situations with élan and grace; even once when facing a loaded firearm. Yet, after reading the encrypted Email late the night before and the early morning drive to Albuquerque, he was anxious; why, he couldn't fathom. He had driven through a MacDonald's in Santa Fé shortly after sunup, where he purchased an "Egg McMuffin," orange juice and scalding hot coffee, all of which he managed to juggle and consume on the Interstate without mishap. He wished he hadn't eaten, since his innards felt bloated.

Scattered throughout the public room in front of him, with its immense, carved-beam supported ceiling, a smattering of people stood, anxiously watching the exit doors that stood as a barrier to the security and boarding areas. Then, as passengers began to emerge, the sound of babble rose. He focused on the job at hand.

No more than two minutes passed when a magazine was dropped onto a padded stool placed immediately outside the shop where Beakman stood. He lowered the book, took a step nearer and peered down at it. It was a copy of the latest *Time* magazine. He looked at the stream of people moving toward the two escalators that lead to the lower floor and the baggage carrels. He saw no one he recognized, and no one out of the ordinary.

He returned the novel to its place on the book rack, picked the magazine up and headed for the nearest men's room. There, he found an empty stall, closed and secured the door, then flipped through the pages. Roughly in the middle, he found a "post-it" note stuck to a page. It read, "faded jeans Harvard sweat shirt red rollaboard blonde hair."

Dangling the magazine in his right hand so that its cover faced out, he rode the escalator down, then proceeded toward the street exit. As he moved past the opening to the short hall leading to the street, he spotted, from the corner of his eye, a woman dressed in the clothes described in the magazine-hidden note. She stood on his right, looking at nothing, as though waiting for someone as several others near her did, a red roller board angled away at her feet, holding the telescoping handle. She did not look at him overtly as he passed. As he went by her, he held the magazine up briefly, as though waving an insect away.

Beakman moved on as the woman turned slowly but deliberately to follow. In the instant after his recognition of the her, he was somehow not surprised. Then that realization, along with a modicum of shock set in, which led him to a flash on internalized anger. He took in and released a deep breath.

He marched on, stopped momentarily at the passenger pick-up curb, looked to his left, then dodged a car to cross the street to the parking structure. He didn't look back, but knew the woman in the Harvard sweat shirt was following. He could hear the clatter of the hard wheels of her baggage on the concrete. When he arrived at his vehicle, he popped the trunk open. He got into the driver's seat, then watched through the rear-view mirror as the woman placed the red bag in the trunk and closed it. A moment later, she opened the passenger door and slipped in. Wordlessly and without looking at her, Beakman started the engine and backed out of the parking slot.

As she pulled her seat belt down and locked it into place, Beakman said, his voice flat, "What the fuck?!" He had yet to look her way as he turned the wheel to maneuver the car out of the densely packed concrete parking building.

She was in her mid-forties, shapely, with an intelligent, pretty face. Her hair was off-blonde, cut in a long page-boy. She looked at him with bemusement, then forward through the windshield. "What the fuck? Some greeting, Beakman."

He was silent until after he pulled up to the ticket booth, handed the cashier a bill, then accelerated away as the barrier rose. "I repeat, what the fuck." He awarded her a brief glance.

The woman brushed away an imaginary particle from her pant leg. "I assume you're crushed by the fact that I'm a woman." She looked up, but not at him. "Incidentally, you may call me Nancy."

Beakman shook his head in disgust. "Look, nothing against you, Nancy, if that's what I'm to call you, but they send a woman?!" He swung the wheel, taking the car onto the Interstate north. He took his hand away from the job at hand long enough to make a questioning gesture.

"It happens."

"Happens?!" He shot her a severe look. "Happens? This is a delicate case, lady. This calls for expertise. Savvy."

She looked over at him, her head cocked. "Expertise? What sort of expertise? Are you such a fucking macho chauvinist pig you believe only someone with balls hanging from his crotch can do the job?"

"Whoa! It's just—"

"Just what, Beakman?! I was sent to aid and abet. Cooler heads than yours calculated that I'd be less likely to be zeroed-in on than a man. I didn't just fall off the turnip truck, mister! Suck it up!" She looked away. "They hired me. I didn't seek them out!"

"Jesus!" Beakman's eyes widened. "Okay. Okay. Jesus." He calmed.

Silence ensued between them, then Nancy said, "Look, I get it. This is delicate. They tell me your guy is unreliable. That you say you believe he's spotted your target. That you've got a large territory to cover. Easy to spot tails and watchers. That the target, a woman, is most likely hunkered down. Ex-pro. Possibly in a place not easy to approach." She looked out her side window at the commercial buildings rushing by. "Hell, I don't have any answers. Control sure doesn't. They want me to go over the thing with you and help out. End of story."

He nodded. "Okay. Sorry." He sighed and slapped the steering wheel with his fingers.

"No problem."

"Control. Have you met them?"

"Not at all. Third party intermediary. I don't know if it's a 'them' or a 'he' or a 'she.'"

He looked at her, taking in her profile. "Makes sense. You're company or a contractor?"

She maintained her vigil as though keeping track of all she witnessed through the vehicle's glass. "I was told to keep that to myself."

"Right." He made a snide face.

"But, because it's you, I'm gonna tell you anyhow, so long as you feign ignorance." She pointed a finger at him.

He grinned. "Mum's the word."

"Contractor."

"True?" His eyebrows went up.

"True. Ex-FBI."

"And your specialty?"

She took in a deep breath and let it out slowly through her nose. "Profiling. At first. Got involved in some wet cases later. Couple of us left the bureau to start our own firm. Detecting, contracting with the feds. Like that."

"Why do you think they brought you in instead of an insider—don't tell me. Because you're an outsider."

"Exactly. I was informed your guy here is no dummy. He pokes around the archives. Stays in touch. Like in the shadows and all that."

"You got that right. Been here before? New Mexico?"

She looked at him. "No. Why?"

He raised his eyebrows. "Big state. Lots of open territory. At the same time, everybody knows everybody. And they notice outsiders. Rugged."

"I've done some research. Doesn't make me an expert, but I figure I'll fit in." She hesitated. "Had you been here before?"

"Touché. No. But I'm a quick study."

"As am I."

"'Nough said. Listen, I'm gonna let you off at the train station in Bernalillo. Take it all the way into town. Santa Fé. Taxi or bus to wherever they've got you staying. Bring a laptop?"

"Yes. Okay. Laptop." She nodded.

"You have the addresses, passwords and all?"

"Yes."

"Okay. Email me as soon as you're settled. I'll set up a place to meet. We can go from there."

"You're on."

Beakman had relaxed, his angst dissipated. He realized, as he drove back onto the highway from the stop at the Bernalillo rail station, that he liked this Nancy. Or whatever her real name was.

Radcliff walked to his mail box at the end of his drive, staying squarely on the relatively dry gravel, given that the recent rains made the edges of small rocks muddy. He retrieved one advertisement, a credit card offer and a bill from the small steel hutment. As he closed the little door, he glanced up and down the paved highway that connected Santa Fé with towns to the southeast. A car sped past as he started back to the house. He noticed that the little, two-door foreign job that had been parked several blocks away on the other side of the highway two days before was no longer there. Beakman had been driving a pickup truck, but that didn't prevent him from changing vehicles. He wondered if he was being watched. It would stand to reason. He looked at his watch.

As he walked back to the house, he looked first at his beloved rebuilt pickup truck, then the door to the shed with the Royal Enfield motorcycle sheltered within. He stopped, looked down, then up, pondering.

He fitted a camper shell over the truck bed and packed it with a bed roll, fishing gear, wading boots and cold box with food. He added a pair of binoculars, a fast digital camera with a telephoto lens, a couple of good flashlights, and a camping lantern. Three different hats followed; baseball, western straw and camouflage floppy cloth hiking. Accompanying those was a back pack. Lastly, he placed the Walther P22 under the seat on the driver's side. Before settling into the truck, he made sure Mandy had plenty of food and water, and set the alarm. Sitting in the truck cab, he called Patsy Romero from his cell phone. She was not happy to hear he might be gone for as long as two days, but she agreed to come by and make sure Mandy had sustenance. He knew he would miss her before the day ended.

Beakman and Nancy met at the Zia Café for lunch the day after she arrived. They sat in one of the booths above the main floor. Since his arrival weeks before, he had begun to partake of the local food, which tended to include "hot stuff." He felt, however, that she would not be ready to acclimate herself to such a strange regimen, so he chose a place that featured standard "American" fare instead. When he saw her enter the restaurant, he was pleasantly surprised. She was dressed differently than when he picked her up at the airport, and looked the part for the city and its environs. She wore a pair of high-grade jeans, a denim vest over a good blouse, and her hair and face were made up such that he found her more attractive. Adding to that, her ensemble accentuated a female figure of which he approved. She carried a thin leather briefcase. She fit in, he thought.

She stood for a moment, pretending not to know where he was, then waved at him from across the big, high-ceiling room, and approached. She slid into the booth across from Beakman, laid the briefcase on the table, opened it, pulled out a business card and handed it to him. She sat back, turned her head to survey the room, then smiled at him.

He read the legend on the card. "Canberry and Martínez, Real Estate Investments. And you're Nancy Mullins?" He spoke loud enough that the couple in booths on either side of them could understand him.

She held her hand out high for him to shake. "That's me!" She awarded him a wide, real estate lady smile. She also made no effort to lower her voice.

He leaned forward and took her hand for a brief shake.

"Well, let's grab something here. After, you can show me what you've got." He looked around the room subtly for the occasional attentive eye, which did not materialize.

She ate lightly, while he, having had no breakfast, and feeling better psychologically, consumed more than he would have normally. She asked about chile, which was not included in her lunch. He had little to offer about it as a novice, except that he was trying to get used to it.

After they finished eating and the crockery was removed, she spread out several slick, four-color brochures for them to pretend to peruse. She also added a map of the area.

Beakman borrowed the pen she wielded and drew a small circle around the approximate location of Radcliff's house. After a bit of phony small talk, Nancy paid the tab, and they left.

They sat in his truck.

"You rented a vehicle?" he asked.

She jerked her thumb. "Escalade. Makes the newly-minted real estate agent look prosperous."

"Trick of the trade." He smirked.

"Right on."

"So, you plan to carry on with this guise? What's your plan?"

"Show me where your guy lives, and the lay of the land, and we'll work something out. Basically, I figure it'll be easier for me to explain my presence wherever I go as a real estate gal."

He nodded. "Good thinking."

"You expect foul play? Is this a TWP caper?" She turned to look at his eyes.

He shook his head. "No. We just need someone he doesn't know. I'm exposed. To him. It's down to a matter of trust." He paused. "Did you bring heat?"

"Will I need it?"

"No, no. But you never know. You know?" He frowned, shaking his head.

She turned toward him and pointed. "Better be the case. And if so, you be prepared to back me up!"

"No problem." He shook his head.

She waited a full count, then, "Why are we—you—after this guy? Is this a wet ops?"

Beakman cocked his head to one side and looked out at the traffic moving along Guadalupe Street. "No, no." His mind reeled from the lie he was telling. He looked at her. "Unless Control has let you in on everything, I can't." He looked at her. "As I said, he knows me. We approached him to find the primary, and he's to report. But he hasn't. We think he spotted him. The primary. If so, for some reason, he's gone independent. Maybe made a deal with the other side. On the other hand, maybe he's making sure, or hasn't found the roost. But time's of the essence. We need more eyes."

"Is he present company? Ex-company?"

"Ex. I can say that much."

"What's with the primary? Why don't you do the job?" She looked closely at his face. "Man?" Her face muscles betrayed doubt.

"What'd your contact tell you?" He cocked his eyebrows.

"Not much." She looked away, then back. "But I have a right to know." She squared herself toward him. "Look, suppose I observe him with someone who might be the primary. If I have doubts about who it is, seems to me I should know more. To be effective."

Beakman took in a deep breath and let it out as he stared straight ahead through the windshield. Without looking at her, he said, "You're right. It's a woman." He hesitated, then he waved his hand. "Scared rabbit." He paused again. "We got to get to her. Before it's too late. The guy you're helping with is the ferret. Or so we thought. We may have fumbled this."

Nancy cocked her head and followed his gaze. "Okay. Whatever."

He shook his head and sighed. "Delicate. Primary's in danger. Need to bring her in—as they say—from the cold. And I'm compromised. I'm out. For that part." He hesitated. "After she's located and secured, I can do escort duty." He pointed at her. "Maybe you."

"Gotcha. So, when do you show me the ferret's place?"

"Now, if you're ready."

"I'm ready. I'll follow you." She was silent, then, "What's his name?"

He started the engine. "Radcliff. Jeremy Radcliff." He looked at her, then reached across the center console and touched her arm.

"Hey, Beakman, we're at the office."

He withdrew his hand. "No offense."

She opened her door and was halfway out when she stopped and smiled at him. "Work first, play later. Right?"

"Right." He grinned openly.

"We'll see," she said. She closed the door and walked away.

Radcliff drove up Holy Ghost Canyon, past the house where he had seen the man and the woman. He went another half mile, returned to the main road, turned left and circled slowly through the Terrero Store parking lot. He eased the pickup down into the river plain and found a spot where he could watch traffic coming and going from the canyon. To his right, up along the stream bank, were two other pickup trucks and a small camper. A man Radcliff reckoned to be in his thirties and a boy of ten walked along the bank carrying fishing rods. A couple of women fussed over smoking camp stoves.

He got out, opened the shell, donned the western straw, and grabbed his camera. He closed the shell, looked about to see that no one was interested in him, then made his way to the bridge that crossed to the canyon. From there, he clambered over rocks, brush and grassy areas still dew-wet to a point where he could sit and see the narrow canyon road. He put the camera to his eye and focused in and out of range along the road. A car headed for the main, state road, emerged from the canyon, and he raised the camera and managed to focus on the driver. He snapped the shutter several times, then lowered the camera to review the digital photos he had taken. Satisfied with the images, he laid the camera aside, pulled an "energy bar" from his jacket pocket, unwrapped it, and bit down.

A little more than an hour and a half after he had positioned himself on a rock to watch the Holy Ghost Canyon road, he glanced at his watch and sighed. He raised his hat just enough to scratch an itch above the hairline, then righted it on his perspiring head. At that moment, he heard the sound of a vehicle engine approaching from the direction of the canyon. As the car appeared, he recognized it as the Jeep he had seen before. He raised the camera quickly, dialed in the focus, and began a rapid-fire series of takes, including as the car passed and as it was visible from the rear. He then examined his product. Three people were in the vehicle; two in front, one in the rear. A man was at the wheel; the others were women. He did not recognize the woman in the passenger seat, but from the group of pictures, he was able to discern that the other woman was, indeed, the target, the so-called "ghost," the Wraith Beakman wanted him to find. The pictures he had were not equal to clear, frontal face shots, but his focus was good, and from what he was able to piece together, he knew it was she, based on the data he had gleaned from the Internet. He lowered the camera, took in a deep breath, and studied the ground at his feet for guidance.

After a few minutes of reflection, he returned to his truck. He put the camera on the seat alongside himself, stowed the other gear, drove onto the highway, then the road into the canyon. He passed the target house slowly, careful to watch unobtrusively, though he suspected no one was there. He went past and found a place to turn around. On the return, he spotted a place within walking distance of the house where he could pull the truck close to the stream, where it would be unlikely that questions might be asked.

He parked, peered out, waited a few seconds, then got out. Standing next to the truck, he looked in both directions along the road, then looked and listened for anyone near the water. Sensing no one, he then retrieved the Walther from under the seat, checked the chamber, and pushed it into the little steel-and-leather holster clipped to his belt at the small of his back. The camera was next. That he hung around his neck by the strap. From the camper shell, he grabbed a couple of energy bars and stuck them into his shirt pocket, and clamped a pint water bottle to his belt. He put his baseball cap on, locked the Ford and moved toward the little river.

On the stream bank, he turned toward the house. From his vantage point, he made parts of it out through the foliage, then began to pick his way carefully in that direction. He found a narrow spot where he forded the stream, leaping from stone to stone to the opposite side. From there, he picked his way along a sloping ridge, then up on it, from where he was able to see the house and the interior through windows along the southern wall. He found a substantial log, brushed dirt, leaves and twigs from its surface, and settled in.

# 21

Nancy followed Beakman's pickup in her Cadillac along the Old Pecos Highway, maintaining a distance of several car lengths. As he passed the Radcliff house, Beakman set his left-hand turn signal on, then off. Nancy flashed her headlamps in response, and Beakman sped up to distance himself from her. As she passed the house, she slowed, looked quickly, taking in as much as she could. They had discussed using their cell phones, but eschewed the idea because their future might be at stake if the operation were ever publically exposed and cell phone records brought to light.

She continued south to the three-way stop with its overhead flashing warning lights, turned around and headed back. Meanwhile, Beakman had driven on to the Interstate and back to Santa Fé. At the house drive, she slowed and drove in, taking in everything as she did. A small red foreign car was parked at a shallow angle to the house. Nancy stopped her vehicle alongside the red car, killed the engine, inspected her face and hair in the rearview mirror, gathered her briefcase, and stepped out. As she walked to the front door, she pulled a business card from an external pocket on the shiny leather briefcase.

No more than fifteen seconds after pushing the doorbell button, the door opened.

Patsy, a table spoon in her hand, looked up at the taller woman. "Yes?"

Nancy beamed. "Good morning! I'm sorry to bother you, but I wonder if I might have a word with the owner. Are you the owner?"

Patsy frowned. "Who are you?" She glanced past the fake realtor at the big vehicle parked next to hers.

"I'm sorry! Allow me to introduce myself. Uh—here's my card. Hi! I'm Nancy. Nancy Mullins. I'm with Canberry and Martínez. Realtors."

Patsy palmed the card and shook her head. "Well, I don't know why you're here, but the owner's not at home." She gestured toward the interior with the spoon.

"Oh—might that be your husband?"

Patsy smiled and shook her head. "No. He's a friend. I feed his cat. Looking after things while he's away." She held the utensil up.

"Oh, I see." Nancy licked her carefully painted lips and began to open the briefcase. "Well, I wonder if I might take a few moments of your time to leave some information with you—for him. May I come in?"

Patsy looked back with a pained expression. "Well, this is not my house, and—"

"I won't be a minute, and I really need to put my materials down. So you won't have to take them yourself." She pointed to the cat-food soiled spoon. "You've got your hands full!" She smiled brightly.

"Well, you're right. Uh—okay. C'mon in." She turned.

Patsy led the intruder into the living room, where she stood, the spoon still in her hand. She watched as the fake real estate agent entered and sat on the edge of a sofa cushion without asking.

Nancy, busy pulling slick brochures and other papers from her briefcase, looked around the room and peered down the hall. "I really like this house. It's just what I was told it would be like. Perfect." She looked up at Patsy and smiled. "May I know your name?"

"I'm Patsy." She frowned. "But what I'd like to know—" She glanced at the card she'd been given. "Is what you want; why you're here."

"Patsy. I like that name." Nancy turned toward her host in a gesture of earnest sincerity. "Patsy, you deserve an explanation. Well, here it is. As you may know, this neighborhood, this area, is considered prime real estate territory. And my company, Canberry and Martínez, is interested in acquiring properties in this area. And we feel this would be one of our top sellers." She spoke in a cheery sing-song.

Patsy shook her head. "I know Jeremy—that's the owner—isn't interested in selling. I can tell you that."

Nancy opened her arms wide and cocked her head. "Well, now, I haven't told you what Canberry and Martínez would be willing to offer, now have I?" She winked. "I'll bet if Jeremy—is that his name?—were to hear our offer and terms, he just might be!" She cracked another wide grin.

"Well, I don't know . . ."

"Patsy, may I ask your relationship to Jeremy?"

Patsy blushed. "We're friends."

Nancy looked at Patsy from under her eyebrows. "And maybe more than that?"

Patsy looked at the floor. "I guess you could say that." She smiled coquettishly.

Nancy pretended to look at a white paper document. "Do I have Jeremy's last name correct? Could you confirm it for me?"

"Radcliff."

Nancy clicked a pen and scribbled something on the paper. "Yes, of course. My information was correct." She looked up, then stood. Could I just peek at the rest of the house? So I can report back? I just love this place!" She accented the word 'love.' "The walls are very thick!"

"It's an adobe. It's—"

"Oh, my goodness! Even better! I must look!"

"Well, I—"

"Patsy, I know this is not your place, and I confess I tend to get a bit overbearing, but when I see a house as charming as this, I just can't resist." With that, she started down the hall, cooing and chatting to herself as she went, looking, craning her neck and pointing.

Patsy followed, then laid the spoon she had been holding on the counter as she passed the opening to the kitchen.

At the end of the hall, Nancy turned to face Patsy. "When do you expect Mr. Radcliff to return?" She brushed at her hair.

"I'm not sure. A couple of days."

"Hunting? Fishing?"

Patsy shook her head. "I don't think he hunts. Fishing, maybe."

"Well, now I'm being rude and nosey. Please forgive me. None of my business." She waved her remark away, then came up close to Patsy. "But you know, I'm a people person, and I like to get to know people, especially clients. Or potential clients." She maintained her cheery smile.

Patsy, overwhelmed, merely nodded with a wan smile.

Nancy hesitated while she stared at Patsy, then said. "Well, my dear, I've taken up far too much of your time." She walked past, then turned. "The spoon. You said a cat?"

Patsy nodded. "Yes."

Nancy held up a finger. "I have a couple myself. Cat person." She pointed at herself. "But listen, if you'd please make sure Mr. Radcliff gets the materials I left. And I'd appreciate a call at his earliest convenience. It's all there." She indicated the paperwork on the coffee table. "It's been really great meeting you!"

As she drove away, Nancy's phony exterior returned to its normal serious demeanor.

Radcliff wished he had worn a warmer jacket, since, as the sun waned toward the west, casting the narrow valley in shadow, the temperature dropped precipitously, and he felt it. The fallen tree trunk he occupied added to his discomfort, forcing him to stand from time to time and stretch. He began to wonder if his quarry would return before he would be forced to call off his watch.

It was dusk when he saw the lights of a vehicle play across the roadway beyond the creek and the verdant ground between. It brightened, danced, bounced, altered, then swung in toward the house he was watching and disappeared, leaving the late grey of the day to take over. He stood, awakened and energized in anticipation. In less than five minutes, lights began to wink on inside. The row of small windows facing him became rectangles of white-orange light.

He raised the camera to his eye and peered through the lens. As he adjusted the distance and focus, blurred forms became clear objects. First a shadow appeared in the window to his left, then a man. He twisted the focus ring, recognized the man he had seen at the wheel of the Jeep and pressed the shutter trigger. The man moved to the next rectangle, stopped, turned toward the window and leaned down. Radcliff figured he was doing something in what appeared to be the kitchen, and snapped again.

He moved slowly along the edge of the stream, treading carefully in the fading light to afford himself a better view of the interior of the house. He studied the ground, barely able to make out where he should put his feet. He moved ten paces, nearly tripping on a fallen branch. As he did, the dead wood cracked and made a report loud enough to concern him, since it echoed off the building across the moving water. He froze, looked around, waited several seconds, and hearing nothing, moved again.

The man had disappeared, but a woman whom he didn't recognize moved across the window set. As he took her picture, she stopped, turned, and appeared to be speaking to someone out of frame. Then she moved on, disappearing behind a portion of wall.

"Freeze. Don't move a muscle. Fair warning. Do as I say."

The voice came from behind him. It was female, but low, authoritative and commanding. He did as he was told, the camera still to his face.

"Back slowly toward me. Slowly. I have a pistol pointed at you. If you don't obey, I will end your spying here, and do it legally, since you are on private property. Tell me you will comply."

Radcliff had a catch in his throat, but managed to croak an answer. "May I lower the camera?"

"Stop there. Answer my question."

He halted. "Yes. Yes; I comply."

"Lower the camera. To the ground. Carefully."

At that moment, a bright beam from a flashlight played across his back, down between his legs and onto the expensive camera as he set it down.

"Now, back this way. Leave the camera."

Radcliff backed up carefully, watching for the dried branch, odd rocks and other possible trip-up objects as he moved. The woman moved aside, giving him room to maneuver. With the light on him, she stepped slowly to the camera, picked it up with her flashlight hand, then turned toward the intruder.

"Now, turn around and move slowly to the point where you crossed. If you try to run, I'll take out a leg. Nine millimeter slugs can really smart. Break a bone. Understood?"

"Understood."

Radcliff, his hands instinctively folded across the back of his head, moved cautiously back to where he had crossed the creek. He held them out high and wide for balance, and crossed the stream.

"Stop there," she said. "Face away from me."

"Okay. Got it," Radcliff said.

She leapt skillfully across, then took up a position to his right, facing him, holding the light on his face. "Who are you?"

"I'm—"

"Never mind. We'll sort that out in good time. Move toward the house. Same rules. Funny business and it's all over but the coroner's inquest. Clear?"

"Clear. I'm moving." Radcliff's mind was reeling. Who was this woman? He thought he knew the answer. It had to be.

Radcliff moved up the steps onto the dark porch ahead of Evelyn, then stopped, facing the door.

"Open it," she said.

He turned half way toward her, then grasped the lever and pressed down. The big, heavy door opened onto the warm interior. He took one step inside onto the flagstone-covered walkway, and without moving his head, scanned the big room and what he could see of the kitchen beyond.

Behind him, Evelyn spoke. "Three paces and stop." As he moved, she closed and latched the door and set his camera on the marble-topped foyer table.

In the kitchen, Cassidy had been chatting quietly with Alex Petersen. At the sound of the door, he turned, expecting to see his sister returning, although through a different entrance, from her nightly sojourn. Seeing the man standing in the living room, he rose, his face screwing up at the sight. In another moment, he saw his sister move to one side of the man and realized she was pointing her semi-automatic pistol at him.

Without a word, he walked the length of the kitchen and down to the living room level. Still silent, he looked at Radcliff, then his sister, then back at her prisoner. Behind him, Alex rose, looked at the strange sight and brought a hand to her face. She gasped, but not so the others heard.

"Cassidy looked at Evelyn. "You know 'im?"

She shook her head slowly, her mouth firm. She used the pistol to point at Alex briefly. "Ask her. The question begged here is, does she know him? And does he know her!"

Cassidy swung around abruptly to look at Alex. He frowned. "Do you know this man?"

Alex went white and nearly faint. She shook her head slowly, mouth open, her eyes darting between Cassidy, his sister and Radcliff. She leaned on the trestle table with one hand, supporting her weight in the sudden weakness that overcame her.

Evelyn took a step toward the kitchen, nose flared, eyes burning. "Yes, she does!" She yelled. "I told you there was something fishy about her, damn it!" She flashed an angry look at her brother, then at Alex.

Cassidy shook his head and looked at the floor. "Calm down, Evelyn. Just calm yourself. We'll get to the bottom of this." He waved his hands at the floor, head lowered. "Just—just calm down. It's under control." He turned to Radcliff. "Who are you, and why are you here?!"

"I—"

Cassidy looked at his sister. "Where'd you find him? Where was he?"

Evelyn gestured. "The other side of the stream. Over there!" She gestured toward the south wall.

"How'd you spot 'im?"

"Heard something. Knew it was human. Took a look." She glared at her brother, then Radcliff.

Cassidy looked at the intruder. "What were you doing prowling around this property?!"

Radcliff, his hands still shoulder-high, rolled his eyes toward Evelyn, then back to Cassidy. "Before we get into that, I suggest you look under my jacket. Rear. Waistband."

He turned his head toward Evelyn as she hesitated an instant, then leapt to Radcliff's back, lifted his jacket and retrieved the Walther.

"God damn it, Mark! That's it! This guy's a pro! She lead him here!" She pointed her gun as well as his in Alex' direction again.

"May I lower my hands?" Radliff asked.

Evelyn swung around to look at the intruder as Cassidy stared at him.

Cassidy nodded. "Yes. Lower your hands. Sit over there." He pointed to one of the big chairs. He looked at the pistol in his sister's hand.

Radcliff turned, made his way to the proffered chair and sat. He looked up first at Mark Cassidy, then his sister, neither of whom had moved. "She has nothing to do with my presence." He gestured with his head toward Alex.

Evelyn stormed over to him and leaned over. She pointed both guns at his head. "Bullshit!"

Radcliff looked up at her calmly. He shook his head. "I don't know who she is, and she does not know me. That's a fact."

Evelyn swung around to look at Alex, who shook her head slowly as tears streamed down her cheeks.

"I don't believe you!" She shouted. She stared at Alex, fire in her eyes, then Radcliff who was nodding slightly, then her brother.

Cassidy went to Evelyn. "Evelyn, give me the gun. His gun. Keep yours trained on him, then please sit. Sit. Please." He held out his hand, indicating one of the chairs. He looked up toward Alex. "Alex, come down here, please. Have a seat. Here, on the couch." He took Radcliff's .22 from his sister, cleared the breach, removed the magazine and set the firearm up on the half wall that separated the kitchen from the living room. He then went to the front door and picked Radcliff's camera up. He turned to the outsider. "Let's start with the name."

Radcliff looked up at Cassidy. "Radcliff. Jeremy. Jeremy Radcliff."

"And what were you doing outside our house, Mr. Radcliff? With a high-resolution camera and a gun?" Cassidy inspected the camera closely.

"Spying."

Evelyn leaned forward in her chair, mouth agape, looked first at Radcliff, then her brother. Alex, confused and psychologically bruised, her mouth open as well, looked at all three people in wonderment.

Cassidy, ever the attorney, reacted little, but nodded and cocked his head. "Interesting. Mr. Radcliff. Interesting. For whom were you doing this spying?"

Radcliff studied Cassidy's face for a few seconds, cast a brief glance at Alex, then looked directly at Evelyn and pointed. "For rogue elements in the CIA who want her dead."

# 22

Alex, her face lined with fear, moved from the kitchen table to Cassidy's side. He instinctively took her hand.

Evelyn jumped from her chair, her 9mm semi-auto Walther leading the way. "Jesus Christ, Mark, kill the lights!" She ran past her brother for the light switch nearest the front door and slapped at it, dousing the entry light over the foyer. She spun around and pointed. "Alex, get that lamp at the end of the couch!" She looked at her brother, who had moved only incrementally. "God sakes, Mark, get the kitchen lights!"

In the subsequent dark, she swung the pistol around to point it at Radcliff, who remained seated. "How many are out there, Radcliff—or whatever your name is?!"

"No one else. I'm alone." His voice was calm.

"Bullshit!" Evelyn moved closer to his voice, nearly tripping over the offset between the walkway and the living room floor, but righting herself in time.

Radcliff looked toward her in the blackness. "I assure you, alone. I came alone. There is no one else out there." He hesitated. "Check it out. Satisfy yourselves. Then we can talk."

"Why, you miserable, arrogant bastard! Why should we believe you?!" Evelyn's voice carried menace.

"You have little reason to, I admit," Radcliff replied, "but you'll see I'm telling the truth."

Evelyn went to one of the two large windows that looked out onto the front yard, swinging her head left and right frantically. She spoke almost under her breath. "God damn it! I wish we had infrared cameras!"

"Think about it," Radcliff said, still softly, "if there was a team backing me up, they would have penetrated this place by now. Why would I be across that stream with a camera if a team knew you were here? They—we—would have busted in here, killed everyone and worried about the consequences later. I'm it, Evelyn. I'm it!" He raised his voice slightly as he turned to her in the dark.

A light came on in the kitchen. Mark Cassidy stood at the end of the counter, silent, his hand to his chin. Alex was in the living area, standing behind the couch.

Evelyn pivoted to look in his direction. "Mark!"

"He's right, Ev. Listen to reason. I don't know what his game is, but he's right. If they'd wanted to take you out, knowing where you are, we wouldn't be arguing about it now." He stepped down into the living room. "Alex, would you please give us some more light? The one you shut off?"

Alessandra moved to the end of the sofa and snapped the table lamp on. She looked at Cassidy and smiled. Her eyes were red.

"Thank you, Alex," Cassidy said. He looked at his sister. "Ev, sit down. And set the pistol aside. Please." He pointed on Evelyn's behalf, then looked at Radcliff. "Now, Mr. Radcliff, is it? Enlighten us." He moved down into the living area.

Radcliff nodded at Cassidy, then looked at Alex and Evelyn in turn. He studied the floor, then looked up. "I told you I was sent to find and assassinate you, Evelyn. That's the simple truth. I found you. I will tell you how. Right now, please believe I'm telling the truth." He glanced at Cassidy, then focused on Evelyn again. "They want you gone. I also believe they'll want me gone once they've taken you out. Of that I have no doubt. Why did they want me to find you? Because I'm retired company, I've been here—well, in Santa Fé—for several years, and I know people and places. They don't. Also, they know enough about the area that they feel they'd be spotted if an outsider did the job." He looked at Cassidy. "May I have some water? And may I stand?" He looked at Evelyn.

"I'll get it," Alex said. She moved toward the kitchen, then stopped and turned. "Hungry? I could fix something." She shot a worried glance at Evelyn as she wrung her hands at waist level.

Radcliff looked up at the woman from Texas. "No, thanks; just water. I had a couple of energy bars. I'm okay." He closed his eyes momentarily.

Radcliff rose from his chair without protest from Evelyn and met Alex half-way as she returned. She handed him a glass, awarded him a weak smile, then returned to the sofa and sat down.

Radcliff took a long drink, then, glass in hand, moved back toward his chair, but stood beside it. "There was another problem. They made a mistake." He set the glass on a nearby occasional table.

"Mistake?" Cassidy asked. He shot a glance at his sister, who maintained her frown.

"Yes. They thought they had found you. A few weeks ago." He looked at Evelyn.

"What?!" she exclaimed.

"They thought they'd found you. They didn't tell me that. I found out for myself." He moved two paces toward Evelyn. "I live here. I get the paper. I was also given access to secret, encrypted files through the Internet." He looked at Cassidy, then back at Evelyn. There was a murder in Santa Fé. A man and a woman."

"Hey!" Cassidy stood and walked slowly toward Radcliff, peering at him intently.

Radcliff looked at Cassidy and cocked his head, his brow furrowed. "What—what did I say?! That's the truth—"

Cassidy stopped, his gaze on Radcliff intense. "What about the murder?!"

Radcliff spread his hands out. "Well, I read the story in the news about the killing—the murders—and when I saw Evelyn's picture—"

"Oh, my God!" Alex jumped from the sofa and ran to Cassidy's side. Tears streamed down her cheeks, her hand over her wide-open mouth.

Cassidy put his arm around her as she leaned her head against his chest.

Evelyn rose slowly from her chair as though arthritic, and paced away, moving in a tight circle. Her mouth fell open as she stared at the bare floor.

"Hey—what's going on?!" Radcliff asked, his arms out pleadingly.

Cassidy leaned in toward him as he held Alex. "Go on, Radcliff. About the murders. Evelyn."

"The murdered woman. Evelyn. They looked alike. They killed the wrong woman." He looked around the room at the others, his eyes wide. "What's going on here?! What have I said?"

"Oh my God!" Evelyn said. Her voice was barely above a whisper. She looked at Radcliff.

Alex began sobbing in earnest.

Evelyn turned toward Alex. She spoke softly. "My god, Alex, you said I resembled her! I'm so sorry."

Alex nodded emphatically as Cassidy held her close.

Radcliff shook his head. "I wish someone would tell me what's happening here." He looked from brother to sister and back.

Cassidy took in a deep breath. "Radcliff, the woman who was murdered, was Alex' friend. The man killed with her was Alex' husband." He moved his head, gesturing toward Alex, who still clung to him.

Radcliff's eyes went wide, his mouth dropped open, and he walked slowly away, then back, his hands out wide. "What?! Jesus. This can't be. Then—why are you—how did you—" He looked at Alex.

Alex shook her head. "I—I don't know. I didn't—"

"This is insane," Radcliff said. "Insane!"

"Radcliff," Cassidy said, "go on." He guided Alex back to the sofa and sat next to her after handing her a kerchief from his pants pocket.

Radcliff was silent for several seconds. "Well, I reasoned that they had killed the wrong woman—and an innocent man with her—and had to find a way to fix it—"

"Radcliff," Cassidy said, interrupting him.

"Go ahead."

"When Alex asked my help after the murders, I spoke with the police. Their assessment was that the murders were, as they put, professional. A professional job, a hit."

Radcliff pivoted, sat in his chair and took another drink from his glass. "That makes sense. They wouldn't leave anything behind. Not a crime of passion, simply a job to do, done neatly and professionally." He glanced at Evelyn, who was nodding her head, eyes closed.

"So you compared a newspaper photo with Evelyn's picture and put two and two together," Cassidy said.

Radcliff nodded. "Exactly. I figured they had blown it, and had to find someone else to do their dirty work. They couldn't stop. The stakes had been raised." He looked at Cassidy. They have your photo, too. I have it."

Cassidy frowned. "They do?!"

Radcliff nodded emphatically. "Yes. They gave it to me."

"Where'd they—"

Radcliff shook his head. "I don't know."

"Jesus. And they chose you," Evelyn said, her voice calm.

"Right. Right." Radcliff looked at each in turn again, stopping with Alex. He shook his head slowly. "I'm so sorry. Alex, is it?"

Alex mouthed a silent answer and nodded, her head still against Cassidy's chest.

"So what's next, Jeremy?" Evelyn asked. Her tone was still filled with distrust.

Radcliff took in a deep breath and released it. "Not sure I know."

"And why did you decide to come clean? And the way you did it? Why the sneaking around?" She squinted at him.

He moved his head again. "I wasn't sure. After I spotted you—and I wasn't sure it was you, I had to be certain. Good photos would have told me, but I had no plan. Hadn't gotten that far."

"How do we know you weren't followed?" She looked at her brother.

"You don't. But I do." He looked at the room. "This is a good safe house. Hard to find, easy to defend. You found me." He smiled. "I watched my back. I doubled back and waited."

Evelyn looked at her brother. "We've had it here. We have to go."

Alex sat up and looked at Evelyn. "I didn't . . ."

"Yep," Evelyn said.

"No," Radcliff said.

"No?!" Evelyn shot him a severe look.

He shook his head. "No. This is defensible. This place." He stabbed his finger toward the floor. "There's time. Let's think this through." He looked at her closely. "If you leave here, you open yourself up to real danger. You know that. You'd never see it coming. The reason you came here in the first place. No. Stay. We'll work it out." He hesitated. "One way in, one way out. From the village north, a virtual trap. Stay." He shook his head.

"We? What about your assignment? What have they got on you?"

"Old crap. Inconsequential." He shook his head and waved the question away. "What you have on them, though, is far worse, I suspect. But I'm not up for assassinations or aiding and abetting. Especially inside the country. I'm not safe. I know that."

"They didn't tell you?"

He shook his head again. "Not directly. An operational code. I remember it, but I'd have to research it. Snippets. But they did say I'd go down with them if you were to testify."

Evelyn nodded her head. "I think I know what it is, and that gives me ideas as to who's behind it."

Radcliff agreed silently.

Evelyn looked at Cassidy. "You're quiet."

"Radcliff's right. To move could be suicidal. When the time's right. Not now."

Evelyn lowered her head and shook it. She looked up at Radcliff with tired eyes. "How'd you get here?"

"How? Pickup. Parked up the road. Near the stream." He gestured.

"I think we all need some food." Cassidy spoke as he gently massaged Alex' upper back.

"I could eat," Radcliff said. "I wouldn't mind a drink."

Evelyn got up and moved toward the kitchen. "What's your poison? Some wine here."

"A beer sounds good. If you got some."

"Comin' up," Evelyn said.

Alex rose and followed her to the kitchen. "What should we fix?" She sounded meek.

Cassidy stood as well. "I don't know. Ideas, Ev?" He also moved for the kitchen.

Radcliff stood up. "Evelyn, how—why were you out there, in the dark, to find me? On the other side of the river?" He furrowed his brow. "Isn't that asking for it?"

Evelyn turned from the refrigerator where she had retrieved a bottle of beer, and began to open it on the counter. She started to speak, but was interrupted.

"My sister has cabin fever," Cassidy put in. "She spends a lot of time prowling around outside. Even after dark." He looked at Evelyn reproachfully, then at Radcliff. "I don't like it, but I'd say in this case, it served us well." He waited a count of three. "I trust you concur?"

Radcliff nodded. "I do. I do, indeed." He moved to meet Evelyn as she brought him the beer. "Thanks." He took a swig, then, "Is there a phone I could use? I'm sure cells don't work up here."

"Over there," Evelyn said. "You're right. No signal." She took a moment. "But I'm sure you'll forgive me if I insist on you telling us who you're calling, and the purpose. I also want to listen in." She looked at Radcliff from under her eyebrows.

Radcliff shook his head. "Not a problem. You've every right. My girlfriend. She's been watching after my cat. Mandy's the cat, a calico. Her name—my girlfriend—is Patsy. Patsy Romero. Nurse. Works at the hospital. And to answer your question before it's asked, no, she knows nothing about this. She knows a little about my history. A flowered-up picture of my past. I'm keeping her clear of this." He waved his hands in a negating gesture.

"Good," Evelyn replied. "Go ahead."

"Thanks." He picked up the living room handset as Evelyn went to the kitchen for the remote.

After a short wait, Radcliff spoke into the handset. "Patsy? Hi. You okay?"

Across the room, Evelyn held the portable handset to her ear with her other hand over the mouthpiece. Alex and Cassidy stood nearby, both still and silent, moving their eyes between Radcliff and Evelyn Cassidy.

Radcliff listened, then, "Well, honey, I told you this business might take more than a day. Right. We're taking a break now. It's going better than I thought. Yes. I'll let you know soon's I get home. Yes, babe. It could be later tonight, but maybe tomorrow morning. Hey, I miss you, too. And

Mandy's okay? Angry as usual, I suppose. Okay. Okay. Bye—What? Who?" He furrowed up his brow, bent forward in intensity, and shot Evelyn a glance as he did. "She said she was with what outfit? Yeah, well, I'll check it out when I get back. Yes, I love you, too. Okay, honey. Night. Sleep well."

He hung up the phone slowly, then turned to look at the others as Evelyn also pressed the "off" on her portable phone.

Radcliff stood for a moment, then moved slowly toward the kitchen after picking his beer up from the chair-side table where he had left it. He looked up. "Is there a Santa Fé directory here?"

"I'm one step ahead of you," Evelyn spoke as she pulled a thick phone book from the shelf above her head.

Radcliff stood beside her, his beer bottle in his hand, and watched as she began to riffle through the yellow pages.

She glanced at him. "What did she say the name was?"

"I think it was something Cadberry and Martínez—"

"Canberry—"

He shook his head. "Never heard of 'em."

"Doesn't mean they don't exist." She flipped to the Real Estate section.

He peered at the pages past her. "I don't see 'em."

She shook her head and closed the book.

Radcliff walked slowly away, rubbing the stubble that had developed on face. "It may be nothing."

"And it may be something," Evelyn said. "Are they watching you?"

He turned. "I'm not sure. But have they brought in a woman?"

Evelyn made a strong motion with her head, her lips compressed. "Wouldn't be the first time." She pointed at her chest as her eyes went wide.

Radcliff looked at Cassidy, then his sister in turn. "You all have no reason to trust me. I propose that you, Mark, come with me—no, follow me—to my house. Or somewhere nearby. I need to scull this out—yes, come to my place. Unobserved, of course, and I'll show you what I have. Maybe you could help me with this Nancy, whatever her name is. See if she's legit. They may be getting desperate. And we need a plan for getting Evelyn out of here and to the congressional committee." He paused. "We'll have to be careful. What do you say?"

Cassidy was slow to react. He turned and looked at Alex, then his sister, who was nodding her head in strong affirmation. "Okay. Yeah; okay."

"I like it," Evelyn said. She reached for Radcliff's Walther that Cassidy had cleared and handed it to him along with the magazine. She smiled at him. "How'd you find me?"

"I told you Patsy works at the hospital. The data on you indicated you were suffering from cancer. I reasoned you were probably taking treatments, and that it might be close by—if you were here. Patsy was good cover because I meet her there often. I spotted you there by accident. I wasn't sure at the time because of your disguise, but I figured you'd use one. The people there gave me nothing, in case you're wondering." He drank from the bottle. "I was there for other reasons, and saw you arrive with Alex." He smiled at the Texan. "When you got out and walked away, you couldn't hide the fact that you're a woman."

Evelyn looked down, then at her brother, then away, nodding silently.

"Which means, in theory, they could do the same thing," Radcliff said. "But, also in theory, they've left it up to me."

"You say 'they.' How many have you met with locally? Here. Santa Fé." This from Cassidy.

Radcliff held the nearly empty bottle out at arm's length. "One. That doesn't mean there aren't more. This woman who showed up at the house could be on the team." He hesitated, ruminating. "I suspect they're keeping it tight, because the caper I believe they're worried about involved a small group. One or two of them are dead, or have gone into hiding, and I doubt if the ones who're left want any kind of field exposure. So, they've handed it off to me, and they're light on the ground. But they won't tolerate too much delay." He looked directly at Evelyn.

"Who's your local contact?" Evelyn asked.

Radcliff moved to the counter and set the empty beer bottle down. "He calls himself Beakman." He thought for a moment, then focused on Evelyn. "Do you have more treatments?"

She moved past him, then turned and looked at her brother. "Yes."

"When's the next one?" Radcliff asked.

"Couple of weeks."

"Can you move? The treatments? To another clinic?"

She looked at him. "I don't know."

Cassidy took a step away from the counter and scratched his head. "We need to find you another clinic."

"On the other hand, maybe we can resolve this before your next appointment." Radcliff traded glances with Cassidy and Evelyn.

# 23

After consuming a sandwich and a second beer, Radcliff walked in the dark to his truck. He was accompanied by Evelyn and her brother. Evelyn was armed and although not outwardly, she was inwardly nervous, trying to dissect the difference between her instincts and rational thought. Radcliff's pistol, the chamber cleared, was tucked into his waistband holster, the magazine in his jacket pocket.

He stopped his pickup just beyond the Cassidy place, engine idling, and waited while Cassidy backed the Jeep out onto the road and got behind him. Cassidy then followed Radcliff to the highway junction in Pecos, waited two minutes, then, assured there were no interested parties, drove back to Holy Ghost Canyon. He was not followed.

Radcliff had drawn a map, with written directions to his place. He offered Cassidy advice about how to approach unobserved, important in view of the fact that his adversaries could also identify their target's closest relative. Following that mandate, Cassidy drove into the yard a few minutes after ten the following morning in a rented sedan in place of his Jeep. He was dressed in a suit with a white shirt, conservative tie and street shoes, a good western hat that hid his sun glass-covered eyes, and carried a leather briefcase. As he approached the house, he stopped, looked around and consulted a note pad, all in the cause of seeming to be at a place out of complete innocence and for a purpose other than the intended. He rapped on the door and stepped back.

Radcliff opened the door. "Yes? May I help you?"

Cassidy handed him a business card. "Good morning. Mr. Radcliff? Are you the gentleman who called about an investment portfolio?"

Radcliff shifted his eyes past Cassidy subtly, then looked at him. "Yes; right. C'mon in."

Cassidy followed him and Radcliff shut the door.

Cassidy turned. "That was necessary?"

Radcliff shrugged. "With the technology available today, who knows who's out there hearing what we say or reading our lips." He gestured toward the living room. "I hope you checked the roadway."

Cassidy walked into the living room, removed his hat, set his briefcase down and loosened his tie. "I watched for parked cars as far as I could see. I made sure I drove in when the highway was free of traffic."

"Good. Here's the card that woman left with Patsy."

Cassidy took it and read the printed message. He turned it over, then handed it back. "These are easy to produce. Do you know if she's genuine or not?"

"Haven't had time. I think I—or if you want to go along—we should go to that address and check."

"Good idea. I can go. You said you had something to show me."

"Yes. In the interest of honesty and transparency, I'm going to show you things that not even Patsy sees. Follow me."

Radcliff took Cassidy into the back room with the computer, floor safe and files saved from his past. He brought up the encrypted web site, surfed to the pages on his sister, and showed him the newspaper article about the murder.

In the shaded room, Cassidy looked at Radcliff. "I believe you." He sighed. "Evelyn is hard to convince, but—"

Radcliff held up his hand. "Hey—I know. She has every right. She's staring down a gun barrel. Almost literally. I don't blame her. I could have been the hit guy."

Cassidy nodded emphatically. "Why the 'Wraith' thing? What's that all about?"

"From what I can gather, your sister was pretty good at getting in and getting out. Not just premises—you know, buildings and so forth—but situations. She's a smart cookie. Like a ghost. At any rate, she earned the nickname."

Cassidy shook his head, smiling. "Wow."

"Yep." He hesitated. "Listen, Mark, I've done a lot of bad things in the name of the United States and the agency, but this is too much. I'm not going to commit murder for these guys. The CIA is supposed to stay out of stuff within the borders. They're over-stepping their bounds. Way out. They gotta' go down. Even if I go down with 'em." He held his finger up.

"I guess you know I'm an attorney," Cassidy said. "If I've anything to do with it, you won't. And I don't think you'll have to be on the run." He poked his finger in Radcliff's direction. "I'll back you. I've got a few friends."

"I appreciate that. I sure don't want to be looking behind my back the rest of my life. Or staring out from behind bars."

They sat silently in the dark room with the single desk light for another half minute.

"You ready to do the real estate thing?" Radcliff asked.

"Let's do it." Cassidy stood up.

After tightening his tie, Cassidy left with his briefcase, and both men carried out the charade of a salesman leaving with a handshake and appropriate words.

Cassidy drove into the center of the city, and parked south of the Plaza in the city lot. His tie and jacket off, wide-brimmed hat pulled down over his shaded eyes and briefcase left behind, he walked to the corner of the La Fonda hotel across from the Plaza. He waited amid the crowd of tourists who drifted about on the sidewalks and criss-crossed the narrow streets randomly. Ten minutes passed before Radcliff showed up in his pickup and pulled to a stop so Cassidy could climb in.

Radcliff eyed the reflection in the rearview mirror, then watched the street and traffic in front. "It's an address off of Cerrillos," he said.

He drove down one of the many short streets that connected at a right angle with Cerrillos on the north side, the one on the fake real estate card. Radcliff slowed as Cassidy examined what numbers he could make out as they moved along.

"Slow down," Cassidy said. "Three-oh-six, three-oh—Stop! Can you back up?"

Radcliff checked his rear, pulled sharply to the right so the old blue pickup was close to the curb, then reversed carefully. "What'd you see?"

"Three-oh-eight. It's a vacant building. Check me out." He handed the map to Radcliff and pointed out his window.

Radcliff peered at the map, checked the street name, then looked up and around, craning his neck. "You're right. Non-existent. So much for our Nancy." He looked at Cassidy, his lips compressed.

"So, what's next?" Cassidy raised his eyebrows.

Radcliff took several beats before he answered. "Not sure." He was silent, then, "I may have mentioned that this woman was rather pushy. She wandered through the house, according to Patsy, asking questions." Both his hands gripped the steering wheel tightly.

"Not unusual for a real estate agent."

"No, but given that her business address is phony, it's obvious she had other reasons for her curiosity."

"Mm."

"What it means to me is that they're not only keeping an eye on me, but are trying to get inside. They probably believe I'm holding back." He paused. "And they're right."

"How do you handle it?"

"I'll bite."

"Bite?" Cassidy furrowed his brow.

He looked at Cassidy. "I'll call her. Arrange an appointment."

"Then?"

"Not sure. Again. Play it by ear."

Cassidy nodded.

"I could use some lunch."

"Yeah."

"Better do take-out. Not a good idea to be seen sitting together in a public place. This is risky enough." Radcliff looked into his mirrors and steered the pickup back into the street.

"I should get back, too."

"Okay. I know a place."

They sat in a parking lot at a big-box building supply store, in a nearly deserted corner, two hundred feet from the nearest other vehicle, and far from the entrance. Both worked on hamburgers. Cassidy had called his sister from his cell phone to see if all was quiet.

"I looked on the company data base before you came. Nothing on our Nancy," Radcliff said after swallowing a bite and slurping at his soda.

Cassidy looked at him, chewing.

"Doesn't mean she's not company, or that she was and is retired. She could be a contractor."

"Contractor?"

"They do it sometimes. If the internal asset count is low, or they want someone from outa' town, like that. Hell, I've hired former enemies. Make a deal. Give 'em money and a ticket. Threats. Get outa' jail free card." He looked at Cassidy, then stared out through the windshield at the blank wall they faced.

"So she could be a contractor?"

Radcliff nodded. "Oh, yeah. In this case, if so, she's probably ex-company."

"But the phony address—"

"Seems sloppy. But if they think I'm on board. Don't suspect. Don't figure I'll investigate. I need to keep it that way."

"Makes sense."

Radcliff sucked on his drink and turned to Cassidy. "Didn't get a chance last night. About—Alex is it? A bit too convenient. How did that come about? Who is she?"

Cassidy, also finishing his drink, swallowed and cleared his throat. "It does seem that way, and Evelyn was convinced after we learned of the murders, that there had to be a connection." He took two beats, then, "I had her checked out. Couple of guys, detectives, one in Lubbock—where she's from—another from a Chicago outfit. Did a thorough digging and a watch and wait. Eyes on the ground. Close in. Business, home. She's clean." He looked at Radcliff, then out the windshield. "I went to the murder scene after she called me. The way she was torn up—"

"Is there something between you?"

Cassidy snorted a chuckle and looked down. "I took a liking to her. She and my sister get on well. She's also spooked by what happened, so she's been staying with us." He raised his head. "I think she likes me."

"She could go home?"

"She could. She did. I had her tailed. I also met with the Santa Fé P.D. guy running the investigation. You might say I took her case. Unofficially, of course. I'm not licensed in New Mexico. Assured 'em she'd be back. They didn't want her to leave." He looked at Radcliff. "She came back. They've pretty well dropped her as a suspect. Speaking of her, I better get back. Makes me nervous to be too far from the place. I feel a bit naked out here."

"I'll drop you. South City lot?"

After tossing their fast-food trash into a bin, and with Radcliff's pickup truck in motion, Cassidy asked, "You may not be able, or want to answer this, but you said you met with someone here? Locally? From the CIA? Any of the people who want Evelyn eliminated?" Cassidy lowered his head so that he was looking at Radcliff from under his eyebrows.

Radcliff, still facing forward, was silent, then, "Yes. I was invited, you might say, to meet with one man. I mentioned him last night. Beakman—which, of course, might be false—but he was, to the best of my knowledge, alone." He shot a glance at Cassidy before resuming the requirement to watch the road.

"Do you think this guy killed those people? Did the murders?"

Radcliff took in a deep breath. "I don't know. It wouldn't surprise me. I think the guy is capable. But I have no proof. They could have brought in an outsider. He—or she—would be on the first plane out after ditching the gun. Beakman may have been brought in after. After the first one took off. Just a guess." He waited a beat. "Somebody had to realize they had the wrong target."

"Would it do any good to put the cops on his trail?"

Radcliff shook his head in a short, jerky motion. "No. If the scene was as clean as you say it was. And things could blow up in our faces—"

Cassidy interrupted, "I was allowed in several hours after the fact, so—"

"But you had no reason—"

"I was allowed to see most of what the police discovered. It was clean. The bodies had not been removed. When I rode with the detective—Griego—he told me they found nothing incriminating. And that was after they'd interviewed Alex."

Radcliff nodded. "Okay."

"Another thing."

"Yeah?"

"When Alex met with the police after her return, they showed her a pen. Ball point. Not cheap. Had the symbol of the Masons on it. Mean anything to you?"

"No."

"It wasn't Alex' husband's."

"Probably a dead end."

They both fell silent.

# 24

It was four o'clock in the afternoon when Radcliff placed a call to Nancy Mullins, a couple of hours after leaving Mark Cassidy near the Plaza. Her voice mail responded, but she called back half an hour later.

"I think you met Patsy when you came by," Radcliff said.

"Yes! What a sweetie! Are you two married?"

Radcliff tried to detect something from her voice, but could not. "No. You might say she's my main squeeze. Is that current these days?" He chuckled, although it was an act.

"Well, I certainly liked her! Listen, I really liked your home. And the place—the setting. Great!" She stretched the word "really."

"I appreciate that, but it's not for sale."

"We could make you a really great deal."

He let out a short, explosive laugh. "Where would I go? What would I do with the money?"

There was silence on the line, then, "Well, Mr. Radcliff, you have a very good point, but then, we have some wonderful properties. Other properties I think you'd love."

Radcliff's mind was swirling. Why was she going this route? She's a patented phony, with nothing with which to work, and sounding as though she did. What would she do if he took her up on her offer? What's her game plan? His own plan began to form. "Well, talk is cheap. We can discuss it."

"Wonderful. Would tomorrow morning be okay? I have an opening. Say around tennish?"

"That would work. Say, I may have something for you."

"Oh?"

"Yes. Ever handle ranches? You know, just plain land?"

"Unimproved?"

"Yes." She had the proper lexicon list on her lips, he noted.

"Sure. We could have a look-see."

He detected a diminution of enthusiasm. "Okay. Not far from here. You got some time, I could show it to you."

"That would be wonderful," Mr. Radcliff.


Nancy Mullins arrived at the appointed time. Radcliff let her in and guided her to the living room, where she sat poised on the sofa, deposited her briefcase on the coffee table, and opened it. She looked up as Radcliff spoke.

"Coffee?"

"Oh, no; thanks. I'm coffeed-out." She awarded him a big smile.

"What've you got there?" He took a step toward her.

"Some samples of other properties that might interest you."

He moved his head in a negative gesture. "Mm—"

She stood. "You know, I had only a brief time when I was here. Could I see the rest of the house? A real tour? I feel we could get you a super price."

Radcliff tried to fathom why it was so important for her to engage in a tour. The only quick answer he could derive was that she needed to case the house for a clean break-in. He looked at his watch. "Could we do it on the way back? Maybe some lunch? I'd really like to show you the ranch property I mentioned. Best time of day—"

She was silent for a moment. Her face changed to a momentary blank stare as she thought of a way to change his mind. She brightened. "Okay! That sounds great! I'll follow you."

Radcliff had turned away. "Where we're going, I think you better go with me in my truck. Could get that shiny Cadillac scratched." He swung around and gave her a wry look and winked.

"Oh, you're right. Of course. And it'd be faster, right?" She waved her hand in acquiescence.

"Right."

With Nancy strapped in, Radcliff backed the pickup, turned, and headed for the pavement. There was little conversation as he joined the Interstate and headed east. They dropped down into Cañoncito, then the rise though Glorieta Pass, and on toward Rowe, where he took the off ramp.

As they came to the stop at the end of the off ramp, Nancy looked up at the steep escarpment ahead. "Where we headed?" There was a note of nervousness in her voice.

He pointed. "Up there."

"Really?"

"Yeah. If you look over there, you can see the road. Quite passable. Locals up there year-round. Cattle, wood-cutting. Hunting."

"Hunting? Really?"

"That's a fact." He shot her a smiling glance, filled with innocence. "Deer."

At the top, as the land flattened out onto the plain in front of them, Nancy craned her head in all directions. "God! I had no idea."

"Something else, no?" He managed the wheel along the rutted dirt road.

At a break in the barbed wire fence which featured a cattle guard, he slowed, turned right and entered a road that was considerably worse than the one they'd been on. They moved at no more than ten miles per hour.

"Are we close?" She looked at her watch.

"Close." He looked down at her wrist, then up. "Gotta date?" He smiled.

She looked over at him coyly. "I don't know. Do I?"

Radcliff remained silent, facing ahead, a trace of a smile showing.

The truck climbed gently as they entered a thickly-forested area, and the road began to wind and narrow, in places tortuously.

"Is this part of your property?" She asked. She bounced in her seat in reaction to the increasingly rough trace.

"A bit more. One more gate and we're there."

Radcliff steered the truck through increasingly rough terrain, then came to a dilapidated gate across the road. It was made of crooked, dried, debarked cedar, rusted barbed wire and featured a loop of old, rusted chain that held it in place. He stopped the truck, shut down the engine, removed the keys, and opened the gate. Back in the truck, he re-started the engine and drove on.

Nancy looked at him, her face a mask of high curiosity. "Why did you do that?"

Without looking at her, he said, "Do what?"

Her voice lowered in an attempt to control herself, she said, "Take the keys!"

"Ah—that. Force of habit. Sorry." He shot her a smiling glance.

"How odd, Mr. Radcliff."

"Hey, call me Jeremy." His face was bright and smiling.

She hesitated. "Alright. Jeremy." Her voice cooled.

He brought the truck to a sudden halt, shut the engine down, and reached under the seat for his Walther, got out, and stuck the gun into his waistband. He looked around, then at Nancy. "Gettin' out?"

"Yes." Her voice had lost strength.

"Leave your purse behind. You won't need it here."

She looked at him from the corner of her eye, without a smile. "I find your behavior rather strange, Mr. Radcliff. Jeremy."

He ignored her remark. "Take a look at this." He pointed.

"What's the gun for?"

He kept his gaze front. "Out here, one never knows. I always pack heat when in the wilderness of New Mexico. Come. Look."

She walked in his direction. Ahead of them stretched the immense valley that contained Cañoncito, and beyond, Lamy and the immense Galisteo Depression.

"Where are we?"

"At the western edge of the uplift the locals call Rowe Mesa." He looked at her, then back at the fantastic scene. "Really Glorieta Mesa on the maps. But they're wrong, too. It's not a mesa. It's a cuesta. Ask the geologists." He waved his arm out in a sweep as though painting the scenery.

She peered at him. "Is this your land? This isn't yours, is it?"

"No more than you're a real estate agent, Nancy. If that's your real name." He did not look at her.

"What?! What are you saying to me?!" She took two beats, then, "I insist you take me out of here! This is over!"

He looked at the ground at his feet, then at her. "Indeed it is. I ask you again. Is Nancy whatever it is—Mullins—your real name?"

"Of course it is! What is this?!" Her torso was distorted in anger and frustration, then she straightened.

"It may be your name, but you're no real estate agent. I checked you out. The address on your card is non-existent." He turned to face her directly and took a step toward her.

She was silent, her resolve having returned. She stared at him, fury in her eyes. She remained in place.

"Kinda' dumb, Nancy. Who thought that up? Figured I wouldn't check?"

She turned away, slumped forward and sighed heavily.

"Who you with? Guess you're not company. Couldn't find you on the data base. 'Course, that doesn't mean anything. Contractor? Yeah. Yep. Contractor. Who brought you in? Probably not Beakman. Charlie? You know 'im?"

She shook her head.

"Who do you know?"

She was silent.

"I suggest you start talking, Nancy. You may not know it—no, they didn't tell you, did they? You're here to facilitate a murder. That's right, murder." He waited. "You didn't know that, did you?"

She took a step back, then turned, her head down. Her face darkened. "Murder? What are you saying? She looked up at him, her mouth sagging.

"I said murder. Homicide. To kill someone. A killing. Assassination. A hit. Wet op. They didn't. Did they? What did they tell you?" He shook his head and sighed.

"What are you saying?"

"I'm saying, you were sent here—for what stated purpose, I sure as hell don't know—I guess to help Beakman with me, to help rid the agency—rogue agents in and out of the agency—of a problem. Used to call it extreme prejudice, I believe. To kill someone. Wet ops. Murder."

"You're serious." She squinted at him.

"Could not be more serious, Nancy. They've already killed some-one. Two someones. Wrong folks. Screwed it up. Was it Beakman or an outsider? I don't know. Do you?" He raised his eyebrows at her.

She walked a small, tight circle, then came closer. "Murder? This is about getting rid of someone?" Her voice was barely above a whisper, her face screwed up in disbelief.

"Depending upon how you handle yourself from now on, I can of-fer up proof. If not, well, I'll simply go to the cops and suggest they look into you and your buddy." He hesitated. "Your call."

"Who is it? Who do they want dead?"

Radcliff paced away, pondering, looked out over the valley, then back. "A woman. A woman, Nancy. They've targeted a woman. They think she's gonna' rat on 'em. Something that happened years ago. An operation gone bad. They fucked it up."

"And you?"

"Oh yeah, it could affect me. That's why they came to me. You know the drill. But I'm not ready to murder someone. Not here. Not on American soil. Sure as hell not for those assholes."

She looked at him carefully. All the acting to make her what she wasn't had faded completely. "You have proof?"

"I want to know if you're ready to listen. If you're not, I'll throw you to the wolves. Are you armed?"

"What?!"

"Do you have a piece on you?"

"What?! No—!"

"Prove it! Come closer!"

She hesitated, then took a step toward him as he moved quickly to her side. He reached out and began patting her down, starting with her ankles, which were covered loosely by the high-quality pants she wore. He then worked his way up, over her waist area, then her back.

"Hey!"

"Don't give me a hard way to go, Nancy! You're in no position, lady! This thing has gotten out of hand when Charlie and the boys call in a con-tractor! Means they don't trust me. And if they don't trust me, then I'm on their prejudice list." He stepped back. "You're clean. What's in the purse?"

She looked at him. "Small caliber."

"Figures. If you run for it, I'll drop you before you take two steps. Understand?" He took a count, then, "Out here, it'd be years—"

"I'm not going to fight you on this. If you're telling me the truth—"

He looked at her. "Did Beakman kill those people?"

"Radcliff—Jeremy—I didn't know. They didn't tell me. I'm telling you the truth!"

He held up his hand. "Okay. Stay here. I'll be right back. Don't move."

He went to the truck, retrieved Nancy's handbag, then came back as he dug through it. He held up a small semi-automatic pistol. He dropped the bag to the ground, cleared the chamber and magazine by manipulating the slide several times, letting the rounds fly out onto the ground, then stuck the gun into his belt line alongside the Walther.

He picked up the bag and handed it to her. "Let's go."

He told her to finesse Beakman, come to his place late that night, and to ensure there was no tail. When she arrived, he hustled her inside and immediately took her purse, set it aside and frisked her. He then told her to sit in the living room while he quickly looked inside the handbag, then set it down. He offered her an alcoholic beverage, which she accepted. He then sat across from her without a drink, and insisted she tell him her life story while he went through her purse, looking at her identification, credit cards and the like.

A half hour later, they sat in Radcliff's office, where he showed her the same evidence he had provided Cassidy.

She sat quietly. "Have you found her?"

Maybe I have, Nancy, and maybe I haven't. What would your reaction be if I said yes? What would you do or say? What would be your next move?" He sat back and studied her face in the semi-dark.

"I don't know. I really don't. I'd have to think about it." She pondered, then, "I know I won't take part in murder." Her voice quality betrayed something akin to depression.

# 25

You got inside the house?" Beakman leaned forward, keeping his voice moderated.

He and Nancy Mullins sat a corner table in the subdued light of the Santa Café. Their dinner dishes had been cleared, and they each nursed the last of the wine from the bottle he had ordered.

She looked around the big, half-empty room furtively, as though what she was about to say was of any interest to anyone else at other tables. "Yes; of course. I got inside. I told you." She sipped her wine.

"You said one of the rooms was locked, and he didn't want you in there?" He squinted.

She nodded. "My impression, yes."

"We need to get in there." His head lowered, one hand holding his wine glass, he looked to his left, then back.

"We?" She was amused.

"Yeah. Okay. One of us." He looked up, then tasted the red liquid in his stemmed glass.

"And I suppose you want me to be the one. Of us."

"I understand you're good at that sort of thing."

She twiddled her glass so that the wine spun slowly. "Wouldn't be the first time."

"Good. So, I need to keep watch."

"Need to get him out of there. He's retired, you know. Sculpts."

"Mm. Right, right." He was quiet, then, "How long you need?"

"Long as possible. An hour should be enough."

"If I'm with you, he's gotta' be with someone else."

"Yeah—"

"Right. But who?"

"Girl friend? Her name's Patsy."

"That'd be best, but how?"

"Let me think about it."

"You know where she lives?

"No. I know her last name. What're you thinking?"

He waved his hand. "Nothing. Just asking."

She pointed her finger at him. "Listen, Beakman, no nasty stuff with the girl! I didn't sign up to hurt people!"

"Don't get your panties in a ruffle. I wouldn't do anything to hurt the girl. Calm down." He tipped his glass up and swallowed the last of the wine.

"Just make damn sure you don't, Beakman! You do, I'm outa' here, and I'll blow the whistle!" She sat back with a stiff gesture of defiance.

He leaned forward. "Jesus, lady! Take it easy! Did I say I was gonna' hurt somebody?!"

She stared at him across the table. "No, but you got hurt in your eyes, pal!"

"The wine's gotten to you, Mullins. Slow down." He looked away, tapping the table with his fingers in nervous frustration.

"We understand each other?"

"Yes! Of course." He hesitated. "But we gotta' work fast. I'll think of something. Soft as a cushion, okay?" He pointed his finger at her, stood, and reached into his jacket pocket for his wallet. "You say you met her?"

"Yes."

"Describe her car."

"No funny business with the car!"

"Thinking out loud. Thinking out loud." His voice trailed off.

She glared at him and hissed, "I mean it!"

He shook his head and leaned across the table at her. His voice a hoarse whisper, he said, "Goddamnit, Nancy, I'm not gonna' chew through a brake line or put a bomb under the hood! I just need to know how to find her. Shit! Let's go!" He threw several large denomination bills on the table and moved toward the door after her.

Five people at two nearby tables looked up at the quarreling couple as they exited the restaurant, then resumed their quiet conversations.

The following morning, over breakfast at Radcliff's house, he briefed Patsy Romero on how she was to react to any message or visit by someone she didn't know. She could expect that whomever contacted her would have something "special" for her and a guest, most likely an expensive event to take place on a particular night that would take up most of her evening and that of her guest. The special event tickets would most likely be a prize, awarded at random, by an obscure organization devoted to those who worked in her profession. Any questions about the organization would probably be answered in guarded terms, with the organization being at a great distance; for example, New York or Washington. Attendant with the prize there might be extra cash; possibly transportation, even a meal at an up-scale restaurant on the same evening.

Patsy looked at Radcliff in silence for a long time, cocking her head first one way, then the other, as a dog, curious about a master's voice, might do. "What's going on, Jeremy? What's this all about?"

He shook his head in a minor way, thinking. Then, "There's no danger. It's all under control. I have to tell you—I'm asking you to you go along with it. I'll tell you later. Please?"

"But—how do you know this might—will—happen?"

He reached across the table and took her hand. "Sweetie, please. Just this once. I really don't want you involved. There will be tickets. And a nice dinner. That's it."

"Jeremy—!"

He shook his head again. "Patsy, please do this. I will be your guest. Okay? Then it's over."

"I don't like this. I think something bad will happen."

"No. Nothing bad will happen." He sighed, exasperated. "Do you trust me, Patsy?"

Her mouth pursed in a smile, her brow furrowed, she said, "I love you, Jeremy, but I'm not sure I trust you."

He curled up his mouth in disbelief, his eyes wide.

She gripped his hand with her smaller one as hard as she could. "I'm kidding! Of course, I trust you! Silly!"

He nodded, his face relaxing to relief. "Good. You okay with this? You and I are gonna' have a good dinner out and a show. Sound good?"

"Yeah! So, what do I have to do? When?" She leaned forward, beaming with excitement.

They kissed.

Two days later, Patsy Romero received a piece of special delivery mail from the National Organization of Nursing Professionals. In the official-looking envelope was a letter stating that she had been selected, along with a few hundred other nurses around the country, from thousands of those in "good standing," to receive a special, one-time gift. That gift consisted of a "night on the town," which included "fine dining," a "great show" at a nearby casino, and a chauffeur-driven limousine. All she had to do was call a certain number and provide her name, nursing registration number and one other proof of identity. She was told she could bring a guest.

Radcliff stood next to her as she made the call that same day. The following Friday, shortly before sundown, a long, black limousine rolled up to her apartment complex. The uniformed driver, innocent of the charade being performed, bounded up the steps to her apartment and rang the bell. Two minutes later, Patsy, attired in an evening dress purchased the day before with money provided by Radcliff, climbed into the back seat of the long car. She was joined by Radcliff in his best suit and tie. The driver turned in his seat and told them to help themselves to beverages in the little bar that pulled out from the front seat assembly. From there, the car headed for Albuquerque.

Beakman picked Nancy Mullins up a block from her hotel an hour after dark.

As she climbed into the passenger seat, she looked at him. "You seem nervous. What are you looking around for? You expect someone to be watching?" She placed a black cloth bag at her feet.

He snapped his head toward her. "No. No. Natural for me. Being cautious."

"Yeah, right, Beakman. But you're so damned obvious." Her face showing disgust, she averted her eyes.

They headed east along Alameda, turned south onto Old Santa Fé, then to the Old Pecos Highway. Neither spoke until they gained the traffic light close to the Interstate.

Without looking at her, Beakman asked, "Got everything you need?"

"What do you think?" She looked out her passenger-side window.

"Jesus Christ, Nancy! What is it with you?! Lately, you've been a real bitch, you know?!"

She hesitated and sighed. "Hey, I'm sorry. I'm nervous. I don't like the smell of this gig, okay?" She glanced at him, then away.

He nodded. "Yeah, I know. "You'll do fine. Just get in there and get out quick. See what you can find. There may not be much, but it's worth a try."

She peered at him. "You're sure he's gone?"

"Oh, yes. He's gone. With his *chiquita*. All the way to Albuquerque. Big night." He smirked.

"Okay."

Beakman drove past the house, then turned back a half-mile away. As he approached the Radcliff drive, he slowed, then pulled off to the side, watching the on-coming traffic as well as that approaching from the rear. When the highway was clear, Nancy opened her door and slid out, pulling the bag with her.

"Got your radio?" Beakman asked.

"Yeah. Check in five. Going in the rear." She closed the door and sprinted away at a crouch.

Beakman pulled onto the highway and headed for the next road to the east, where he drove a quarter mile, then pulled into a wide, dark section. He shut the engine down and killed the headlamps. He retrieved a small, hand-held radio from the glove compartment and snapped it on.

He pressed the transmit button. "B1 here. You copy, N1?"

There ensued a high-pitched hiss, then. "Copy, B1. N1. Over."

"Standing by."

Nancy moved to the side of Radcliff's place, near the shed where the Royal Enfield stood ready. She found the spot where Radcliff had placed a stool for her and settled in. From her position, she could see the road. As her eyes became accustomed to the night, she was able to see if anyone approached.

She waited another two minutes, then she keyed her radio on. "B1, N1, come in."

"B1 here. Go."

"I'm in. Over."

"Copy, N1. Happy hunting."

Nancy put the radio aside, dug into the black bag, pulled out a candy bar and tore the wrapper away. She sat back and bit into the sweet.

Forty-five minutes passed before she picked up the radio. "B1, N1."

"Copy. Go."

"Extracting, B1. May have pay dirt. Over."

"Charmed life, N1. See you in five."

"Copy. Over and out."

Beakman once again drove well past the Radcliff drive, then circled back to where Nancy waited in the shadow of a large cedar next to a sage. He slowed, and she jumped in, pulling her door shut as he moved away and back onto the pavement.

He looked over at her. "What'd you find?"

She reached into her blouse and retrieved a piece of paper. She held it out, then dropped it into her lap. "A map."

"Map?"

"Yeah."

"Of what?" He screwed up his face.

"Not sure. Looks fresh and local." She cocked her head toward him. "What'd you expect? What're you after—or who're you after, anyway?"

Beakman drove the pickup through the traffic light next to the Interstate, then pulled to a stop in the safety lane alongside the curb. "Let me see it."

She handed it to him.

He snapped on the front dome light and studied for a few seconds, then looked up and out through the windshield. "Yes," he said.

"Well, what is it? What does it mean?"

He nodded slowly. "Yes."

"Well, what?!"

He looked at her and smiled. "Pay dirt, indeed. You've earned your keep, Lady Nancy!" With that, he turned the light out, put the transmission in "Drive" and accelerated away.

"I repeat, what now?!"

He glanced at her. "Well, for one thing, how about you and me?" He smiled.

She hesitated. "What about you and me?" Her voice was icy.

"Well, hey, you said—"

"What I said, Beakman, was not a guarantee." Her voice was low; sincere.

"Yeah, well, alright." His voice trailed off in disappointment.

"Thing is, I was hired to do a job. It didn't come with the proviso that I sleep with you."

"Who said anything—?"

"Tut-tut, buddy. I wasn't born yesterday." She wagged her finger at him.

He shook his head. "Yeah. Okay. Fine. Sorry."

She waited, then, "Are we okay? Professional?"

"Yeah. Sorry."

"Okay. Good. I have somebody. And I don't go outside. Make sense?"

"Sure. Sure. I get it. No offense." Both hands on the wheel, he shot her a glance accompanied by a manufactured smile.

"None taken. I'm flattered."

Beakman pulled to a stop in front of the hotel lobby. "Great job, Nancy."

She turned toward him, bringing her left leg up onto the seat. "Shut off the engine. I have a couple of questions."

He reached out and killed the engine, then looked at her with curiosity.

"What's going on? Why am I here? Why couldn't you have broken into that house?"

He thought for a moment. "We needed somebody from the outside. I have some exposure, and I can't do my job—you know—stay around without botching the job."

"Yeah, okay, but what *is* the job?"

"You know better. Isolation. Don't mix the trails. Too many ways to connect the dots. They must've told you."

She nodded and looked down. "Okay. Sure. So, what's next? What do you want me to do?"

He sighed, pondering. "I think you've done it. I checked. Best you move on. Leave it to me. I can wrap this up quickly. Now."

"You're telling me to leave?"

"You can stick around. See the town. The area. Lots to see. But I can take it from here."

She brought her leg down and faced forward, then smoothed her pant legs. "Naw. If we're done, I'm outa' here."

"Need a ride? Anything?"

She shook her head. "I'm fine. Re-trace route and all that. Take care of those for me, okay? Better dump 'em." She pointed at the black bag on the floor. As she did, she checked her memory, making sure she had removed the candy wrapper and stuffed it into her pants pocket.

"Sure. I'll take care of it. Lost and gone forever."

She extended her hand. "Nice working with you, Beakman."

He took her hand. "Same here. Take care." He withdrew his hand. "They're paying you well?"

She smirked. "Oh, yeah." She opened the door, slid out, faced him with a small wave, then turned and was gone.

He watched her walk into the lobby as he cranked the car's engine to life.

# 26

Since the time was after one in the afternoon, the Atrisco Café was lightly attended. Two men sat on stools at the bar, drinking draft beer and grazing on chips and salsa.

Radcliff sat across from Beakman in a booth next to the line of southern windows that faced the sunny parking lot. Each had a plate of food and a bottle of beer in front of him.

Beakman toyed with his food, then after drinking from his bottle, said, "So, Jeremy, how goes it? Where are we? Time's a-wastin'."

Radcliff swallowed a bite and looked up. "I'm working on it, Beakman."

Beakman, who had picked up his fork, set it down hard and looked directly at his table partner. "Listen, Radcliff, we've got to finish this thing! What's the problem?!" His voice was a hoarse whisper.

Radcliff looked around to see if anyone had reacted to Beakman's sudden wrathful expression, took a moment, then said, "Well, you listen to me, pal! This assignment is not easy!" He looked around again. "Goddamnit, This woman's not easy to find. Fact is, I have a line on her, and I'm working it, but it's not a sure thing. So you just back off, you hear me?!" He was breathing hard, and took a count of three before he raised his bottle to his lips, his eyes fixed on Beakman.

Beakman shook his head in one, jerking movement. "Okay. Okay. Sorry. I guess I thought you could perform some magic. Sorry."

Radcliff looked around again, then lowered his head and leaned forward. His voice went soft. "I'm working it. I have a lead. I'll have something soon. You can tell the troops."

"Listen, I know it's a bitch, but I've got these guys on my ass."

"Well, tell 'em to cool it. I'm doing my best."

Beakman only nodded.

Finished, he paid the tab with cash, and they left, Radcliff first. Little was said between them as they stood for a minute on the sun-drenched sidewalk. As Radcliff walked away, Beakman stared after him, his face disturbed under his dark glasses and broad-brimmed Resistol hat.

Beakman went to the map store on Montezuma Avenue and bought three representations of New Mexico. He took them back to his room, spread each out in turn on the bed, and compared areas he thought might match the lines and notes on the piece of paper Nancy had given him after the break-in. Feeling he had made a good comparison, he drove away in the small foreign car he had rented after turning the pickup in, a fact he had hidden from Radcliff.

He stopped at a fast-food restaurant, purchased two sandwiches, a milk shake, coffee, French fries and a fruit pie, then headed for the Interstate. Following the colored accent tracings he had made on his published map, he took the off ramp to Pecos, then drove along highway fifty, watching each and every vehicle he passed, as well as keeping an eye on one following and one in front. At the intersection in Pecos, he stopped, consulted the map, then headed north.

Unfamiliar with the two-lane highway that wound north along the Pecos River valley into increasingly steep, rocky terrain, Beakman peered at every road, house, and vehicle he saw. Much of the time, he was in shadow, since the time was well into the middle of the afternoon. When he reached the bridge that crossed the river several hundred yards short of Terrero, he slowed even more, feeling he had arrived at a crucial point. He drove on and into the wide parking lot at the store and pulled to a stop. With the engine running, he studied the map, the note paper and the area, craning his neck around. He finally decided that the two bridges, one old and one new, were at the point where his search changed direction.

He put the map, partly unfolded, on the seat next to him, put the transmission into Drive and returned to the river crossing. Driving slowly, he turned into the narrow, badly eroded trace that pointed west into the depths of the mountain. He read the little sign on the right which read, "Holy Ghost Canyon." The paper Nancy had handed him did not contain that phrase anywhere that he could find, but the initials "HG" next to the last, crudely penned line told him he was on the right track.

His heart rate was up. Dry-mouthed, he found himself angry with Radcliff, and thought of the warm milk shake in the paper sack from the fast-food place. His heart also raced because he realized he might be close to a resolution to a case that had baffled and eluded him for weeks. To hell with Jeremy Radcliff. He had a bundle awaiting him offshore. He could smell it now.

He drove another quarter mile, found a wide spot alongside the road, and pulled over. He reached for the sack, retrieved the shake, fitted a straw into the plastic cover, and drew in a mouthful. Holding the paper container against the steering wheel, he looked around. He saw no one and no vehicles. He put his window down, and heard only the soft rustling of leaves in the deciduous trees along the banks of the creek, and the water that rushed by in it. Oddly, he felt peaceful, but the sensation was mixed with a rising sense of fear. He put the drink into a cup holder in the center console and picked up the map. A small square on the left of the line he figured he was on, that which represented the road, was marked with a question mark. But where was the house the square stood for? He looked again. A smaller square jutted out from the larger. An arrow pointed to it. At the tail end of the arrow was the remark, "new garage?"

The engine still running, he engaged the transmission, checked the outside rearview mirror, and pulled out onto the decaying tarmac. He drove slowly along the winding road. Two minutes later, he spotted a big house on the left. In front, closer to the road, was what appeared to be a garage. It seemed newer than the house, since the wood siding looked fresher; lighter in color. He knew he had found the place Radcliff had marked on his crude map. Exhilarated, but nervous, he drove slowly on, careful not to appear to be watching. Then, it suddenly dawned on him: would Radcliff notice that the simple drawing was missing? He had forgotten to ask Nancy where she had found it. It was too late. He would deal with Jeremy Radcliff. He had his marching orders.

He drove on another mile, then turned and headed back down the inclined road. When the house, now on the right, came into view, he looked quickly for a place to park. Seeing no other vehicle, he stopped, put the car into reverse, and backed to a wide spot at the edge of the crumbling, patched asphalt. There, he pulled the car as far into the foliage as he could, pointing it at a steep angle to the road. He reached under the seat, pulled out his Glock 9mm pistol, checked the breach, and stuck it into his belt line. Then he took a sandwich from the sack and the remains of the shake, the bag of cold, limp, French fries, and got out. He stopped, turned, and reached inside for his jacket and a pair of seven-power binoculars from the back seat, then started toward the house. When he was within a hundred feet of it, he crossed to the opposite side of the road and clambered up a leafy incline to a grove of trees where he could watch the house. He set the food aside and reached into his shirt pocket for two wallet-sized photos. One was of the Wraith, Evelyn Cassidy, the other of her brother, Mark. These he propped up on a small branch, backed with green leaves, such that he could see them from his vantage point. He put the binoculars to his eyes and scanned the property across the road. The garage doors were closed, and he saw no activity in the house. He then set the field glasses aside, put on his jacket against the chill mountain air, and saw to his late lunch.

It was dusk, and Beakman was half asleep, propped up against a tree trunk, when he was alerted to sound from across the road. He jerked forward, grabbed the binoculars and scanned the scene on the opposite side of the fraying tarmac. One of the two garage doors of the house was closing, but he was able to make out the distinctive shape of a Jeep from its rear. He scrambled to his feet and moved to his left to an opening in the trees and above the dense underbrush. With the field glasses trained on the windows along the front porch, he watched diligently for any movement. A minute later, he was rewarded. A woman crossed from window to window, then a light came on. He realized immediately she was not his target; rather she was shorter and heavier than Evelyn Cassidy, and her hair color was different.

The woman left the room, and it was more than two minutes later when a man entered the same area. Beakman twiddled the focusing knob on the glasses. He picked up the image of the man he had gotten in Seattle and looked closely in the semi-dark, then back through the binoculars. He was certain. It was the brother.

"Shit!" He exclaimed. He put the magnifier to his eyes again. "Yes!"

He dropped the field glasses and looked down. He sat down in place, then raised the binoculars again. Still no Evelyn. He looked at his watch under the light of a small flashlight. He wanted the other sandwich, and needed the coffee, both in his vehicle, but was uncertain about moving around. They surely would have the place under watch. He sat back and closed his eyes, pondering his next move.

Deep in thought, he heard another sound. This was of someone stepping on branches, or twigs on the ground; a single crack of snapping wood. It came from across the road and to the right of the house. He sat up and peered. Unable to see little, he used the binoculars again. He moved them back and forth. With their superior light-gathering capabilities, he was able to discern trees, rocks, foliage, then a human form. He stood and focused in. It was a woman, but dressed as a man. Her form was different than that of the woman he had seen in the house. It had to be she, he reasoned.

The glasses held by one hand, he fingered the Glock at his belt line, then withdrew his hand. Both hands holding the field glass again, he watched as the woman moved several yards from the house, then back toward it. In another few seconds, she disappeared, apparently, he reckoned, into the house. He reached into his jacket pocket, pulled out a four-inch long suppressor, pulled the Glock from his belt line, and screwed it onto the threaded adaptor at the end of the gun barrel.

He slipped and slid down to the road, then, watching carefully, moved cautiously toward the house, staying on the opposite side of the asphalt trace. When he was directly in front of the house, he moved gingerly across the road at a crouch, the Glock in his right hand, pointed at the ground. It was then he could see three people in the room behind the large windows. He stopped, still bent over, and watched as they stood and talked briefly. He recognized the other woman, the brother, Mark Cassidy and his sister, Evelyn. He moved closer until he was at the verge of the road and the front of the property. The binoculars he held in his left hand at chest level.

"Stop there, Beakman!"

The harsh voice came from the darkness behind him, along the road's edge. Beakman recognized the voice immediately. He froze.

"Drop the weapon. Do it!"

Beakman, without looking, did as he was told, silently. The Glock semi-automatic dropped to the ground with a thud.

"Now move three steps forward, your hands on your head."

The voice was getting closer as Radcliff walked up to within ten feet of Beakman. He was holding a sniper rifle up high against his shoulder, his right cheek against the stock, the barrel pointed at Beakman. Beakman obeyed, allowing the binoculars to dangle from the strap around his neck.

"Don't look around," Radcliff said. The rifle still trained on Beakman, his eyes on his prisoner, he knelt, picked the long pistol up and stuffed it into his waist band.

"I figured something like this, Radcliff." Beakman stood still, his hands on his head. His voice was a defeated croak. He was lying. His surprise was stupefying.

"Really? I don't believe you. If you had, you wouldn't be in front of me with your hands in the air. Now move, slowly, up onto the porch. If you pull anything, I'll kill you and think of a reason for doing so later. Make no mistake."

"No worries," Beakman said. He walked slowly to the porch, mounted the steps and stopped. "Now what?"

Radcliff followed him up, his weapon still pointed at Beakman, now at hip level, then moved to his side. He tapped on the window with the knuckles of his left hand, but kept his eyes on Beakman.

Inside, all three people looked toward the porch windows.

Cassidy jumped up immediately, made for the front door and opened it. "Catch a coyote, did we?"

"Turn and face me, Beakman," Radcliff said.

Beakman turned.

"Lower your hands behind your back."

When Beakman lowered his hands, Mark Cassidy bound them with a plastic tie-wrap.

His gun still trained loosely on Beakman, Radcliff spoke to Cassidy. "Better make sure he has no more weaponry."

Cassidy frisked Beakman, which included testing both ankles, then removed the binoculars from around his neck.

"Clean," Cassidy said. "Inside?"

"Inside," Radcliff said. He lowered the rifle.

Cassidy got behind Beakman and guided him into the house. When he was three feet in, Beakman stopped and looked down into the big living area. Cassidy set the binoculars on the foyer table. Alex was seated on the sofa, while Evelyn sat in one of the over-stuffed chairs. The two women stared up at Beakman, almost expressionless. Evelyn then looked at Radcliff, nodded and smiled. Radcliff set the sniper rifle aside, cleared the Glock, set it down on the foyer table and pocketed the magazine.

Cassidy took Beakman's arm and guided him to a bare wooden chair at the end of the sofa, placed there for his expected arrival. "Have a seat, Mr. Beakman."

Beakman, his eyes roving around the big room, almost fell into the seat, given that his hands were secured behind him, causing him to nearly lose his balance. He had been seated a few seconds when he heard movement behind him. He turned to look. His eyes went wide and his jaw became slack as he watched Nancy Mullins come into the room.

She looked at him as she stopped on the walkway. "Hello, Stanley."

"Jesus! What the f—!" He looked at her, then shot a glance at Radcliff and back, turning his torso uncomfortably. His mouth was open half-way, set into a feral snarl. Then he dropped his head and looked at the floor, shaking his head slowly.

Nancy moved down into the living room, then turned and faced Beakman. "You lied to me, Stanley." She looked at the ceiling for a moment. "Well, maybe you didn't lie, but you sure didn't tell the truth. To me. I was to help find this lady here so you could arrange her permanent disappearance? Uh-huh. Radcliff clued me in." She pointed vaguely toward Evelyn.

Beakman, leaning forward in his uncomfortable chair, peered up at her. His face had calmed to a mask of surprise and uncertainty. "The break-in. Did you actually—"

Nancy smiled ruefully. "Of course not. Charade. The map was for you to get here. Good work. Congratulations." Her tone was snide.

Beakman looked at her silently, then dropped his head again, shook it and sighed.

Cassidy looked toward the opening to the kitchen. "You can come in now."

Beakman sat up and looked around at the man who entered. Again, he expressed surprise and deep concern as he looked at Radcliff for answers.

Sergeant Griego stepped down into the living room. "Release his hands, will you?"

Evelyn stood, handed her brother a pair of diagonal cutters, then he and Radcliff went to Beakman. As he leaned forward, Cassidy cut the plastic tie wrap and removed it.

Beakman brought his hands to his front and rubbed them as he looked around, then concentrated on Griego. "Who—?"

Griego walked to within ten feet of Beakman, pulled a small stone from his pocket and said, "Catch," as he tossed the rock.

Beakman instinctively reached out and caught the stone with his right hand.

"Thank you Mr. Beakman," Griego said. He stepped forward. "Please." He held out his hand for Beakman to hand the rock back. "Now, let me see the back of your right hand, please."

Beakman hesitated. "Say! What the hell is this! Who is this guy?!" He pointed, looked around, then up at Griego. He pulled his hand back and dropped it into his lap with the other.

Griego pulled his windbreaker aside to reveal the gold detective's badge. "I'm Detective Sergeant Griego. Len Griego, of the Santa Fé Police Department, Mr. Beakman. Now, if you'd be so kind as to let me see the back of your hand." He let his jacket close, then stood directly in front of Beakman, his hands clasped in front of his belt, his feet well apart. He looked down at the man in the chair, his face calm, but serious.

Beakman slowly held out his right hand, palm down.

Griego leaned over and studied it closely, rolling it from side to side, changing the way the light hit it. "How'd you get this scar, Mr. Beakman?"

Beakman tried to pull his hand back, but Griego held it tightly. "What scar?"

Griego pointed to a small area on Beakman's hand. On it was a narrow, whitish scar an inch and a half long, just behind, and parallel to, the knuckles. "This scar, Mr. Beakman." He tapped it.

"I—I don't remember. I don't know. Probably doing some work around the house. I have a shop—"

Griego released Beakman's hand, turned, walked away, then turned to look at the man in the chair. "Where do you live, Mr. Beakman? Where's your home?"

Beakman hesitated. "Washington, DC. Why?"

Griego studied the floor for a moment. "Why are you here? In New Mexico? Santa Fé? Are you a tourist? Looking for a job? Moving here?"

Beakman shook his head and looked away at nothing. "Visiting. Visiting."

"Visiting who, Mr. Beakman?"

"Friends. I'm visiting friends."

"And in your spare time from visiting friends, you prowl around remote canyons in the lower Rockies with a pair of binoculars and a hand gun?"

Beakman looked away, silent.

"Are you willing to submit a DNA sample?"

Beakman frowned deeply and shook his head in a short, rapid motion. "Why? What for? What's this all about, anyway?!"

Evelyn had regained her seat, Cassidy had moved toward the front door and turned, Radcliff stood to one side of Beakman, and Alex was on the edge of her seat on the sofa. Her eyes darted between Griego, Beakman and Cassidy, her demeanor one of wonder and deep interest.

"I'll tell you what this is all about, Mr. Beakman. Stanley. Recently, there was a double murder in our fair city. Santa Fé, that is. The victims were a man and a woman. A close relative of one of the victims is in this room. Right now. Want to know who that person is?"

"I—" He swung his head around and settled on Alex for a second, then looked back at Griego.

Griego nodded with emphasis. "Right, Stan." He pointed at Alex, who began to tear up. "That lady, there. Mrs. Petersen, of Lubbock, Texas. Her husband was one of the victims, Mr. Beakman."

Cassidy went to Alex, stood beside her and massaged her shoulder. She reached up and laid her hand on his, her other dabbing at her eyes with a tissue. Evelyn watched and smiled.

"Wait a minute! What's this got to do with me?!" He started out of his chair.

Griego took a step toward him, as Radcliff moved closer as well. "Stay seated, Mr. Beakman!" Griego scolded as he swept his jacket aside to show Beakman the holstered pistol high on his hip.

Beakman sat down slowly. He glanced at Alex. "I'm sorry for your loss." He looked back at Griego. "But I had nothing to do with it! I know my rights, goddamnit! This is ridiculous! I want to leave. Now!"

Griego moved in closer to Beakman. "Not yet, Mr. Beakman. We have reason to believe you're involved."

"What?! Me?! Why the hell would you think that?!" His face flush with anger, Beakman glared at Sergeant Griego.

"We have certain information that leads us to that conclusion. You see, I—we—have reason to believe you're here to do some dirty work. What the hell are you doing sneaking around in the woods outside this house?!" He paused. "I'll ask you again. Are you willing to give a DNA sample?"

Flustered, Beakman hesitated, his eyes flitting about. He tried to hide the act, but he looked down surreptitiously at his right hand, which, along with his left, was shaking. He bore in on Griego again. "Yeah. Sure. Why not? What do I have to do?"

"You'll come with me. We'll take a swab, and you'll be placed in protective custody. You're not under arrest, but you're to remain close, and you won't be allowed to leave. For now. If you should try, you'll be placed on an APB with a bench warrant. Am I clear?"

Beakman, sullen, nodded. "Yeah. I understand. Okay."

Evelyn cut in. "Sergeant Griego, you looked at his hand. The scar. Why—?"

Griego turned, lowered his head with a frown, then looked about the room. He took a deep breath and released it. "We have reason to believe that the shooter, the person who shot and killed Betty Nolan and Ted Petersen—" He looked at Alex, then continued, "We believe that person was most likely wearing gloves, but—" He paused, then, "We think that person, the shooter, was right-handed, and that when they finished shooting Mrs. Nolan in the bathroom, they allowed their gun hand to drop." He held out his right hand, made a gun with his fingers, then swung it down along his side. "There's a small nail sticking out from the door stop. The door stop on the bathroom door. We think the shooter's hand brushed against that nail, and that nail cut through the glove the shooter was wearing, causing the shooter's hand to bleed. Even in that short time, a small drop of blood was left behind. Enough for a DNA test." He looked down at Beakman who was studying the floor.

Griego took a pace back, turned, pondering, then faced Beakman. "There's more. We're working with federal agencies in this case. If you cooperate—with us as well as them—things could go better for you. If not, and it's found that you're culpable in any way, your future could be very dim. Get my drift?" He looked over at Radcliff, then at Cassidy, who remained at Alex' side.

Both men acknowledged him with a nod.

Beakman turned his entire body to look hard at Radcliff, then moved his head slowly toward Griego. "I think I do. Yes."

"Good," Griego said. "Stand up." He walked to Beakman. "Turn around." He pulled a pair of handcuffs from the rear of his belt. "Hands behind."

"Hey! Why this?!"

"For your safety as well as mine. Just cooperate."

Beakman did and Griego cuffed him.

"How'd you get here? Where's your vehicle?" Griego spoke to Beakman from behind.

Beakman pointed with his chin. "Up the road."

"Keys in here?" Still behind him, Griego searched Beakman's jacket pockets and came up with a set of keys. He looked at Radcliff. "You headed back?"

Radcliff nodded.

Nancy stepped forward. "So am I."

Griego held out the keys. "Why don't the two of you take his car to the rendezvous. One of you can take it back to town, while I transport him."

"That'll work," Radcliff said. He took the keys from Griego and motioned to Nancy.

"Let's go," Griego said. With that, he took Beakman by the arm and led him from the room.

# 27

Charles "Charlie" Henshaw arrived at the Albuquerque Sunport in early afternoon. As he walked into the large, open area outside the security hall and the long, wide corridor between the gate and greeting areas, he was being watched.

Beakman stood in the same magazine stall where he had waited for Nancy Mullins. His eyes were hidden behind his large, dark glasses. He held a magazine up at nose level, peering at the approaching CIA agent. As Henshaw passed and stepped onto the down escalator, Beakman merely followed with his eyes. He took the magazine to the cashier, paid for it, then walked across the lobby. He dodged streams of arriving passengers who were dragging roller boards or were burdened with backpacks and "carry-ons." Many jabbered with friends and relatives who had come to greet them. He selected a drink and a sandwich from a food kiosk, then took a seat at a table in a seldom-used area nearby. He glanced at his watch, opened the magazine, then sipped on his cold drink. He ignored the sandwich.

Beakman did not know who they were, and he was careful not to look around as though searching, but he knew he was being watched. He had been informed that two men in plain clothes would follow and watch him. One was an FBI agent; the other a state policeman. He was also told that if he tried to escape or to thwart the plan as agreed to with the federal and state authorities, that he would be arrested immediately.

Henshaw dropped down to the baggage area on the escalator, walked three yards into the unfamiliar open space, studied the signs guiding him to the baggage carrels for his flight, and turned in that direction. In another five minutes, he had his leather overnight bag, and made for the exit. He went to the taxi rank, got into a cab, and was driven away.

An hour and a half later, Beakman, after using the men's room once, wandered away from the table. The sandwich abandoned, he took up his position at the novelty stall across from the food kiosk. This time, he perused the books offered, purchased a candy bar, and wandered about, looking at gew-gaws as he ate the confection. He looked at his wrist watch again, then donned his dark glasses. He picked up a newspaper, paid for it, then turned toward the passenger exit doors and watched as people began to stream through them. Two minutes later, he spotted Dennis Powell.

Powell walked past Beakman, recognizing him from the corner of his eye, but didn't acknowledge him. When he got to the top of the escalators, Beakman fell in behind, the newspaper in his hand. Powell continued to the baggage carrels, retrieved his roller board, then sought a taxi outside. Beakman went to the parking structure and his car. An hour later, he picked up Charlie Henshaw and Dennis Powell at two different Albuquerque hotels; Powell first, then Henshaw. Both men were dressed casually, and both covered their eyes with dark glasses, as did Beakman. None wore a hat. Beakman had left his Resistol in his Santa Fé motel room.

With Powell seated in front, Henshaw crawled into the back seat. Beakman didn't look around at his passenger, nor did Powell, and all three were silent. Beakman checked his mirrors and exited onto the street.

After the car joined traffic, Henshaw spoke from the back seat. "Where we headed?"

Beakman said, "Place where we can talk."

He steered the car toward the Interstate, headed west, and found a lonely dirt trace off the frontage road, old Highway Sixty-six. He pulled the car to a stop and shut the engine down. He wondered where his tag team was, since he saw nothing and no one. They were good, he thought. He was careful not to alert Henshaw and Powell to his secret knowledge.

Powell opened his door and got out first, followed by Henshaw, then Beakman. All three men walked away from the car, silently, in different directions. Beakman looked west, while his two visitors looked east, toward the Sandia Mountains and the city sprawled below it. All three kept their dark glasses on.

"Some view," Charlie Henshaw remarked. His arms were folded across his chest. He was not as tall as Beakman, but taller than Powell, with a slight paunch. His hair was thin salt and pepper. He wore a dark blue cloth jacket over a light blue shirt. His collar was open.

"Sure is," Powell agreed. "Big country." Powell, not as old as Henshaw, looked older, with less hair, which had mainly gone white. He wore a brown leather jacket over a white shirt. He wore no tie.

Beakman turned and joined them, such that all three stood side by side in a row, staring east and down into the valley of the Rio Grande.

Henshaw swung his head about. "And no one nearby. Good choice, Beakman."

Beakman merely nodded.

Henshaw moved, walking around Beakman, studying the ground as he went, his arms still folded. "So, Beakman, what's this all about? What's this bullshit with Evelyn Cassidy wanting to make a deal?"

"She's dying of cancer, Charlie. She's under a cure regimen, and doesn't want to appear in public before committees. She's sick, tired and wants a deal." He looked at Henshaw from under his eyebrows.

"Tell us again." Powell said as he moved toward Beakman.

"She wants you guys—me, too—to call off the dogs. In exchange, she'll lose her memory." He shrugged and looked at both men in turn. "On paper."

"So why come here? Why'd she want us in New Mexico?" Henshaw asked. He pointed.

"She wants direct, eyeball confirmation," Beakman said. "Assurance," he added.

"Tell us again how you found her. Or how what's his name—Radcliff—found her."

Beakman looked at Henshaw. "He hasn't detailed how he did it, but he said he was able to find her because of the cancer thing."

"Cancer thing!" Powell reacted, squinting. "What's that got to do with it?!"

Beakman looked at him. "She's being treated locally. Can't travel."

"Shit!" His annoyance was palpable.

"Take it easy, Dennis," Henshaw admonished.

"Yeah, right. Sorry." He turned away.

Henshaw grasped both his hands behind his back as he turned to look at Beakman. "Okay, so what's next? And where does Radcliff fit it?"

"We go see the Wraith. Evelyn. Radcliff will head it up. The meeting. He's the go-between."

Both Powell and Henshaw were silent and looked at each other.

"Wait a minute, Beakman," Henshaw said. "Radcliff was supposed to get rid of her. How is it that she's still around to make deals?!"

"I told you!"

"Humor me. Tell me again."

"Charlie, he went in after he zeroed in, but she got the drop on 'im."

Powell peered into Beakman's eyes. "What?! The asshole let her take him?!"

Beakman glared back at Powell. "Yeah, Dennis! Why you think they called her the Wraith?!"

"Jesus!" Powell stalked away several steps and halted, his fists balled.

"So, she takes him, disarms him, then says she wants a deal?" Henshaw asked.

"That's the story." Beakman shrugged.

"Did Radcliff tell her who was behind him?" Henshaw asked.

"Didn't have to. She knew it was you guys." Beakman paused. "That's why they called her—"

"Yeah, I know. The Wraith!" Charlie Henshaw shook his head and paced away.

Powell came back. He looked at his watch. "Okay. So, when?"

Beakman stepped toward Powell. "Too late today. Tomorrow's better."

"I don't like this," Dennis Powell said. "I don't like it at all."

Henshaw got up close to Radcliff, glanced at Powell, then, his voice low, said, "I don't care about her cancer, and I don't care about her offer. This woman is fuckin' dangerous. It's too risky, Beakman, and you're a fool to even consider it." He drew in a deep breath, pinched his nose, looked around, then back at Beakman. "Now I'm going to tell you how this is gonna' come down." He jabbed Stanley Beakman's chest. "You've been there? To where she's holed up?"

Beakman nodded, chastised. "Yes."

"Okay. What's the lay of the land? Is she alone?"

"Her brother's in and out."

"He the lawyer?" Powell asked, as he moved in closer, happy with Henshaw's direction.

Beakman looked at him and merely nodded.

"So, what's his take? His part? He wants her to negotiate?"

Beakman shrugged. "You know lawyers."

"Yeah," Henshaw said. "And the surroundings. House? Apartment? In town? The sticks? Where?"

"The sticks. Almost wilderness. Lots of trees. Nobody around. They're pretty much isolated. I think they're scared—both of 'em, and they want to deal." He shrugged again and raised his eyebrows. "They want an end."

Henshaw, up close, pointed his finger at Beakman's face. "We couldn't come in packing, so you're gonna have to provide heat. Delay the meet. Stash some armament close by the place. Make it good, I want some automatic stuff. Tech nine, that kinda' hardware. Or similar. Stuff we can grab as we go in. Can you handle it?"

"Jesus, Charlie! You don't want to negotiate?" Beakman whined.

Powell stepped up to Beakman and grabbed him by the throat. "You son of a—!"

Beakman reacted, tried to throw Powell off, and nearly lost his balance in the process.

"Goddamnit, Dennis, back off!" Henshaw snarled. He pushed Powell away, then looked around, and south toward the highway. He observed cars and trucks plying the Interstate in the distance, but nothing and no one close by.

Beakman massaged the affected area of his neck, glaring at Powell, who pirouetted away, muttering.

Henshaw got in close to Beakman again. "Get this, Beakman; we're going through with this! There's no way we're going to let her stay around.

Maybe she's got one foot in the grave, but we're gonna' help her into it. And the brother's got to go, too. He knows too much. And Radcliff. He's a loose end and unreliable. Now you straighten up, damn it! Understand?!"

"Radcliff?! Jesus, Charlie, that's heavy! He'll stay cool. How we gonna' make this look good?!"

Henshaw reddened. "Damn it, Beakman, we don't have a choice! You have any goddamn idea what'd happen to us if this goes Justice's way?! Do you?!"

Beakman nodded, still nursing his neck. He sighed. "Yeah. Automatic weapons."

Henshaw looked at Powell, then back at Beakman. "Good boy," He patted Beakman on the shoulder, circled away, then back. "And a good job. We're almost home." He pointed again.

"Do me a favor, okay Charlie?" Beakman said.

"Yeah?"

"Keep your mutt off me." He motioned with his chin toward Powell.

"You got it."

"I mean it. Or he'll be next."

Powell looked at Beakman with a smirk.

"Okay," Henshaw said, waving the remark away. "Off to Santa Fé? I need to check out."

Beakman pondered, then said. "I think you should stay here. Give me some time to gather the tools."

Henshaw and Powell both looked at Beakman in silence.

"You might get exposed. In and out's better. Okay?"

The other men looked at each other, then nodded in unison.

"Okay," Henshaw said. "We'll wait. But let's get on it. We're here under cover as it is. In and out."

"No slip-ups, okay?" Powell said.

Beakman looked at Powell and rubbed the bridge of his nose slowly with his middle finger.

# 28

Beakman drove to Albuquerque at midday, picked up Charlie Henshaw and Dennis Powell at their respective hotels, then headed back to Santa Fé. In keeping with maintaining a low profile and security, he brought along two take-out lunches, one for each man. The menus were according to their wishes.

Beakman kept a sharp eye out for his tail, instinctive after many years of training, and in one case, of dire necessity. In this instance, it was benign, but he was curious and fretful nonetheless.

All three were relaxed to the extent that they didn't fear anyone knowing of their destination and purpose. There was minor apprehension on the parts of all, but unspoken and well hidden, again by training and experience. Not one of them said a word until they were well onto the Interstate north.

Powell, in the back seat, having finished his lunch, and after taking a last sip of his drink, spoke first. "What about Radcliff?"

Beakman looked into the rearview mirror to catch Powell's image. "What about him?"

Powell looked away, taking time to dissipate his irritation. "What about Radcliff means is he going with us."

"Yes," Beakman said. "I told you. Go-between."

"Right," Powell growled.

Henshaw finished chewing, balled up the paper his sandwich had come in and tossed it over his shoulder into the back without looking. It missed Powell, bounced off the seat and dropped to the floor. "Make sure you clean this car after we're gone," he said. He wiped his mouth with a paper napkin before it met the same fate as the wrapper. He watched the highway through his dark glasses and the windshield. "Does he know what we're going to do?"

Beakman snapped, "I wasn't born yesterday, Charlie! Of course not! It would give him time to think. He's suspicious as it is. He'd blow it."

Henshaw nodded silently.

From the back seat, Powell said, "So, how we gonna finesse this? Where're the guns, and how do we get 'em without alerting him?"

"I've got it worked out. He'll go in first. We follow."

"The way you planned and worked out the other thing?" Powell's head bobbed with insinuation.

Beakman didn't answer.

"I'm gonna' ask a favor of you two love birds," Henshaw growled. "Lay off each other 'til this is finished. Then you can duke it out and go your separate ways."

"Yeah, okay," Powell mumbled. He looked out his side window.

Beakman did not react.

With the same passenger configuration when Beakman brought Henshaw and Powell up from Albuquerque, he pulled into the Albertson's parking lot on St. Francis Drive. He circled the lot once, then stopped alongside the marked parking slots on the north end. Radcliff stepped out of the shadows, ducked to peer into the car, then walked around to the driver-side rear door, opened it and slid in. He said nothing as he got in, nor did any of the three other men.

They were on the Interstate when Charlie Henshaw broke the silence. "Nice to see you, Jeremy." He didn't look back.

"Same here, Charlie," Radcliff answered. "Want your coin back?"

Henshaw smiled. Naw. You keep it. Souvenir."

"Right. I'll have it set in purple velvet and display it on my mantle."

"Only way," Henshaw said. He brushed imaginary dirt from his pants.

"Yep."

"I don't like this," Powell said. He turned to look at Radcliff beside him. "What guarantees do we have?"

"You're Powell, right?" Radcliff looked at him in the dark of the back seat.

"We can save the introductions, Radcliff. Or do you prefer Jeremy? I'd like an answer to my question."

"Jesus. You're a friendly prick, aren't you?" Radcliff asked. He looked away, took a moment, then, "She's willing to sign on the dotted line. Her brother's a lawyer. He's prepared a document. It's written such that if she goes back on her word, she goes down, too. Everybody gets a copy."

Henshaw turned to glance at Radcliff. "Really?"

"Really."

"Have you seen the document?" Powell asked.

"Yes. Ask Beakman."

"Beakman?" Henshaw asked.

Beakman nodded. "I've seen it."

"You have a copy?" Powell asked.

"No. They wouldn't release it," Radcliff said.

"That's bullshit! I don't like it!" Powell snarled.

"Take it easy, will you, goddamnit?!" Henshaw snapped.

"How do we know—?"

"You don't," Radcliff said. His voice was controlled. "But they also know that if what they have is unacceptable, you know where she is, and could call in a strike. Fast. They're trapped where they are. One way in; one way out. A shooting gallery."

"Shit," Powell muttered.

"They don't want any more trouble. She's mellow. Cancer does that to a person."

"And what if it's the other way around?" Powell asked. "We're trapped, too!"

"Take the next off ramp, Beakman, and head back." Radcliff said.

Beakman looked up into the rearview mirror at Radcliff's outline in the dark of the back seat. He let up on the accelerator pedal, and the car began to slow.

"Hold on, hold on," Henshaw said. He waved both his hands. "Stay on course, Beakman. We'll go through with this charade. Of course they don't want trouble. Blood and guts all over the place? Right?" He looked around at Powell.

Powell rubbed the back of his neck and smirked in the shadows. "Yeah, Charlie. Okay."

"Everything's cool," Henshaw said.

"Cool, cool," Powell said. He hesitated. "Where is this place, anyway?"

"Mountains," Beakman said.

"How long?" Henshaw asked. He glanced at Beakman.

"Twenty minutes give or take," Beakman said.

As the car carrying Beakman, Radcliff, Henshaw and Powell moved up the narrow highway between Pecos and Holy Ghost Canyon, Powell swung his head around, looking back out the rear window from time to time. Henshaw was less nervous, but was more apprehensive than he had been when they left Santa Fé.

Beakmen wondered if they still had a tail, and if Radcliff was in on it. He watched the rearview in vain.

"Jesus, where is this place?!" Powell ranted.

"Few more minutes," Beakman said. "Remind me, okay, Radcliff?"

"You got it."

Two minutes later, Beakman slowed and made a left turn into the canyon after Radcliff tapped his shoulder. As they moved slowly along the bad road, the only light was from the headlamps of the car. Then Beakman braked, brought the car to the left side of the road, and pulled in at an angle to the house. He waited five seconds, looking around, then shut the engine down.

All four men peered at the house, then variously, they studied the surrounding territory. The light coming from the living room onto the porch was dim and yellowish, as though only one lamp were on.

Beakman turned his head to speak. "Radcliff, go in first. Tell 'em we're here. Better to not spook 'em with all four of us trooping in. We'll wait outside until you give us the high-sign. Wave from the front door."

"Okay."

Radcliff got out, closed his door softly, then moved for the porch. There, he went to the nearest window, turned and gave a thumbs-up. He then knocked on the door. Five seconds later, it opened, and the men in the car saw a man standing inside. It appeared there was conversation, then Radcliff waved and went inside. The door closed behind them.

Powell got out first, moved around the back of the car and came up to Beakman as he was exiting. Henshaw got out and came around the front, watching the house as he did.

"Where's the hardware, Beakman?!" Powell's voice was a hoarse whisper.

Beakman moved past him toward the trunk. "Stashed inside." He opened the trunk, then looked toward the house. "Hurry!" He spoke in a loud whisper.

He reached into the trunk to roll out a heavy canvas sheet. He knelt and handed Powell a Smith & Wesson 9mm semi-automatic pistol and a magazine. He gave Henshaw the same type of pistol, then picked up a Glock 9mm and magazine for himself. He stood up. "Best I could do. Couldn't get full-auto on short notice."

"Okay, okay," Henshaw said nervously. "Magazine?"

Beakman handed him a magazine, which Henshaw quickly inserted, pulled the slide back and let it snap forward. Beakman did the same with his, and Powell set his magazine and slide as well.

"No silencers?" Powell asked.

Beakman said, "Hard to get this quick. Look around. Nobody. Who's gonna' hear a few gunshots? Okay, let's do it."

With Beakman in front, the three men moved quickly to the porch, up the steps and to the front door. He looked around at the other two, nodded, then burst through the door. They stood in a triad on the flagstone foyer, looking down into the living room, then to the short hall and the kitchen beyond. The big area was empty, and there was no one in the kitchen.

Beakman looked at the other two.

"What the—!" Powell whispered.

At that moment, Radcliff entered from the kitchen, and walked slowly toward them. Powell pushed past Beakman and raised his weapon, pointing it at Radcliff. He waved his pistol toward the living room. "Where are they?!"

Radcliff stepped down slowly into the living area. "They'll be in. Keep your shirt on." He looked back as he reached the rear of the sofa, where he stood and turned. "What's with the hardware? I thought we were here to make a deal?"

"You know good goddamn well what it's about, Radcliff!" Powell snarled.

"Where are they?! Tell 'em to come out!" Henshaw snapped.

Radcliff looked toward the kitchen. "Come on out."

The three men holding the guns watched as first Evelyn, then Mark Cassidy, followed by Alessandra Petersen, whose hand he was holding, entered the walkway, then down into the living area. They all watched the three armed men with trepidation.

"Who the hell is she?!" Henshaw shouted. He pointed, his arm outstretched at Alex.

Cassidy, who had moved down into the center of the living area with Alex at his side, spoke. "She's a friend, Mr. Henshaw. Objections?"

Henshaw moved several steps toward the kitchen end and faced the group assembled on the lower level. He looked at Beakman. "She wasn't part of the deal!" His gun hand wavered. "And how'd you know my name?!"

Cassidy shrugged. "Well, she's no threat. I know who you are. Why the arsenal?"

Powell stepped down onto the living area level. His face was screwed up into an intense frown. "It is what it is, and that's because the deal is, no one leaves here alive but us! There is no deal!" He glared at Radcliff. "What the hell you doing down there?!"

Radcliff shook his head. "There's supposed to be a deal, Powell." He was calm.

Evelyn Cassidy sat down in the over-stuffed leather chair at the far end of the room.

"Shoot her, Beakman!" Powell shouted.

"You're so anxious, you do it!"

Powell opened his mouth in a small circle of disbelief, then clamped it shut as he pointed his gun at Evelyn and pulled the trigger. The hammer slammed down with a loud click. For a full second, Powell didn't realize what had happened. He looked at the pistol closely, operated the slide, which ejected a round and cocked the weapon. Again he pulled the trigger. He heard nothing but a metallic click.

"What the fuck!" he shouted. He looked at the gun again, then crazily at Beakman, then at Henshaw, who was speechless, his mouth open, his face pale.

Henshaw reacted by raising his pistol, pointing it at Evelyn and pulling the trigger. There was no report. He looked at Beakman. "Why, you son-of-a-bitch! What the fuck is this?!"

He swung the weapon wide, trying to hit Beakman's head. Beakman dropped his pistol, ducked, blocked Henshaw's arm, grabbed his wrist with one hand and his throat with the other, and pushed him backwards. Henshaw staggered back with the weight of the taller man pushing him. The Smith & Wesson left his hand and sailed away, hit the half-wall dividing the kitchen area from the living room and dropped to the floor with a clatter.

At that moment, the front door swung open and four men, wearing dark blue jackets burst in. Three of them, wielding semi-automatic pistols, took up a defensive crouch stance. Their weapons were pointed, at arm's length, at Powell, Henshaw and Beakman. The man who remained standing shouted, "FBI! Drop your weapons! Drop your weapons! Now!"

Beakman released his grip on Henshaw, turned and raised his hands. Henshaw staggered away, his eyes bugged out, and raised his arms high. Powell wheeled around, threw his weapon away and moved backwards, his hands over his head.

One of the men shouted, "Against the wall!"

The FBI agents all rose from the defensive stance and began herding their prisoners against the west wall, along the raised walkway. All three were forced to spread their legs and were patted down.

The agent nearest the door spoke. "I'm Martin. We're agents of the Federal Bureau of Investigation. These men are under arrest." He held his badge out, then hung it on his jacket pocket.

Sergeant Griego walked in through the still open front door.

Martin turned to him. "Griego."

"Martin," Griego replied. He closed the door.

The FBI agents patting the three men down had them lined up in a row along the walkway. Henshaw was on the kitchen end. Powell was in the middle, with Beakman on the foyer end.

As the agent handling Powell reached for his handcuffs at his waist at the small of his back, Powell acted. The agent used his left hand to grab the cuffs, with his pistol still in his right. Powell lowered his head, looked around to his right, and saw the agent's loosely-held gun. He pulled his hands free from his back where the agent was holding them, and wheeled around to his right. He wrenched the pistol from the surprised agent, pushed him away, raised the gun and fired twice in rapid succession at Beakman. The first slug penetrated Beakman's left side; the second missed and went through the front door, leaving a large, clean hole from the 9mm projectile.

In an instant, both Griego and Martin, the senior FBI man, had their weapons raised and pointed at Powell. They fired a hail of bullets at the man, hitting him in the stomach, chest, and his left leg. Powell flung the agent's gun away, spun backwards, hitting Henshaw, then collapsed onto the floor.

The agent whose gun he had taken lost his balance and fell backwards into the living area, onto the floor, landing on his back. He rolled to his side and sprung to his feet in time to see Powell sink to the floor, close to death.

Alex screamed from the edge of the sofa where she was sitting. Evelyn bolted from her chair. As she did, she pulled her 9mm Walther out from under the cushion. In three seconds, it was back in its hiding place as she realized her help was not required. Cassidy, who had been moving toward Martin and Griego, halted and took a feral stance, hunching over, aghast at the gun play. Radcliff, who had been standing behind the sofa, also reacted defensively, wishing he had his pistol before realizing it was all over. The agent who had been handling Beakman crouched beside him and began to investigate his wounds. The agent behind Henshaw finished cuffing him, turned him around and ordered him to slide to the floor and sit.

Henshaw dropped his head to his chest and shook it slowly.

As Martin went to assist the agent with Beakman, Griego rushed to the portable telephone on the table next to Evelyn's empty chair. He picked it up and began punching the universal "911."

Evelyn joined Martin and the other agent at Beakman's side. Alex followed and knelt beside the bleeding man. Martin stood, backed away, pulled a portable radio form his belt and spoke into it.

An ambulance arrived forty-five minutes later, and Beakman was carried out on a stretcher. Griego accompanied his prisoner after he and Martin conferred outside. Henshaw was led away by the FBI agents, who placed him in a waiting van. Powell's body was placed in the rear.

# 29

Two weeks later, on a late afternoon, Evelyn, her brother Mark Cassidy and Alex, Jeremy Radcliff and Patsy Romero, all gathered in the Holy Ghost house living room. They all held stemmed glasses of red wine.

"Here's to you getting well, Wraith!" Radcliff said. He raised his glass.

Evelyn nodded modestly as the others laughed, raised her glass to Radcliff, then sipped as did the rest. "Wraith," She mused.

Cassidy patted Alex' knee and stood, wine glass in hand. He looked around the room. "The meeting with Justice went well," he said. "We were assured by their representative and the FBI that there'll be no need for a congressional hearing, and that there are no charges pending. Henshaw is going to be off the streets for a long time. Jeremy's in the clear and can go back to Patsy, Mandy and clay!" He raised his glass. "More than anything, though, my sister can relax and go out and about."

Radcliff leaned over and kissed Patsy on her cheek. He looked up. "And you?" he asked.

"Well, Alessandra here—Alex to you—and I are thinking about a Caribbean cruise." He beamed down at her. "Then it's back to damp Seattle. I've asked my west Texas lady to go with me. Get away from all that sunshine and dust!" He paused. "But who knows?"

Alex looked up at Cassidy, put her glass aside, rose, put her arms around him and looked up into his smiling face.

Patsy turned to Evelyn. "What about your treatment? You know I'm at the hospital."

"Now that my brother is abandoning me, I'm thinking about moving into town." She smiled and drank from her glass. "I'm sure I'll see you there."

"That'd be great!" Patsy exclaimed. "You'll have to come to dinner with me and my hunk, here!" She squeezed Radcliff's hand. "He's a pretty good cook!"

Evelyn smiled and raised her glass again, this time to Patsy. She sipped, then looked first at her brother, then Radcliff. "What happened with Beakman's scar and the DNA test."

Cassidy nodded and glanced at Radcliff, then moved toward the fireplace. He held Alex' hand, and she went with him. "There was a match. Beakman was the shooter. But he made a deal, as you know, otherwise he wouldn't have been able to be free to lure Henshaw and Powell up here."

"Don't forget the recording I made when he recruited me," Radcliff offered.

Cassidy pointed at Radcliff. "Right. The closer."

Evelyn shook her head. "Sad, in a way. Maybe it's poetic justice the poor guy died of his wound." She stood up. "Hey, I'm damned hungry! I'm gonna' tuck into some of Patsy and Jeremy's green chile stew they brought! Who wants to join me?"

Cassidy raised his glass again with one arm around Alex. "Here's to Holy Ghost Creek and wet dresses!"

www.ingramcontent.com/pod-product-compliance
Lightning Source LLC
Chambersburg PA
CBHW011405010726
47495CB00009B/2790